THE WIND AND THE RAIN

THOMAS BURKE

British Library Cataloguing-in-Publication Data
A catalogue record for this book is available from the
British Library

THE WIND AND THE RAIN

A Book of Confessions

BY

THOMAS BURKE

Thomas Burke

Thomas Burke was born in Clapham, London in 1886. His father died when he was very young, and at the age of ten he was removed to a home for middle-class boys who were "respectably descended but without adequate means to their support." Burke published his first piece of writing – a short story entitled 'The Bellamy Diamonds' – in 1901, when he was just fifteen. However, proper recognition came in 1916, with the publication of *Limehouse Nights,* a collection of melodramatic short stories set amongst the immigrant population of London's Chinatown. *Limehouse Nights* was serialized in three British periodicals, *The English Review*, *Colour* and *The New Witness,* and received positive attention from reviewers and a number of authors, including H. G. Wells. It also sparked something of a controversy, however, and was initially banned by libraries due to the scandalous interracial relationships it portrayed between Chinese men and white women.

It was these portrayals of London's Chinatown that Burke is best-remembered for. However, there is some degree of confusion over how much of Burke's writing was based in fact; as literary critic Anne Witchard states, most of what we know about Burke's life is based on works that "purport to be autobiographical, yet contain far more invention than truth." Whatever the truth, there is no doubt that, in his day, Burke was regarded as the foremost chronicler of London's Chinatown at the turn-of-the-century. Burke told newspaper journalists that he had "sat at the feet of Chinese philosophers who kept opium dens to learn from the lips that could frame only broken English, the secrets, good and evil, of the mysterious East," and these journalists almost uniformly took him at his word.

Burke continued to use descriptions of urban London life as a focus of his writing throughout his life. Off the back of *Limehouse Nights,* Burke published the thematically similar *Twinkletoes* in 1918, and *More Limehouse Nights* in 1921. However, he was a prolific author who tried his hand at a number of different genres. He semi-regularly published essays on the London environment, including pieces such as 'The Real East End' and 'London in My Times', and during the thirties even tried his hand at horror fiction. Indeed, in 1949, shortly after his death, Burke's short story 'The Hands of Ottermole' was voted the best mystery of all time by critics. Burke also influenced the burgeoning film industry in Hollywood; D W Griffith, for example, used the short story 'The Chink and the Child' from *Limehouse Nights* (1917) as basis for his silent movie, *Broken Blossoms* (1919), and Charlie Chaplin derived 'A Dog's Life' (1918) from the same book.

To

WILLIAM McFEE

CONTENTS

THE WIND AND THE RAIN

THE WIND AND THE RAIN

CHAPTER I

CAUSEWAY

THE road is long, says the Eastern sage, but it
has many corners; and my London road has
corners at Limehouse Causeway; at a court in the
heart of Bermondsey; at Caledonian Road; at
Greenwich; at Paddington Station; at "The Barge
Aground"; at Lyons' tea-shop in Holborn; at Bel-
gravia; at Gracechurch Street; at Brick Lane; and
the Borough High Street; each corner a symbol of
those other symbols of life which we call facts.

At the first corner I see a little store in that street
where China has settled on the coast of London
and brought grace and bitterness to the midnights
of court and alley. Over the doorway of this store
is a gas-lamp painted with the chop of Quong Lee.
It is a side-street shop, no different in structure from
the side-street shops of any working-class district;
small and low, with many panes to its window; but
its side-panels are fantastically gay with Chinese
script, and its window is crammed with the mer-
chandise of legend. Blue jars of ginger. Coloured

11

canisters of tea. Tins of fruit and fish and syrup,
lifted above the tinned goods of other shops by their
ribbons of ideographs. Crooked weapons and statu-
ettes of coral and jade. Dishes of dried fins, of
lychees, longans, seaweed and water-lily flour. Tea-
pots built into cradles of cushion and wicker. Banners and masks and punk-sticks.

Before that window a child stands by the half-
hour, poring upon the ideographs, then (as now)
fuller for him of hidden beauty than any painted
picture. About him is a narrow street, and through
its mist move the calm faces of Canton and Malaya.
There are open doors showing long, dark passages,
and at the end of them the glow of a lamp, half-
seen figures, the smell of sweet scent and dirt, the
faint music of guitar and drum. Above his head
hangs the lantern of Quong Lee, and beyond the window sits Quong Lee himself, gazing out as the boy
gazes in.

Quong Lee wears steel spectacles and the hair
at his temples is grey. He wears a blue linen suit,
loose sleeves, a skull-cap of black silk, and a long
queue. (The Republic is not yet heard of.) He
has the husky voice of those who have lived long
in the sunshine. His teeth are pink from long
chewing of betel-nut, and his skin has the appearance of having been fine-combed. All day and all
the evening he sits in the corner-seat of his counter,
gazing through the window with unwinking eyes,
as though carven. He seems to be a part of the
immutable. His temper is fixed, aloof from the disturbance of delight or distress. He seems as set as

his ginger-jars, as permanent and tranquil as the expressionless face of his seven-stomached Lord of Right Living.

But it was not so. Fluent as his road had been, it had a sharp corner. His shop is there; his lantern is there; maybe his spirit is there; but the English law had not the child's feeling for the perdurable, and all that the child now has of him in material shape is an old silk cap, tasselled with devil-chasers.

.   .   .   .

Many years later I was sitting in the Ivy Restaurant with a young composer who a month or so earlier had arrived. He was at the top-side of his hour. He sat before me, under the stare of the other tables, tingling with nervous force, ruffling his dark curls, flashing with mignon gesture, and talking sardonically about himself. People came to us at intervals without apology or introduction. An actor of the higher drama, dark and reticent, offered him a white hand. A queen of drawing-room comedy bowed. A bearded dramatic critic gave him a glance that, coming from him, was a benediction. A novelist with owlish eyes shook hands and inspected him without speaking. A London Gossiper, the Captain Gronow of our day, stood over him, slim and saturnine, dropping languid epigrams. His agent came across, and we found a chair for him, and at last lunch was ordered. People stared, as though anxious to see (at least) what the man was eating.

At this point I suffered the feeling that I have suffered at every corner, where in the moment of turning, one stands still and sees oneself and the occasion set apart, as a picture or statuary, exhibited under glass. It seemed fabulous that I should be sitting in that place, careless of the clock, careless of the bill, undismayed by the surroundings, and in the company of those, who, ten years ago, to my eyes walked on clouds. Me—in the Ivy. Was it really me sitting there? Me—the Hardcress kid, brought up to be humble, and to order myself lowly and reverently towards the Nobility and Gentry, and to remember that I had no rights except what charity conceded to me; a lesson so stamped into me that it has become a part of my character. A queer thing, this Me. I was the Causeway. I was the one room in Carfax Street. I was the Big House at Greenwich. I was the Orphanage. I was the Dark House in Caledonian Road. I was the City Office. I was London Bridge. I was the Old Kent Road Lodging-house. I was. . . .

At that moment a *mousse* of chicken was served, and as I looked up from my plate I caught my young friend's eye and, speaking without thinking, I said: "Pearce and Plenty, Goswell Road. Eh?" His eye flickered. The faint grin of his that plays shield to his quivering spirit flashed across his face, and he asked:

"How do you know?"

I said, "Your face. You've got the marks of it. One never loses them."

He said, "Funny! I used to go to that one. And it's just what I was thinking when you spoke. Only I'd never have said it."

As the lunch went on we telegraphed each other. "Lockhart's, Charing Cross," says he to the asparagus.

"Good Pull Up, Newington Causeway," I said to the Pêche Melba.

And when M. Abel himself poured the liqueurs, " 'The Old Foresters.' Tuppence a basin."

I knew that his road had many corners, and I could see that he was fumbling after them. He came out at last with the phrase with which even serious philosophers must begin and end—"Life's a queer thing," and stopped. Then went on, and for ten minutes the conversation was a string of sententious burbling. "All accidents. Here we are, sitting here, a few years after Pearce and Plenty. What extraordinary accident brought us here?"

"Lord knows. What accident made you a composer?"

"Couldn't say. One of a dozen moments. Being miserable, for one thing. Wanting to tell people what I felt about things. Meeting a man at Kennington Oval. All of 'em were corners, but where I turned off I don't know." He stopped and drank coffee. "We're all decorated with accidents. Assemblies of parts, like a South Sea nigger, with this man's hat, t'other fellow's cuffs, and somebody else's umbrella."

"But did you want to be a composer?"

"Never entered my head in those days. Music was always part of me but I wanted to be—oh, all sorts of things—expensive things. But composer. . . . First of all, I reckon I wanted two pairs of boots instead of one pair that let water. I wanted books. And theatres and concerts. And all the time I was really working—at silly, useless work—I never got near those things. No money, no hope, stupid people all round us, and always—just out of reach—music and books and the people who did things. Now I'm doing work that is sheer enjoyment, they'll give me everything I want. And all an accident. Not the thing I foreshadowed for myself. Never is, is it? What made you a writer?"

"I think I can answer that. It goes back to a moment when I was ten years old, looking in a shop-window. I began writing at sixteen. Not because I wanted to write, or thought I could write, or for the joy of writing, but with one purpose. I've been at it ever since. Just trying to express one moment in a London side-street. I've never done it yet. But one goes on and does other things by accident. Eh?"

"I know. I had something like that once. One of those things that stick with you, and somehow get into your work."

"I'd like to hear it."

"Why, it was. . . . Oh. . . . But *you* know. The moment when everything comes close to you and you understand everything. When you——" He hovered for a word, then used face and hands, miming: "I can play it but I can't explain it. I'd rather hear about yours. The accidents and all that."

"Yes, but the only important thing in any story is the gaps. And gaps never register. The growth

spaces—when you change colour and style and find
yourself different without knowing how it happened.
You think that love or success or disaster are the big
moments, but, looking back, you see it was the little,
unnoticed street-corner moments that mattered.
And they're hard to get at."

"I know. Like thinking. You start thinking
about, say, blankets, and a minute later you find
you're thinking of the nebular theory; and tracing
back you see that it was an orderly progression of
forty separate steps. . . . But, blimey, we're getting into deep stuff. Let's talk about Pearce and
Plenty!"

. . . .

Well, at the time of my visits to the Causeway, I
was living with Uncle Frank in Poplar, and I was
happy there. We lived in one room of the upstairs back of a small house in Carfax Street.
It was a street of uniform bald houses of four
rooms and scullery. Its parlour windows bayed
out to the street, without the grace of one yard
of green or the gentility of a gate. Some of the
houses, at that time, in a spasm of discontent with
their estate, had turned themselves into shops,
and had made a bad job of it, being neither good
shop nor honest house, but though it was down it
grinned. Always there was the noise of dogs and
babies, and the cheery calls of neighbour to neighbour and the occult cries of coal-man, winkle-man,
milk-man, and balloon-and-flag man. There was no
melancholy in Carfax Street. Wonderful people
lived there, too. We had a riveter, a French pol-

isher, a turner, a screw-maker, a glass-bender, a carver and gilder, a wheelwright—all of them magicians with their hands; men who could *make* things. Whenever I heard them talking of their work, I settled my future on the work that was being talked about.

Ours was a jolly little home. The length and breadth of home was exactly five of my paces; I had often marched to war across it with a sword made by Uncle Frank from a broken trowel and a stair-railing. On one side, next the cupboard, was the bed. Against the window was a little deal table with two "leaves," both sadly warped, and two chairs. On the right of the fireplace was the pine chest of drawers, containing Sunday clothes and uncle's treasures; and on the other, the coal-box, the water-can, and the wash-stand. Over the fireplace hung an illuminated scroll in red and gold lettering: "Presented to Mr. Reuben Battershell on the occasion of his leaving 'The Galloping Horses' as a token of esteem and respect in which he was held by his following friends"—and over the bed a coloured supplement on art paper showing Wilson Barret in *The Sign of the Cross.*

In the past Uncle Frank had been an innkeeper, but he was then gardener at a big house in Greenwich. It was always the Big House, and its owner, except in moments of petulance, The Lady. He still kept the signboard under the bed—"The Galloping Horses."—Reuben Battershell. Free House —and it served him as rosary in desolate hours.

"Hi, cock. Fetch out the ole signboard. Let's

'ave a look at 'er. Ha! That was a House, me boy. I wasn't touching me 'at to nobody then. No fear. I made that House, me boy. Got it cheap. It'd gone down. Doing nothing. In three months, me boy, I couldn't take the money fast enough."

"Why ain't you got it now, uncle?"

"Never you mind, me boy. As you get older you'll learn that there's ups and downs in everything. And no counting on 'em neither."

I loved Uncle Frank, and it hurts me to-day that I can only remember him as a shiftless figure of fun whom nobody for a moment took seriously. The farcical gestures alone remain—the nods, the winks, the finger at the nose, the rude words, the schoolboy foolery that sorted so ill with his short, round figure. I want to remember the other things —the years of service and companionship, the self-denial and care and thought. And I can't. I do not think of him sitting up with me all night through a sickness, and working all day and sitting up all the next night. I think of him treading on a rake in the garden and hurting his nose. I think of him falling downstairs over Miss Paske's cat. I think of him coming home one Bank Holiday wearing a long yellow nose. I see him halfway inside his Sunday shirt, swearing because he couldn't find the sleeve-holes. I see him always ludicrous in ludicrous situations, always laughing at himself, always facetious in serious moments. I want to think of him with reverence, but the moment I think of him I laugh, and then am ashamed. But perhaps it doesn't matter. Perhaps a laughing remembrance counts as high for his welfare as a solemn requiem.

I loved Poplar, too. It had rich company and kind streets and laughter, and ships and water. These things—a work of art and a work of nature—carry beauty and the feeling of adventure wherever they go. They lend colour to the people who have to do with them; and a wet day or a grey twilight is less troublous to the soul if brown sails, red funnels and great spars break up its melancholy. Over the wall of East India Dock lay the world. The world was even with us in the streets, for around the dock and on the point opposite the Tunnel gathered men from all the seven seas. The feeling of travel was always with us. There were ships' chandlers and junk shops and foreign sailors' homes, and the very newspaper shops displayed books on ships and navigation and signalling. Always there were movement and the light and space of neighbouring water, and the bells and whistles of departing ships, and grave-eyed sailors to light the poorest alley with the nobility of the sea and the strength of the human heart.

I say I was happy with Uncle Frank and the rough and gusty life of Carfax Street; but often there were those moments of restlessness known to all children—moments of mystery half-perceived—which I couldn't understand, and which I couldn't take to Uncle Frank. I divined that he would be beyond solving them, and would think I was ailing. It was then that I would escape down the road and wander in a street of no-time and no-place; a street of spices and golden apples, where men, dark or lemon-faced, wearing the raiment of pantomime, swam through the mist or held the walls in living statuary. There lived all wonder and dismay, and the rewards that come to us in dreams. What drew me to it I do not know, but I loved to be there, to touch shoulders with its shadows, or to stand at the window of Quong Lee filled with a Want that I could not name. I was out of the world of the common things that I knew, lost in a world to which I had no key; a world that, I felt even then, held, behind all its colour, something pale and cold and pitiless; the marble stupor of those who have lived a thousand years and have a thousand more to live, giving no revelation, but turned always inward, solitary and self-sufficient.

I could not, of course, shape it or say it to myself; I could only distress myself with the feeling, and loaf about the Causeway out of tune with myself and my pals of Carfax Street. Although I lived at the waterside, ships and the water had none of the interest for me they had for other boys. Even at ten years old I was interested more in people than in things. But, like all land creatures, I would often go down to it, and stand on the wharf for an hour, staring at the water and the boats, and wondering what it all meant and whether Quong Lee's shop-window would explain it.

And then, one evening, as I stood in the Causeway staring through his window at him, Quong Lee raised a hand and beckoned. For a moment or so I did not move. I was struck suddenly shy and apprehensive. Then he beckoned again, and I understood that he was inviting me in. This was the moment I had waited and wooed him for. Dare I? I would.

With a sense of desperate adventure, as of cutting myself off from the friendly world, I went in. He smiled. I smiled; though not easily: I was trembling. Then he turned in his seat behind the counter, opened a jar, speared in it with a wooden skewer, and held out to me a piece of ginger.

Again I hesitated; and in the moment of hesitating the thing happened. In that moment I knew a joy sharper than any I had known, and with it came a sense of time arrested and crystallised; a sense of eternity; a fancy that always, behind the curtain of time, this thing had been; that always Quong Lee had been sitting in that shop in that street; that for all time he had been holding out a piece of ginger and I had been standing before him, with the pins-and-needles of emotion in the back of my neck, holding out my hand to him. With it came, too, something more than joy; something that I know now was at once joy and knowledge and understanding and serenity. The Secret. I knew then all the beauty and all the evil of the heart of Asia; its cruelty, its grace and its wisdom. And I felt that whatever else might move or change, whatever comings and goings there might be, Quong Lee and I would not change. Always he would be sitting on a stool behind the counter of that shop, beckoning to me, and always I would be holding out my hand.

Then it was gone. I took the piece of ginger and

ate it, smiling from a full mouth, back in the world of time* and place; but a world with a difference. Something had happened to me; something beyond the fact that I had got into Quong Lee's shop; and I knew that shop-windows would never be the same again. I had achieved contact, and the Causeway would be for ever part of me. I had turned my first corner.

When I had eaten the ginger, grinning idiotically all the time, he beckoned me to come round the counter. I went; and he showed me his calculus, his bowl of ink, his writing-brushes, and the pad of flimsy paper on which he made out his bills. He showed me a green-and-yellow Buddha. He showed me a temple carved from six inches of ivory. He took down from the wall one of the many masks with which it was covered—flamboyant affairs of reds and blues and whites and golds—and put it over his face. He showed me prayer-papers and a joss and a pair of chop-sticks, and marvels of banners and pipes writhing with decoration.

And all the time I grinned, not knowing what it was all about or what I was supposed to do or say, or why I was invited in; but thrilled, wildly thrilled, and in love with this shrivelled old foreigner. We all laughed at foreigners then; Foreigners were so Funny, and none so Funny as the Chinkies. But though, with the others, I had laughed at them, I could not laugh at Quong Lee. I found in him— or put there—the essence of all the things I had felt or seen in the Causeway and in the water. I loved Uncle Frank, but I had never caught myself loving him. I loved him as I ate my breakfast or washed my neck. But this was different; this was sharp feeling. I felt that he had picked upon me, above all other boys, as worthy of his notice, and I wanted to do something for him, to cut a figure before him; to earn his esteem. But I just stood there, sizzling and grinning, until he speared another piece of ginger and pushed me to the door.

I ran home. I ran all the way home, and went straight indoors. But I didn't tell Uncle Frank or anybody about it Uncle Frank wouldn't have liked it, and I knew how the chaps would laugh and chi-ike me for chumming up with a silly old Chinky. So I kept quiet. The outer door of my secret world was half-open, and I must keep it so that I might slip in and out. I could not live in it; the life for me was the life of Carfax Street; the little ordinary things; but I hugged it as one hugs a hiding-place for one's special treasures which are too precious to be shared.

From those first few minutes with him my life changed, and his shop became my other home. The world was lit up. Until then I had seen things only as things. Now I saw life and meaning (though what meaning I did not know) in every common sight and object of the streets. Evening after evening I went there, looking through the window until I was invited in; and once in, I was free to roam about the place, to eat ginger, and to play with the writing-brushes, while he sat and smiled, or taught me how to write certain characters with the brushes—Courtesy, Kindness, Tranquillity. I

was ten; he was as old as the Mountains of the
Moon. And he was my friend. At no time was our
friendship demonstrative. Though child and man
may often talk seriously, on level terms, we could
not talk, for at that time he knew only the pidjin
of the shopkeeper's counter. Even later, when he
learned more words, he could never make a sentence; he would throw out four or five words, and I
had to make the sentence myself.

It was at my fourth visit, I think, that he suddenly coughed, "Huh!" and said: "Why you 'ere?"
When I understood the question I said: "I'm
lonely." I don't know why I said that. It wasn't
true. I had dozens of friends, young and grown up,
about Carfax Street. It was a silly thing to say, but
it came out; and his reply seemed to me even sillier.
He said: "Huh! All time you that. All time. One
time plenty people you. No can. All time that."

For twelve years, in all times of sorrow or perplexity, I went to him, and I was not lonely. While
talk was impossible, talk wasn't necessary. He
knew. A barren friendship, perhaps. It had nothing of service or sacrifice or common interest to en-
due it, or the casual fellowship of mutual minds,
mutual creeds, mutual race. He showed neither
pleasure nor irritation at seeing me, nor delight in
my company. If I came or stayed away, it was no
matter.

But for me it was richer than any friendship I
have since known. From every one of his silences
I took away something soothing and exhilarating.
I felt that while I was in that dusty, acrid shop

nothing could touch me; nothing could exalt or grieve. The world of blessings and bruises was beating around and against me, but its waters fell from me. I knew in that shop what some people seek in church and others seek in taverns. Those silences were glimpses; repetitions of that moment when he held out the ginger and I looked through his window as through the window of that Northern King. Every new life is moulded upon the pattern of the old. That pattern is a star whose points touch the outer rims; and it is in the passing of these points that we meet those moments that are our corners and know ourselves. That was the meaning of his friendship; through him I peeped and saw and understood the beauty and sorrow of things. He opened the outer door, and for one moment he showed me the inner door and gave me its key.

But I could not turn it. And though I have tried and tried, I never have turned it. Never has the magic of the artist guided my hand to help me to show what I knew in that moment when the ginger was held out to me.

CHAPTER II

POPLAR

IT seems that in those days, things were always happening. Life was a shower of coloured stars —Christmas Days, Sundays, Bank Holidays, tram-rides, 'bus-rides, Saturday-night shoppings, impulsive feasts, parties in the kitchen of the Lady's House, birthdays, big queer men coming to tea— always some burst of illumination; with, of course, the Board School and its playground steady through it all; myself moving by steps from first to the fifth standard; and outside it all, but touching it—Quong Lee. But now one day is much like another. There are no Treats, no reckless celebrations, no Golden Letter days. The very byways held then the flash and ring of heroic enterprise, into which one could dramatise oneself.

The Saturday-night shopping with uncle. First Chrisp Street and the breathless rivalry of the naptha'd stalls, and from far away the forlorn wail of "Sweet Lavender." Then the warbling traffic of the main road. Then Limehouse Church and Salmon Lane, where life was at full pitch, and into a burst of pageantry. Salmon Lane was all glow and cheer, marvellous with unknown people from unknown homes, and sweet faces, and schoolgirl

27

frocks and hair, that came from nowhere, passed, and vanished into nowhere. Commercial Road, dark and (then) almost shopless, menaced and invited with hints of its end in the strange, cold City; and the tangle of carts and cabs and 'buses at the cross-roads gave one the feeling of being at the heart of the world's business. But often I would go home with a feeling of mild despair at the thought that I could never, never get to know more than one here and there out of the millions of romantic figures that passed by.

Of the Board School, near Canton Street, where I got my earliest learning, I have only faint memories; but I made there the discovery that in any school playground there are just as many liars, thieves, swindlers, cowards, degenerates as there are in any adult community; and I could never understand why grown-ups treated us children with such sweetness and devotion. I was as good a liar as any of them when there was no other way of serving my occasions; and I managed to get a fair supply of pennies for sweets until Uncle Frank suddenly and markedly stopped leaving odd coppers in his Sunday coat. In the ordinary course I seldom possessed a whole penny. Halfpennies were the standard for children then, and if somebody at the "Barge Aground" did give me a penny, uncle took charge of it and doled it out in two coins. There were two sweet shops in our street, and each shop had its regular supporters, and these remained faithful to that shop with reasons for the faith that was in them.

"You go to ole Mother Pratt's. She gives good weight. Always lets the scale go down bang."

"I dunno so much. Morton's is best. They got all sorts o' things at Morton's. Pakwak, pop-corn, nuggets, 'ard-bake, nib-stick, locusts an' barbers' poles an' fig-toffee, an'—oo, all sorts o' things. She's only got two or three sorts."

"Ah, but ole Morton's so grumpy. An' 'e won't make a farden's worth. An' 'e won't give yeh time to choose. Ole Mother Pratt do. 'Sides, she throws in one or two other sweets sometimes— when she knows yeh."

"I don' care. I like Morton's. Lot to choose from there. An' better, too. My father says it's better, 'cos 'e on'y keeps Barrett's sweets. An' Barrett's sweets is Pure. It says so on the boxes."

But I stuck to Mother Pratt, and would spend a quarter of an hour at her window, and five minutes in the shop, laying out my halfpenny in a farthing's worth of this and a farthing's worth of that.

Of course, being poor, we suffered greatly at the hands of the Interferers and all those old women and earnest young men from the Universities who want to leave the world better than they found it. For such people the East End of London was their hunting-ground. No pious youth from college ever seemed to think of doing a little Settlement work in Curzon Street or Portman Square. Always it was the defenceless, voiceless poor who were the victims of the whims and theories of the educated; and what with the District Visitor, the Provident Visitor, the School Board man, the curate, the Infant Welfare Visitor, and the Settlement Worker, our homes were far more public than any public-house. In addition to the distresses incidental to our estate, we had to provide charity-fodder for earnest youths, pink from college and filled with zeal for our welfare. They hadn't the grace or the intelligence to perceive the impertinence of their intrusion in offering us spiritual enlightenment and social example. They did not know, or, if they knew, forgot that throughout the world it is the peasant class that sings and laughs and dances; aristocracy, social or intellectual, cannot sing or dance; cannot be expressive. There is something about culture that saddens and deadens, and the futility of these Social Workers in attempting to teach us how to be happy would have been amusing if it had not been exasperating.

The conditions under which some of my people lived were disgusting, but they carried some blessed armour that lifted them above their conditions. The more foul the environment, the more people will fight, the more they will laugh, and the greater is their capacity for joy in little things. We fought for beauty, for a kipper for tea, for a new pair of boots, for education, for a better job; our self-appointed teachers knew nothing of these battles. The courage and patience with which our people faced constant penury and distress, the grace of soul and the feeling for having things "nice" that persisted in the face of ugliness surely should have shown them that we should be the teachers and they the scholars.

It was the stupidity of these people that most angered Carfax Street. They were rich in commonsense, whose other name is fear. Impudently they would lecture us on how to run our homes, and lay out our money, and rear our babies; impertinently they would berate us for spending ten pounds on a wedding, or the whole of the insurance money on a funeral. They had not the finer sense to see that in this matter we were artists feeling for the light. These are the wooden minds that berate the artist for wasting his time in painting pictures that don't sell, or composing music, or writing lyrics while they might be earning round sums in business. Why does he do it? they ask. What's the good of it? How much better off is he? What has he got to show for it? Well, God knows, and a few people on earth know why the artist starves himself for the joy of painting; why the poet writes poetry that doesn't pay; why the composer continues to compose though he is never performed; why poor people will go short for a month in payment for the one golden moment of the full-dressed wedding; why men try to swing Indian clubs for a hundred hours. The spiritual force behind each of them is the same force—a force which commonsense will never know, or, if it did know, would profane.

My sharpest recollections are of meals. Dinner I took, after morning school, with Mrs. Lazenby in her kitchen. Uncle had his at the Big House, sent out from the kitchen to the potting-shed. Breakfast and tea we had together. Uncle got the breakfast and the six o'clock tea—cocoa and bread and dripping—and if, after school, I couldn't wait till six, there was usually a bag of Broken Mixed biscuits from which I was served by Mrs. Lazenby, or a slice of cake from Miss Paske, the upstairs-front lodger. Saturday tea was a Meal, dressed with a kipper or bloater, saveloy or faggot, or trotter; and in winter we could make toast at the fire, and, by shifting the table three inches forward, have it all snug and pretend we were the Swiss Family Robinson round the camp-fire. I remember now that the things I specially liked—bloaters and kippers— didn't agree with Uncle; he never "fancied" them, and I had to eat his portion.

Sunday afternoon in summer meant a blow on the tram or 'bus through the City or down Burdett Road; and sometimes a grand two-penn'orth on the Thames steamers. Every Sunday had its surprise.

"Where we goin' this Sunday, uncle?"

"Vernon 'Ill, cock."

"Where's that?"

"Cuh—long way out. Further 'n Barking."

"What we going there for?"

"That's where the murder was lars week."

"Murder? Ooh!"

"Ar. Killed an ole man, they did. Broke into 'is 'ouse an' 'it 'im on the 'ead till 'e was done in. A shocking murder, me boy. An awful murder. One o' those murders that make yeh wonder what the world's coming to. Almost too 'orrible to read about. A murder like that ought never to a-bin committed."

"We going to see where they done it?"

POPLAR   33

"We'll be able to 'ave a look at it outside, I
dessay.   Mister an' Missis Gossick is comin', an'
Mister Fremantle.   Be a nice little trip if it's a fine
day."

That Sunday afternoon remains as a spot of horror.   Mr. Fremantle, the green-grocer, was in good
form.   Crime was his hobby, and his reconstruction
of this atrocity, step by step, the methods employed
by the criminals, the awakening of the victim, the
meeting, the assault, the escape, the probable course
taken by the men—this recital turned the London
through which we rode into a city of monsters.
Every street down which I looked, every window of
every house seemed to harbour murderers.   This
thing that had happened once might happen again
anywhere.   And when at last we took train and, after
long travel, got out at some station whose name I
did not discover, the platform and the porters looked
as though they had something to do with it.

Vernon Hill itself was no ordinary London hill;
it was a hill at the world's end, but just within the
world, fit, I felt, for just such horrors as Mr. Fremantle had depicted.   It had murder in its very
shape.   When we came to the house, a commonplace
large villa, and stood with a crowd of cyclists and
walkers looking at it, it seemed to my heated fancy
to have been made for what had happened.   It held
the sense of sin that I have always felt in woods and
hills and Nature's solitudes; and I saw that sunlight
in a flower-garden can hold all the terror of murder
at midnight.   What with Mr. Fremantle's descrip-
tion and the pictures of crime that I had seen

in the *Police Budget,* which was displayed with
the middle pages open in the windows of newspaper
shops, I could see the business in action. I made
my own portraits of the men, and saw them running
through the garden. From the *Police Budget,* I
knew just how murderers stood when murdering or
escaping—in heroic pose, body flung forward, limbs
extended, faces distorted; and always they wore
caps, pulled down over the ears, and mufflers.

I saw it all. I did not dream about it that night,
but for weeks afterwards it lived with me; and even
to-day, when walking through Vernon Hill, I am
sensible of un-ease, of something twisted about
Vernon Hill; that, though it looks like any other
suburb, it is not; it lives with something dreadful;
not with supernatural horror, but with the stronger
horror of this world.

.   .   .   .

Sunday evenings of winter I went with uncle to
the parlour of "The Barge Aground," and was fed
with lemonade and heart-cakes, and fussed by the
company. I sat among big men, big tables, and
big chairs. The giant of them was Mr. Sturt, the
landlord, who was always my friend.

"Well, cocky, 'ow yeh comin' up? Woddud yeh
do with a nice 'eart-cake—eh?"

"Find a good 'ome for it, sir." I was always
taught by uncle to "speak up," but I have never
since been able to do it.

"That's the style, young 'un. I reckon 'e'll git
on, Uncle Frank. No flies on 'im—eh?"

"Ar. I 'ope 'e will. 'E's got a 'ead on 'im."

"What yeh goin' to do with 'im?"

" 'E's goin' ta be in the City, ain't yeh, cocky? An' make money an' be a young genterman."

"Yes, uncle. An' 'ave a 'ouse like the Big One at Greenwich. An' a gardener of our own."

"Strewth! 'E ain't modest, is 'e?"

Mr. Sturt blew from his Sunday Ecclenzia. "Ah, don't do to be too modest these days. Push and Go. That's what you want these days. I dunno, though. . . . Don't seem to be much of it in the young 'uns to-day. Billiards and football is all they thinks of now. An' music-'alls. An' 'ow to do least work for their money. Look at my pot-man—third in a month. Just *won't* work. Don't seem to *want* to get on. No Go in 'im. Give me the old 'uns fer Work. Wodder yew say, Uncle Frank?"

"Ar. Between you an' I, they dunno what work is to-day. I didn't keep 'The Gallopin' 'Orses' without findin' what Work is. Up at ar-pars four, pullin' up the pints fer the 'arvesters; an' never in bed 'fore twelve. On the go all day."

The parlour—called The Wheelhouse—was reserved always for the "reg'lars"—an assorted company held together by Mr. Sturt, who mixed the power of the policeman with the tact of the skilled chairman. Each had his accustomed seat, and each as he came in rumpled my cap as a mark of fellowship. In the far corner sat an elderly fellow, of seared face, who played the double-bass at the local hall, with a young man who played the drums. They never addressed each other, seldom spoke;

but they were inseparable; sat together, took the same drink, the same number of drinks, came in and went out together, silent and content. Round the wall sat Mr. Fremantle, the life and soul of the party, first in and last out, beaming upon the world, taking insult or sarcasm friendly-wise, and expounding criminology, whether he was listened to or not. Next him an engineer from the docks with hands as hairy as his face; then Uncle Frank and myself, and by the door the police-station house-keeper, a giant of five feet eleven, once a seaman, who fed me with wonderful lies about India and the Pacific.

At eight o'clock The Wheelhouse was at work.

"Read what the Bishop o' London said the other day about pubs, Mister Gassler?"

"Ah. I did."

"What yeh think of it?"

"Think of it? If you arst me, 'e dunno what 'e's talkin' about. If a man can't worship God and try to live like Christ without going into a church, 'is worship ain't up to much. I look at it like this— you can worship God just as much in the street or in yer bedroom as you can in any o' these churches. They're shows—that's what they are. It's a job— and for the high-up ones it's a dam well-paid job, too. Don't they charge money for the best seats— just like in a theatre? What do yew say about it, Uncle Frank?"

"Well, Mister Gassler, my views is pretty much yours. I look at it this way—if Jesus Christ come back to-day, would 'E or would 'E not be above

comin' in and 'avin' one with us in The Wheelhouse?
Eh? I'll bet ten to one 'E wouldn't. But the
Bishop—if 'e come in, 'e'd come in with a sort of
pretendin' to be one of us, but all the time not doin'
it properly. And as fer sittin' in a stuffy church
on a fine Sunday—I say any feller potterin' round
'is back garden an' lookin' after his flowers is doin'
'isself and other people a dam sight more good'n
what 'e would do in church. Nobody can't look
after a garden and not feel—well, you know, feel
better, like. A garden makes yeh think. Eh,
Mister Sturt?"

"I reckon you're right, Uncle Frank. What I
say is—as long as you live clean and don't do no
'arm to other people, you won't 'ave a very black
mark against yeh. As the book says—in love and
charity with all men. Church ain't got nothin' to
do with livin' clean an' payin' yer way an' doing as
you'd be done by. Between you and me—I mean,
between you and I, there's plenty o' people that
'aven't got any religion at all, and they lives as
straight as them what goes to church. Why, sometimes, when I've closed up, ar-pars twelve, I go out
for a bit of a stroll, an' when you look up at the
stars, an' everything all round you all quiet—an'
the river—an'—an' you know—(Hi, miss! Your
Jug Bar there. People waitin'. An' swab yer
counters down. Let's 'ave things as they should
be.) As I was sayin', if a feller can't feel anything
then, 'e won't feel it listening to some feller from
college tellin' you what 'e thinks about the Bible.
Why, even in this bar, while we're all friendly, and

not speakin' against our neighbours, but sittin' 'ere
sociable—what does the Book say?—Where two
or three are gathered together. It don't say where
they're gathered. As I see it, it means that when
men get together, peaceable and friendly, wishin'
each other well, that's just the same as any prayer-
meetin'. Dammit, gel, will yeh swab that counter
down?"

Through all this I sat silent, feet dangling, eyes
wide, mouth open, head going from right to left as
the debate moved. What the debate was all about
I did not know, and was puzzled that such magnificent men could be interested in such argument. But
when the station housekeeper talked of the doings
in the Causeway, I was so entrapped that some of
his stories I could recount to this day, word for
word, pause for pause, as they came from his lips.

Once or twice the meeting-place for Uncle and
the boys was changed, and I was taken to the bar
that is known and talked about in every port in
the world. I liked it better than "The Barge
Aground"; it had more movement and colour.
There were stuffed birds, marvellously winged.
There were banners and spears and arrows from
the Islands, poison-darts from Burmah, strange
animals and fishes from Borneo and Java; and
there were Malays and Indians and West Indians
and sad-faced men from East Africa, and women
and young girls from the streets around, and solemn
English seamen who had not a trace of the Bank-
Holiday creature which my picture-books presented
as Jack Tar. And sometimes there was music; the

famous concertina was brought out, and I sat shivering to soulful renderings of "Men of Harlech" or "Home Sweet Home."

Sometimes Uncle Frank's friends came round to tea in Carfax Street; but never more than two at a time; with four people in the room one couldn't stretch one's feet out. Some I liked. Others . . . There was a man named Gassler, who came round to play draughts with uncle. Gassler wasn't fat, but he brought with him a feeling of fat and damp. He said he liked little boys, and he messed me with Sunday-School-teacher embraces, and tried to get me to call him Uncle Gassler, which I never did. He had a reputation in the chapel set as good company, and told the sort of roguish story that clergymen tell—only at greater length. Just as I would take a piece of toffee out of my mouth, and put it aside for a minute to make it last longer, so Gassler with his stories; and all through the stories he'd be messing me about until, by tugs and writhes, I escaped from him. Uncle Frank always covered my retreats from him, and if Mr. Gassler hadn't been a draughts-player, I don't think uncle would have had him in the room.

"Ah, there's my Stanley-boy. Come an' give Uncle Gassler a kiss. And who was the little boy I see in the Causeway the other night—eh? Little boys oughtn't to go into the Causeway at night. All sorts of things might 'appen to 'em there. I knew a little boy once that the Chinks got 'old of, and—ah! . . . I'll tell yeh something."

He told us a horrid story; but I knew it was true.

Others beside the station housekeeper knew things. Always there were whisperings, warnings, about that bright and bitter quarter. Knife-fights I had seen, and gaming-house raids, and police encounters, and black-and-yellow battles, and girls going into the backs of the shops late at night. But there were rumours of women, of killings. There was the night when a girl from Carfax Street was found under the arches dead; and a Malay stoker, John Ram Boona, was charged at Thames with murder, and hanged. There was the night when two Chinese were found dead on the doorstep of an English skipper, and nobody ever knew how they died or why they were on his doorstep. There was a second-mate who one night walked out of the "Ship in Port," was seen crossing the road, and never was seen again. There was little Mary Rusper, who ran away from home and lived with the Chinese for two years before she was found leading the life of a king's favourite. There was Sway Foo, who was put to sleep in Narrow Street by a maddened father. There was Lily Marshall, in the seventh standard of our school, who went off to Cyprus with a black man. Open talk was made among us boys of the opium and other joints, and the things that men and women did there. Once a big boy, who had just left school, took me round to the back of one of these places, and showed me how to climb up a gutter-pipe to the first floor, and look through a crack in the shutter. This same boy had an elder brother, who worked on the Island, and this dashing fellow had been pointed out to me, with, "My brother. 'E goes to the Causeway two'r three nights a week an' *smokes!*"

But whatever stories came to my ears, and though I listened with frightful care, I accepted them as things that were true about other Chinese, but unthinkable about Quong Lee. They made no difference to my feeling towards him, and did not once interrupt my visits to the Causeway.

The double-bass, Mr. Creegan, was a regular visitor, and came every alternate Sunday. He was serious and proud, and one felt that he was entirely good. Uncle said he was a Gentleman Born. He played in a shabby hall near the East India Dock, and had spent his life playing in shabby halls. But he brought dignity to his shabby calling, and had the air of one who has moved among great things— though he had moved only from music-hall to music-hall, and from one back room to another back room. From him I had tentative lessons on the violin; and when Uncle Frank asked: "What good's that goin' to be to 'im?" Creegan said: "No harm in it. And there might be. . . ." He never explained what there might be, but I felt, with some gratification, that he took me seriously. He talked, not facetiously or soapily, as other visitors talked, but as man to man. About books and music and things. But I wasn't awake to them, and he never moved me, as the wordless Quong Lee moved me. He inspired admiration, but nothing else.

What these two derelicts—the Gentleman Born, stored with fine books and musical scholarship, and the ex-publican and gardener—found in each other, one cannot say.   But Creegan came regularly and seemed happy in talking with uncle and with me. Among the insecure these incongruous friendships persist.   The settled and comfortable give care and thought to their choice of friends, picking from their own sort, and their range is limited; the wanderers take them as and where they find them.

Creegan was tall and swarthy, with fierce eyebrows.   An hour after he had shaved he looked as though he hadn't.   He rolled in his walk.   He wore always a long, ragged overcoat, a wide-brimmed, soft hat, and a Gladstone collar; the sort of figure one saw hanging about Wellington Street and the Strand a few years ago.   He talked in gasps, and his voice tingled and rumbled.

After each visit had ended uncle sat chuckling.

"Way that feller talks . . . Very interestin', though.   Very interestin'.   But wi' me it's in one ear and outa the other.   What was all that 'e was sayin' about waterfalls?"

"Why, 'e said that listening to the music of Mo—— Mo-something-or-other, was like standin' in a wood in the summer listenin' to waterfalls what you couldn't see."

"Eh?   What's waterfalls got to do with music?"

"I dunno, uncle.   That's what 'e said, though."

"An' what's it mean, anyway?"

"I dunno."

"Taa!   'E got that outa some book, I reckon. 'E's a rum 'un, 'e is."

It was with Creegan that I saw my first music-
hall.

Great stuff!

The crowds of people coming in. The babble
and parade. The glow of the lights on the golden
fittings. The blue curtain, charged with wonder,
and inscrutable. The smell of oranges and scent
and shag. The uprush of the curtain.

Above my head—I sat with Creegan—magnificent creatures pranced and pranked and glittered.
At my side Creegan's great instrument surged and
throbbed to the order of his wrist. Here was
another window, showing me another new world,
peopled with bright beings as alien to our shabby
streets as the Queen herself. How glorious to
stand up there in public view, radiantly at ease, for
the envy and delight of those pale people in front!
That night I did dream when at last I could sleep.

Mr. Creegan delivered me to Carfax Street some
time past midnight. Uncle Frank was sitting up
for me.

"Well, cock, 'ow d'yeh like it?"

"Oo, uncle! Oo, there was a man come on
dressed up like a tramp, an' sung a song about 'is
wife who was alwis eatin' biscuits in bed, an' a Lady
come on all pearls an' di'monds an' things an' sung
a song—I don't remember all of it, but at the end
of each bit she sung, 'Come, Fly With Me Over
the Sea,' an' ooh! another lady come on dressed
like a coster, with a barrer of geraniums, just like
Mrs. Grayson what keeps the fish-stall top of
Salmon Lane, an' sung a song—I can't remember

all of it, but with a tune like this . . . an' finished
up with 'Three Pots a Shilling,' an' a man come
on—Mr. Creegan said it was a man—dressed like
the lady at Greenwich—grey 'air an' cap an' lace
dress, an' says she's the Angel from Islington, an'
'avin' a Devil of a Time, an' said, 'Chase me, boys,'
an' then a gentleman come on in evening dress an'
sung a lovely song about a skylark, an' then there
come on two men all dressed in silver and did tricks
an' caught each other on their necks an' . . ."

"Strewth, cocky, you got a memory. Now when
I come out of a music-'all it's all gorn direckly I
get out."

Every evening, after a wash, uncle went out for
a walk with one or other of his pals, leaving me to
do my home-work, and then go out on my own until
half-past eight. Usually being "out" meant mar-
bles or tops or cherry-oggs or jump-the-wagger at
the corner, but when those unaccountable moods
came upon me, these things lost their zest, and I
turned to my other world across the street, and in
that shop I forgot half-past eight, and there was a
Jaw. But Jaws were common things. The house
was full of them day and night. Our Mr. and
Mrs. Lazenby downstairs quarrelled as less salted
spirits converse. Life, for them, was a string of
Mafeking nights, and the earnest Workers who
pitied them and strove to bring them to live in
amity would have flatly disbelieved anybody who
told them that their days were full of joy. Mrs.
Lazenby had five children, all "out in the world."
Lazenby worked when he would, and at other times

played the flute, whose melancholy tones went well with his spare face and figure. The flute was at once the cause of most of the rows, and his solace after a row. Nothing jarred him. Enamel sauce-pans aimed at his head, boots, brushes, house-flannels—all these things he dodged impassively, only asking why the hell they couldn't live like other people.

There came an August Bank Holiday when both husband and wife showed their quality. The row started in the street, when one of the married sons tackled his father, in full publicity, about his "goings-on." I was playing at the corner when it began, and soon we boys were in the audience, and picked up the story.

"You talk to yer father like that?"

"Talk like that? 'Ow should I talk? 'Tain't respeckful to mother. Way you go on. *I* saw yeh, Treatin' them two women in 'The Stag.' An' I'll see she knows about it, too."

"Oh, will yeh?"

"Yes, I will."

"Oh? Yeh will? You bin drinkin', ain't yeh?"

"No, I ain't. I don't take after me father. I know what I see. An' everybody else knows about it. Talk about it, they do. You took one of 'em to 'The Queen's' th' other night. Goin' about with women. Draggin' our name down. Mother's gointa know about this. To-night, too."

"Look 'ere, Artie, don't you be a fool. It's a long time since I give you a 'idin', but . . ."

"You give me a 'idin'? *You!* I'd like to see

yeh try it. Go on. Try it. That's all. Try it.
If there's anybody arstin' fer a 'idin', it's . . ."

There was a smack on Artie's cheek that rang
down the road. Then they closed. They wrestled
—into the gutter, against the wall, through the
door. For three minutes we heard crash and bump,
clatter and ring, the fall of china, and hot words.
Then somebody in the crowd saw the matter seriously.

"They'll be murderin' each other. 'Ere, Jenny,
I see Missis Lazenby in Mason's, up the road.
Run an' tell 'er—quick."

Jenny ran, and in two minutes Mrs. Lazenby
arrived. She went indoors, and we waited. But
she was scarcely gone before father and son came
tumbling out, feeling at their necks, panting, and
Mrs. Lazenby followed them.

"I'd like to know what next? Father an' son
goin' on like this. An' me just cleaned up the
kitchen an' all."

"Well, it's 'im."

"What's 'im?"

"The way 'e treats you. 'E goes about with
other women. 'E treats 'em in 'The Stag.' Takes
'em to 'The Queen's.' An'—an'——"

"Well?"

"Well, I ain't goin' to 'ave it. I ain't goin' to
stand by an' see you treated like nothin'."

Mrs. Lazenby ran a finger under her nose, and
jerked her head. "Artie, you're a good boy, but
I wish to Christ you'd mind yer own business. I
ain't lived with yer farver forty years without

learnin' something about men. If you ain't never
no worse'n 'im, you won't 'ave much to worry
about."

"Yes, but 'e goes with women!"

"Gawd, boy! Think I'm blind? Think I don't
know yer farver? Know 'im a dam sight better'n
you do. Now 'fore you go 'ome, you just set to
and put me kitchen straight. All this fuss. After
I just cleaned it an' all."

In The Wheelhouse of "The Barge Aground"
that evening—Bank Holiday counting as Sunday—
I told the story in gasps to Uncle Frank and one
or two listeners. A few minutes later Lazenby
came in, and Mr. Sturt greeted him.

"Evenin', Mr. Lazenby. 'Ad a good Bank
'Oliday?"

"Oh, just the usual, y'know. Quiet."

Every evening, on his return from his walk,
Uncle Frank would make a recital of his adven-
tures, and for me he could invest a walk to the Iron
Bridge with the quality of a grand tour.

"Where ya bin, uncle?"

"Ark a mo. Lemme git me pipe on. . . . Ah.
. . . Well, first me an' Mister Gossick took a bit
of a stroll to Canning Town, to 'ave a look at the
new bridge. Thousands o' people there. Thousands. Fine thing it'll be when it's ready. Then
we 'ad a ride back as fur as the Church. Thousands o' people round the shops. We 'ad a look
in the Penny Bazaar. Wonderful things, them
Penny Bazaars. Wish they'd 'ad 'em when I was
a lad. The things they got there fer a penny. . . .

Everything you can think of, pretty near. Makes yer wonder 'ow they can do it. The big grocer's there—Hackett's—they got a silor boy in their winder—all made out o' sugar. Wonderful bit o' work. You'll have to go an' 'ave a look at it t'morrer. An' Biddle an' Mallom's, they got one o' their winders furnished just like a lady's drawin' room. Everything there—even the flowers—an' the right flowers, too. You'd almost think you was lookin' into some one's private 'ouse. Strordnary 'ow they git things up nowadays. I dunno 'ow they think of 'em. Give us a light. . . . Well, then we stopped at 'The Star,' an' outside 'The Star' there was a organ and a feller singing. Fine voice 'e 'ad, too, an' very pretty thing 'e was singin'. Don't know what it was, though. We stopped an' 'eard 'im fer a bit, until 'e come round collectin'. Then we went inside, an' who d'yeh think was inside?"

"I dunno."

"Mister Creegan. Just 'avin' a quick one 'fore 'e went in to work. We 'ad a word or two with 'im. Then 'e 'ad to go, an' 'e 'adn't bin gorn a minute 'fore—who d'ya think come in?"

"I dunno, uncle!"

"Mister Sturt!"

"Mister Sturt?"

"Ar. Mister Sturt. Just takin' 'alf an hour off. An' 'e arst us both if we'd do 'im the pleasure of 'avin one with 'im."

"An' did you?"

"Damme, boy, use yer wits. Doncher know
manners? When a genterman arst you. . . ."

"An' after that?"

"Well, after that, we come out an' 'ad another
bit of a stroll, and meets Mr. Conelly. Just come
orf 'is boat. Berthed four o'clock. West India
South. Got a lovely couple o' lobsters with 'im,
'e 'ad. Knocked 'em orf at Gravesend."

"What's a lobster like?"

"One o' these nights, p'raps you shall 'ave a
lobster fer supper. When the old devil gives me
a rise, an' Lord knows when that'll be. Well, then
we calls in the chemist's to git some cough mixture
for Missis Gossick, an' then we stopped at the
corner o' Wade Street, 'cos there was a cockle stall
there. No—cockles ain't good fer young 'uns.
Keep y'awake all night. Well, we 'ad a saucer
each, an' very nice, an' then I called in at Monk-
well's to see what about that load o' gravel they
was sending over to Greenwich, fer the 'ouse, and
give 'im a bit o' my mind, and told 'em where they
could put it if I didn't get it t'morrer. 'Anging up
my work fer two days. The feller didn't arf go
red. Oh, an' there's a noo shop opened at the
corner o' Wisbey Street—grocer's—an' they give a
packet o' biscuits with every 'alf-pound o' tea. So
as we're wanting some, I bought 'alf a pound, an'
there's yer packet o' biscuits, an' don't say yer uncle
don't think of yeh.

"Now eat yer biscuits an' say yer prayers an'
wash yer 'ands an' git to bed. I'll just toddle

across to 'The Barge' an' see 'ow Mister Clayton's gettin' on wi' them cuttings I give 'im."

Although I went to bed at nine o'clock, I was usually awakened by uncle's return, and lay awake for half an hour listening to the night-sounds of the world outside. From downstairs, a *gnurr-gnurr-gnurr* of low-toned argument; the chucking-out of "The Barge Aground"; wordy flourishes silenced by Mr. Sturt; the grind and scream of the docks station; the rumble of late 'buses; the hooting of boats going out; whistles and wails; the ring of running chains; voices crying; sometimes a stampede of boots; ending always in the homeward march of the younger revellers from the hall, with mouth-organ or concertina. Down the middle of the road they went with concerted numbers or choruses, colouring the alleys with song and filling me with a sentimental desire to weep. You do not hear it now—that march and song—floating bodiless out of the night. To-day we live under the curse of the negative. Those orderly lads with their concertina and their rhythmic feet, moved to music by the solemnity of the stars, are now labelled disorderly. It seems that the more democratic we grow the more we try to conform to nurse's idea of the Little Gentleman, and pay tribute to gentility's god—Restraint.

In those days I knew nothing of the thing. I was a vagabond, content with vagabondage, and despite the Vicar's and the Greenwich Lady's opinions about Uncle Frank's fitness for the charge of a growing child, Uncle Frank let me alone and so made me happy. He didn't worry much about my soul, but certain rough moral instruction he did instil, accompanying his precepts with ribald, and sometimes indecent, anecdote.

"Teacher said, uncle, that you always git what you want if you want it 'ard enough. But that ain't true, is it? Else we wouldn't be poor. We'd 'ave a house."

"It is and it ain't, me boy. Ya see, what you want ain't always good for ya, and if ya keep on wantin' and prayin', an' don't get it you can depend you ain't meant to 'ave it. Or else when ya do git it, it ain't what you thought it was. Look at Missis Spurling. Always prayin' to God to send 'er a pianner fer 'er daughter, 'cos the people upstairs 'ad got one, and was swankin' about it. 'E did, too. It come through the upstair floorin', which was on'y plaster, just as she was undressin' an' sent 'er ass-over-tip through the door."

When I got to know the Lady at the Big House at Greenwich, I found her teaching of somewhat severer form. After my first appearance at a kitchen tea, she began to Take An Interest in me. I had learned from uncle that one must submit to these people, so I played up to her. I was "good" at religious knowledge and had a memory. Quick to see what line of conduct caught on, I stored myself with texts, and being able to bring up half a dozen whenever called upon, I gained a character for spiritual grace and turned it to account.

"Now, look 'ere," said uncle, before we started for the first tea. "First thing she'll do to yeh is to ask for a tex'. An' you better be careful what sort o' tex'. Something out o' the New Testament is best. Now s'pose I'm the lady. I send for yeh. See? Hopkins, the parlour-maid, brings you in. Whadder you do? You don' say nothin'. You wait fer 'er to speak. But you bow. Put yer 'and to yer forrard and bring it down—slow. See? Like this. Then you wait till she tells you to come nearer. Most likely she'll say, 'What lesson in school d'you like best?' You say Scripture—quick. See? An' then she'll say—I wonder if you can repeat a Tex' from St. John. An' then you out with it. There's nothing to giggle at. This is serious. If she takes a fancy to yeh . . . why, when the time comes fer you to start in the City, she could do a lot for yeh. Git you into a bank, p'raps."

Certainly the lady knew how to do things, or those teas wouldn't lie so pink in my memory. The summer teas were served in the garden, and lasted from four o'clock until eight. On these occasions dinner was cancelled so that the servants might be free to attend their guests. Cook made special cakes, and there were strawberries and cream, and cherries and biscuits, and jam and Swiss Roll, and ices. After tea we children said our texts to the lady, and then there were bats and balls for the boys, and skipping-ropes for the girls, and the garden was given over to us. Never since then have strawberries held such luscious flavour, flowers such sharp colour, new-mown grass such fragrance. Bread no longer tastes piquant; the smell of milk and the perfume of roses are not what they were.

I had no feeling about that Big House then. Its cool elegance, the whisper of silk dresses that was its voice, and its creatures of comfort and convention, who seemed never tired, but always at level pulse, as though life were one long June afternoon —these were as much beyond my experience as the stars; and I neither envied nor questioned.

At Christmas, tea was served in the kitchen— fire glowing, dish-covers gleaming, the air dressed with odours of sauce and savoury, and the table with crumpets and jam-tarts and toast and crackers, with the tea-party spirit and best clothes to point it all. After the visitors, young and old, had been in to see the lady and receive their Christmas presents (bound volumes of *The Cottager and Artisan* and *The Friendly Gleaner*) we pulled crackers and sang carols, and Uncle Frank asked decorous riddles and (following precautions that the door between Up and Down was firmly closed) another boy and I sang comic songs.

And then the journey home by the ferry to the Isle of Dogs, and across the Island, thick with funnels and masts and high walls and flares; and lonely patches that looked lonelier under the light of a single lamp. After my first tea I found that I had made a hit. "You spoke up fine, cocky," said uncle. "I could see she was pleased with yeh. 'Tisn't orfen any o' the kids can manage more'n two tex'. What did she arst y'about?"

"Asked me what church we went to."

"And woddid you say?"

"Said sometimes one, sometimes another."

"Taa! 'Er and 'er church. She can stick 'er church . . ."

"Uncle!"

"Well, it makes yeh wild. Look what church does fer 'er. Nice old cup o' tea, she is. Makes 'er 'ard on everybody what don't do like she does. Grr! It makes yeh say things you wouldn't say. Comes to me when I'm at work and arsts me if I remember what The Book says about gardens. That's why I keep a Bible in the pottin'-shed. She thinks I read it in me dinner-hour, an' it keeps me the right way up with 'er."

"But isn't that deceivin', uncle?"

"Well, an' whose fault is it? Eh? Let 'er ketch me sittin' in the pottin' shed readin' the Bible when I oughta be workin' fer 'er. . . . My Gawd, there'd be a rumpus! It's people like 'er makes people ippacrits. If we was honest nobody'd ever git a job with that sort. If she knew I went to the 'Barge' she'd put me orf to'morrer. An' if she knew I ever kep' a house of me own. . . . But there—you mustn't go thinkin' disrespectful of 'er. After all, she's a Lady. I s'pose she's got a right to be a bit funny if it amuses 'er. An' now you better git orf to bed, 'cos you'll 'ave another late night t'morrer."

"T'morrer? Another party, uncle?"

"No—not a party, exackly. Just a bit of a treat. It's Derby Day t'morrer. The races down at Epsom. Me an' Mister Gassler are goin' fer a ride down as fur as 'The Elephant.' If you be'ave yesself, you'll come, too. Then you'll see what Derby night is."

I did see.   Derby night in South London, in the
days of the horse, was as high a festival as Christmas
or Easter Monday.   Then the world came out, old
and young, to line the main road from Newington
to Tooting, and cheer the homeward procession and
make robust frolic; and the procession played up
to its massed audience with grotesque equipment
and insane song and music.   It was an impromptu
pageant that marshalled itself in successive schemes
of interest whose climax was never reached.
Clowns, niggers, dudes, costers, harlequins, pierrots,
dust-men, and red-robed devils filled South London
with all the popular choruses on cornet, concertina,
tin-whistle, coach-horn, clarinet, accordion, fiddle,
"bones," guitar, ocarina, mouth-organ and jew's-
harp.   Along the road came four-in-hands, donkey-
barrows, victorias, hansoms, drays, lorries, waggon-
ettes, milk-floats, governess-carts, dog-carts, each
ablaze with flags and bunting and streamers; cab
horses wearing women's hats, donkeys' fore-legs
in trousers, and everybody out of his right mind.
Only those vehicles containing the bookmakers were
out of the scheme.   Bookmakers have this much of
aristocracy—they betray neither victory nor defeat.

There, in that carnival, was revealed the majesty
of civilisation.   I have often wondered what Quong
Lee would have thought if he had seen it, and
measured the white man's guffaw against the cold
grace of festival in his own benighted country;
western wealth against the poorest dragon-bearer.

And the audience, and the squirts and the ticklers,
and the blow-outs and the rattlers and the squeakers

and the monkey-nuts and the confetti and the coloured ribbons and the air-balloons—the fluttering
hair—the bold eyes—the audacious hats and flying
frocks, and the Things Said. . . .

.   .   .   .

All the time, behind this day-to-day life of Carfax
Street and the Big House and school and Cockney
outings, there was that other life—the street across
the way, that queer shop and that queer old man
from Abroad. It was a life of the spirit, without
event; yet every hour spent there was a shining
hour, more charged, it seemed, with movement
than the life of events. It was all outside my experience or understanding, but I could feel the
movement; and when there I was consciously *awake*
and sure of myself. Through the shifting world of
fact around me—boys leaving school, uncle's friends
moving away, old friends reappearing—it stood still,
the fixed star. And when my world went to pieces,
I comforted myself with the knowledge that that
street of unknown people, my city of escape, was and
would be there. When Authority had done with me
and allowed me to come back I should find Carfax
Street still there; but the faces I knew would be gone,
and the doorways and windows would hold strange
faces, and Carfax Street would be one of thousands
of streets with nothing to say to me. But because
all faces but one in the Causeway were unknown,
their passing would not change the street at all, and
I should always find the perfume I had left.

.   .   .   .

With my success at "Tex," I was quickly made

free of the Big House, and on Saturday mornings I
was allowed to help Uncle Frank in the garden.
My fourteenth chapter of St. John (word-perfect)
knocked the Upstairs, and my comic songs won the
Downstairs. The lady learned that I liked reading,
and strengthened my literary taste with *Christie's
Old Organ, Jessica's First Prayer,* and *Alone in
London.* Cook fed me with snacks from the oven;
the kitchen-maid wavered between mother and
sweetheart, and parlour-maid treated me in her
pantry with luxuries from the dining-room. In that
kitchen, clean as a nun's cell, and stressing the nun-
nery spirit with its severely framed texts, I spent
many cheerful hours, helping cook with the vegetables, marvelling at the skill and delicacy of her
stout hands, and at the exquisite business that went
to preparing anything that Gentlefolks were to eat.

I had my dinner with Uncle Frank in the potting-
shed. We sat on upturned baskets, I in the shirt-
sleeves of work, Uncle also in shirt-sleeves, battered
straw hat and green apron. After dinner I was sure
to find something waiting in the pantry. Most
clearly I remember asparagus. The very sound of
the word was rich: even to-day it is associated in
my mind with Society, Big Houses, Late Dinner,
Evening Dress; and I remember that the first time
I had a sovereign of my own (when I was about
nineteen) I went to a restaurant where asparagus
was to be had, and lunched on asparagus and roll-
and-butter and came out a millionaire.

In the parlour-maid's pantry I learnt much of
Manners. Until then my ideas of good behaviour

were woolly; the one clear thing was that everything I did was wrong. All Uncle Frank's friends
had offered instructions in the matter. All were
anxious to see me grow up a little gentleman; but
their counsel was conflicting.

"Y'know, Cook, I want to bring 'im up polite
and nice-be'aved. I want 'im to—hi! yeh little
snipe, ain't I told you to *break* yer bread, an' not
bite it."

But Miss Paske, on the first-floor front, always
assured me that ladies *cut* their bread and butter;
they didn't pull it in two; that was vulgar. The
Parlour-maid told me that ladies held their tea-
cups with two fingers and thumb, and did not grab
them with the hand, and though, in following her
advice, I broke a kitchen cup and swamped a table-
cloth with tea, she encouraged me to persevere.
From Mr. Creegan I learned that gentlemen always
got up when a lady entered the room, and when she
left, and always held the door open for her. From
Cook I learnt that ladies never used their fingers
for anything when eating, and that gentlemen never
wiped their plates clean, and, if their spoons
wouldn't pick up a certain morsel, they didn't chase
it all round the plate; and nobody ever asked for a
second helping.

The manners of Gentlefolks must have sadly
moulted since then. Years later, I sat at lunch next
to a noble lord—tenth of the line—who sloshed—
yes, sloshed—asparagus all over his beard and the
table-cloth. I sat with a great Leicestershire Lady,
who licked her fingers while eating artichokes. I

heard a military baronet of old family call to a footman "Bring that back—I'll have some more." And I saw a great County name drink tea out of his saucer, merely saying that it was hot and he was thirsty.

But I knew that all that was said to me in the basement of the Big House was meant for my guidance and improvement, and I listened and modelled myself upon it. I found equal pleasure with cook, who was placid and whimsical; with the parlour-maid, who was alert and had the easy restraint which, to my mind, made her indistinguishable from the Ladies upstairs; with the housemaid, who was docile and instinctively a servant; and with the kitchen-maid, who was all jerks and giggles. All had some quality that seemed to me just the sort of quality I would like to have; and with them and the gentlemen at the "Barge Aground" I had so many models of character that I assumed twenty different moods during the day.

I loved the Big House and its people then, but now my feeling is diluted. It became one of my "Corners," and in this way.

Cook called me from the garden one Saturday morning, and sent me to uncle to demand a cucumber for the lunch salad. When I went back to the garden, and was crossing the lawn, which had been clear when I went in, I saw, for the first time, the Lady's grandchild, Miss Cicely. I blundered upon her round a corner, and nearly committed sacrilege by touching her with my swinging hand. She was of my own age, and was sitting by the window of the morning-room. Finding myself in the presence of a girl of the Gentlefolk class I dared no more than a swift eye. She sat bowed over a book, her face hidden by a lace hat; her brown curls pendulous, her figure, in a white silk frock, all sweep and droop, and one slim leg thrown over the other. As I passed, she looked up and said, just as though she were talking to an equal, but in a lady's voice: "Hullo—you!"

Uncle was near at hand with a rake, and made a sign with it. I caught the cue, brought my hand to my forehead, let it sweep out and down, and said, "Good-morning, miss."

She said: "Where are you going?"

"Get cu-cu-cumber for c-cook, miss."

"I'll come with you."

If only I could have looked forward fifteen years, I should have said: "No, I'm damned if you will. Stay where you are, Lady, and keep your place." But I didn't. She came with me—then and every Saturday—until the last Saturday of my life of freedom.

She came with me as playmate, and after we had delivered the cucumber, she showed me corners of the shrubbery, and permitted me to play hide-and-seek with her, and climbed trees and threw me down unripe fruit, and showed me how to use a skipping-rope, and told me confidential things about her aunts in the casual tones of friendship; and I played my part and kept my place.

I knew that it was just an incident. She was a Lady, and I was the gardener's boy. She repre-

sented something so rare and gracious that real
play was impossible for me; I could not push her, or
catch her in hide-and-seek or take my chance from
the rules of the game; and when she asked me to
give her a leg up a tree . . . She was so far beyond
my world that if I thought of her at all it was only
distantly, as I thought of the fuchsias and rhododen-
drons: and we got on well together. But with one
act of hers she made me think of her, and made
me see myself illuminated from above. I was the
gardener's boy, and proud of my position. Gardeners' boys had their place in the scheme of things.
I could tell other boys of my Saturday-morning
job, and make them respectful and envious; and
I could tell them of the games that I and Miss
Cicely played. But I did not tell them of the last
game whereby she made me see a world transfigured, and gardeners' boys as creatures crawling.

We had played hide-and-seek in the shrubbery,
and on the call of the lunch-bell she had gone indoors through the morning-room window. As I
crossed the lawn a few minutes later, on my way
to the potting-shed, she came out again and called
"Hi!" and whistled and jerked her head. I ran
to her. Her arms were loaded. As I came up,
she opened her arms, and dropped on the grass
before me a toy-engine with three wheels missing, a
doll without arms, a humming-top with no peg, a
paint-box with no brushes, and one cube of paint, a
clockwork windmill, wanting two sails, four lead
soldiers, badly chipped, and a toy gun without a
trigger.

She said: "You can have these. I don't want them."

On the way home Uncle Frank said: "What's the matter, cock? Got the toothache?"

I said "No," and laughed; and directly he had gone for his evening stroll I went to Quong Lee, and sat in his shop for two hours, and somehow I felt nearer to him than I had been the night before.

If the waste patch behind the potting-shed of a big house at Greenwich is ever dug up by its new owner, he will find, about a foot below the surface, some half-dozen broken toys.

Chapter III

ORPHANAGE

GETTING into a Home is almost as hard a business as getting out of one. They lure you by pretence of refusal. There are forms to be filled, personal inspection by the Committee, examinations by two doctors, vote-holders to be wheedled and placated, questions to be answered. Child vaccinated? If so—when last? Ever received parish relief? What school standard? Any hereditary sickness? Any of the family ever been criminally convicted? Guardian's name? Guardian's age? Guardian's occupation? Name of guardian's employer? How long employed by present employer? Child suffer from winter cough? Character by local schoolmaster? Character by local clergyman? What other references, if any?

All these questions had to be seriously answered before I was even considered as a candidate for the Good Home which the Lady had found for me. She found something for everybody around her; usually something that they didn't want. For me she found a Home, and though Uncle Frank, I think, was not altogether grateful, he submitted. He sprang it upon me one evening after tea. He looked at me across the table, grinned, and smacked his hands together and rubbed them. "They're fine places," he said. "It'll be a Fine Thing for you, me boy."

"What will, uncle?"

"This school that the Old Girl's been talkin' about."

"What school, uncle?"

"Why, it's a—it's a Big School. And she thinks she may be able to git you into it. She's taken an Interest in yeh. It isn't certain, o' course. There's a lot waitin' to git in. But it'd be a Fine Thing for yeh, if she could." He rubbed his knees. "They're grand places. Better'n these Board Schools. You'll learn French—an'—an'—short'and—an'—an' chemistry, an'—an'—— Why, it'll be like being at a young gentlemen's boarding-school. Like Eton and 'Arrow, an' that sort o' place." He smacked his hands again. "It'll be the making of yeh. Wod yeh think of it. Eh?"

I didn't know what I thought of it. In the first shock, I was dismayed; then, as he went on, interested. Dismayed at leaving Uncle Frank and the streets and the fellows and Quong Lee, and all the things I had grown up with; but interested by the picture of making a Fresh Start: beginning life on my own, like.

Going away to school had a ring about it that connected me with the heroes of the stories in the halfpenny and penny boys' papers, which, though written for boys of our class, dealt entirely with the doings of boys at schools of the Rugby and Winchester type. Certainly it would be something new and would mark me in Carfax Street as one in touch with adventure. I should be lonely, perhaps, and unhappy, but I should be a figure of interest.

"You'll git a lot there that I can't give yeh. Every attention you git, just as though you was a gentleman's son. It's a grand place. I seen pictures of it. All in its own grounds. Beautiful buildings. Out in the country, too. Country air and—and—games, and—and good food. It'll set yeh up every way. Be the makin' of yeh."

He went on in this strain until I was sure that I was going to heaven; and by the end of the evening the thought that possibly I shouldn't get in filled me with dismay. Next morning I told all the boys about it. I strutted. I was going to a boarding-school—a considerable cut above the Carfax Street Board School. As the Lady and the Vicar reported the daily growth of votes in my favour, uncle's tones grew more and more emphatic. "Strewth, it'll do wonders for yeh. Course, you won't 'ave the liberty like you 'ave at 'ome. There's drawbacks to everythink. An' there won't be no 'olidays. But you can write 'ome once a week, and friends is allowed to visit twice a year. You'll be there till yer fifteen. An' gittin' the best of everything. The Best of Everything. P'raps you won't like it at first, but later on you'll thank the Old Girl for it. Football teams they 'ave. An' cricket. An' swimmin'-bath. An' all nice boys, they tell me. Much better than you'd be 'ere. When you leave they find good places for yeh—in the City. Not like yer pals 'ere, that 'ave to go into shops when they leave school."

After three months of canvassing, it was announced that ten out of the forty applicants (I was one of the ten) had been approved as eligible, and were elected for admission to the School. Two days later a document arrived ordering Uncle Frank to deliver me to the School on the following Monday. I lived through days of apprehension and excitement. Something in uncle's tones made me not so sure about the delights of being shut away in a sort of boarding-school for five years; but the thing was adventure, and I played up to it. I was Going Away into unknown perils and interests, and if at night I shivered, in the morning I thrilled. There was enough movement, anyway, in the last few days to keep me on my perch—farewell visits to be paid to Mr. Creegan, to Mr. Sturt, to the company of "The Barge Aground," to the servants at Greenwich, to the Vicar, to my school-teacher, and to Quong Lee. On the night before the journey, Uncle Frank spoke as seriously as he could ever speak.

"Well, me boy. . . . Don't know that I got much to say to yeh. 'Cept to keep yesself clean an' don't cheat an' don't tell lies—'less you feel it'd be right to tell a lie—an' don't run away when you oughta stand up, an' don't do things you don't want to 'cos other chaps do 'em. See? You'll know what I mean when yeh get there.

"But anyway—you ain't a fool. You'll get on all right, I dessay. I dessay you'll—— Oh, it'll be a Grand Thing for yeh. Now, if ya wanta go out an' see any of yeh pals, yeh can, an' if yeh wanta stop out a bit late, yeh can. I'll just step across to

'The Barge' an' find out the best way down to the
School."

There was only one person I wanted to see that
night. He knew nothing of this, for I had not seen
him since the Saturday when I stayed two hours
with him. I went to him and told him, in gibberish,
of the adventure of to-morrow. "Quong Lee—I
go away. Go long way long time. Going school
long time." I had to repeat this many times before
he understood. Then he looked at me; said "Huh!"
and put a long, wrinkled hand on my shoulder.
"You come again—huh!" I nodded half a dozen
times. "Oo, I will. Oo, yes. Yes." He nodded
once. Then he reached to a shelf, took down a
large jar of ginger and offered it to me. "You go.
Ao! You be—you be. . . ." He seemed to be
seeking a word; then spoke rapidly in Chinese; said
"Ao!" again, and sat down in his usual corner, and
looked out of the window; and I sat down on a tea-
chest with my jar of ginger and thought about
things.

Next morning Uncle Frank had one of his moods
—grumpy, and muttering to himself about inter-
fering old geysers, and where he'd stick them if he
had his way; but when we were on the 'bus for
Paddington his enthusiasm for the School returned
and he kept it up all the way.

The Hardcress Home for Orphans stood outside
a village in the West Country, but it does not stand
to-day. After a life of some twenty years it ceased
to get support and quietly closed its doors and made
way for humaner schools. It was conducted by three

elderly gentlemen of the "country" sort, and it maintained forty boys and twenty-five girls. It looked something between a cottage-hospital and a prison. It was enclosed by high walls of the gray stone of the district, and its buildings were of the same stone, "commonsense" buildings without one touch of grace for the eye. From the entrance-gate a stone parade ran to the main building, and a plot of grass in the centre of the parade stressed the atmosphere of cold and stone.

Elders and children, on arriving, were received at the entrance by a tall man in a pilot-jacket, who waved us inside to a class-room furnished with a row of chairs and a large table.

In the schoolroom sat the three old men who ran it, and there I saw uncle for the first time in the manner that befitted one who had kept his own Free House; alert, respectful, but independent. A gentlemanly uncle. All traces of the gardener or the jester of The Wheelhouse were gone. Even the managers saw that they were dealing with a man, and seemed to me to give him level consideration, where they gave beaming assurance to the nervous, cringing mothers.

Mothers and guardians, with the fortunate children who were to enter the Home, sat along the wall; and as names were called from a printed list by the drill-sergeant, mother and child were led to the table for the formal reception of the orphan. The grey heads and red faces of the old men gave the schoolroom an air of fine wines and cigars; the stained glass windows affirmed it.

One by one the children were received, handed over to a monitor, and led through a narrow door into Hardcress. I was fifth on the list. The old men nodded and smiled at me. A secretary took my docket from uncle, and entered details about me in a massive ledger.

"Well, young man, you're going to be one of us now. I hope you'll be happy here. We're just a happy family, you know—except those who don't follow the Rules. It all depends on yourself whether you're happy. So long as you follow the Rules and obey you can't go wrong."

The monitor, a boy of thirteen, beckoned me, and I went with him through the narrow door, while uncle was directed by the drill-sergeant to one of the smaller rooms, where dinner for the parents was served. I was taken first to the bath, and after the bath, a doctor went over me. Then to a barber, who cropped my hair to the scalp. Then to a dormitory, where two apple-cheeked servant girls were fitting other boys with suits. I was told to undress—quick—and they took away my Sunday suit—Norfolk jacket and knickers—and my Sunday boots and collar and bow tie and straw hat—every material contact with my past life; and left me with a pile of Hardcress clothing. These were an undervest, a flannel shirt, a suit of stiff grey cloth (trousers, and a jacket that buttoned to the neck, to save collars and ties) thick socks and clumped boots. "Now you're all right. Now you're a proper Hardcress boy. Now back you go and get your dinner."

I was taken by my monitor to the dinner-room and was sent to a long table with the other new boys. Dinner was served by a kitchen-maid from a side-table which held a pan of mince and suet-pudding and three long loaves cut into two-inch slices. On either side of these were piles of plates, which monitors held to be filled, and then delivered along the table. My monitor seemed a nice chap, but not like the boys of Carfax Street; rather thick and quiet. This monitor sat down among the new boys, and tried to get us to talk, but we only stared at each other, some shyly, some with a "Who are you looking at?" air. Two of them wept. The monitor nudged them, and spoke in an accent that was wholly new to me. "Cheer oop, young 'un. Tidden so bad when you git use to it. You'll git t'loike bein' 'ere soon."

I was not at ease, and not in tears. I was just dazed by the newness of everything; but something in the atmosphere gave me doubts of the monitor's prophecy. I had seen myself in a mirror, as I came down the main stairs, and I had seen the other boys and girls in the outer yard. They looked Queer. There was something about them that put them outside my range. The boys in their coarse suits, shaven heads and blank eyes; little girls in long grey frocks with circular stripes of yellow—although these children ran and jumped they were not as the children I had known. Something was wrong with them. They moved clumsily. Like sheep. Already I began to be a different boy, as though my own self had been destroyed, and I were

possessed by some new influence. Knowing nothing
of Thomas Carlyle, I began to feel the significance
of clothes, and to find a uniform a strait-jacket.
Wherever I looked I saw other boys just like myself, and the first effect was deadening. Taking my
clothes away, they had taken Me, and I felt naked,
as the system required, and ready to wear such
spiritual garments as they chose to force upon me.

After dinner we were marched to the schoolroom
for a final farewell. Uncle Frank was again
grumpy. He looked down at me, and at my bald
head, and at my suit. " 'M. Ha! I s'pose you'll
do. I s'pose you'll be all right.

"You can write 'ome oncer week an' 'ave letters
oncer week. Don't forgit to write an' tell me everythink. You'll . . . prob'ly you'll. . . . I dessay . . . .

"Oh, you're sure to 'ave a good time. It's a fine
place. They took us all over it. Wonderful man-
agement."

" 'M."

"Ha!"

At four o'clock a bell rang. "Friends all out!"

Slowly the mothers disengaged themselves from
their children and went away through the high
door. There was a murmur of talk, bubbles of
sobs. Those near the door turned to wave a five-
year farewell to the group that stood staring awkwardly after them.

"Well, goo'-bye, cock. Don't fergit to write.
They don't allow you any pocket-money, else I was
going to . . . Well, goo'bye!"

I stood with the others and watched him plod through the door. It was only when the door had swung on him that my daze began to clear and I felt the truth of Hardcress. I began to understand that for five years I should be shut away from streets and shops and people and gardens, and would see only the faces now around me. I looked about the stretching hall. The bigness of it, the gaunt spaces, the limp smell of ink and books, the official air and aspect that the old men had suddenly assumed, seemed to shut out all light. I felt then, what I had felt ever since, in whatever company I find myself, that I didn't belong there. I couldn't place myself with those queer, raw boys from Lancashire and Devonshire and Birmingham and Cardiff and Norfolk. Those boys who were not crying seemed lifted by the novelty of the occasion; but I was only apprehensive, already hating the place, sensitive to its chill and its hollow noise.

My eyes went hot; my throat dusty; and I had one flash of a window in the Causeway and an old man holding out a hand to me; but the flash was faint and many miles away; out of the world. Others began to form groups and make tentative talk, but nobody came to me. I stood alone, awkward and hapless, and was too shy and too listless to approach the groups. I stood there, feeling a sheep already, conscious of hands and eyes and feet, and fearing that any movement I might make would draw upon me the attention of those very official old men.

But I stuck it. I had neither the nerve nor the

stupidity to do what young Fosdick did; the boy who was to be my friend. While looking sideways at the strange faces all about me, I picked out his face as one that seemed more of my style than the others. I felt that if I wanted to talk to anybody, that would be the boy I would like to talk to. He looked to be eleven or twelve, slim and dark, with rapid eyes. His hair was sleek and jet-black. Mentally I gave him the word "refined." He was standing quite still against the wall, where he had stood since his mother left, when I saw him edge away, and slip behind one of the supporting pillars. I wondered what he was up to; whether he had gone there because he wanted to cry and was ashamed to be seen or—— then there was a shout, a scutter of feet, the flap of the door, and he was gone. At the noise the drill-sergeant turned:

"Haalt! That boy, there—halt!"

Then, with flying coat-tails, he followed, and the boys drew into one group, staring at the door with wide eyes. The drill-sergeant was gone for two minutes. He came back alone, and none of us saw Fosdick for two days.

"Fall in! Boys on the left. Girls on the right.

"Fall *in!* Can't you understand? Get into line —two and two. That's better. Now then—you there—fumbling with your fingers—what're you dreaming about?"

The voice was a bark, and I felt that I would take great pains to escape a bark like that about my own person. Then I went hot and pale. "Will that idiot wake up? You! You! Pinch him, somebody—that one with his mouth open. . . . Oh, he's alive, is he? Come here!"

I crawled into a sea of floor, shamed before the grinning boys and the peering girls.

"Name?"

"Eh?"

"Say Sir. Name?"

"Sir. Name."

"Tch! What
                    Is
                        Your
                            Name?"

At last I understood, and answered. Then the uniform loomed over me, and spoke slowly. The voice was not cruel or aggressive or nasty; I could have borne that. It was a disembodied voice; the sound-box of a gramophone.

"Hold your head up, boy. And don't forget that word, Sir. Now, you're at school now, not at home. We don't want dozers here. You'll keep awake here, remember. Sharp to the word of command. Understand? Now—fall in. Smart!"

I crawled in.

Reading from a list in his hand the sergeant assigned us to one of two Blocks; then we were dismissed to the playground to mix with the regular boys. A fresh examination, but more friendly and in many accents, awaited me.

"What's yer name? Where d'ya live? London, eh?"

"Ey, there's three on 'em fro' Loondon this toime."

"What part?"

"Poplar."

"What Block you in?"

"B Block."

"Played football?"

"A bit."

"Cricket?"

"No."

"You'll haave to heere."

They turned to each other. "Looks all right, eh?" One joined the group from outside and pushed his way in. "This the kid they say's from Poplar? What part's yours?"

"Carfax Street."

His face shone. "I know it! Reckon you know the Causeway—eh?"

"Oo—yes."

"An' the Island? An' Salmon Lane?"

"Not 'alf!" The coming of this boy took the edge off the chill. I warmed to him. I should not be entirely cut from my own world. He was a freckle-faced yellow-haired lad, all droop and splutter and amiability, and he spluttered all over me for news of Poplar. "You know Longford and Haydon's—the drapers, I reckon? Eh? They still 'ave their Christmas Bazaar? An' all their winders all dressed up in snow and Christmas Trees? Cuh! Wouldn't 'alf like to be there now. I ain't seen it fer three yers. I on'y got two more now, though. Then I leave. My name's Cosgrove. We lived in Canton Street. Think you'll like bein' 'ere?"

"I dunno."

"You'll be all right. 'Taint so bad. Not reely. When you git use to it. I'll look after yeh. There's games an' things. An' we git letters oncer week. An' twice a year they take us fer a walk in the town. You in B Block? That's mine. My name's Cosgrove. Come an' walk round the Big Yard. What's Narrer Street look like now? Cuh! I wish I was there! Cosgrove's my name; don't fergit it."

The drooping arm went round my neck, and I was led away, paraded round the Big Yard, and introduced. With the touch of that arm I had a feeling of safety and comfort, and when it was withdrawn, or when this boy was not in sight, I had the feeling of being beset my many perils.

"Comes from Poplar. Near where I live."

A big boy, a senior, came along, stopped us, and looked down at me. Cosgrove looked up resentfully but sheepishly. The big boy knocked his arm off my shoulder, and stood looking at me. He looked at me for many moments, while Cosgrove stood aside, awkwardly, as a child stood in the corner. Then he squeezed my face in his hand; said "You'll do, young 'un," and passed on. Cosgrove came back to me, spluttering.

" 'Ere—don't you 'ave nothing to do with 'im. I couldn't say nothing, 'cos 'e's a senior an' a monitor. Don't you let 'im say nothin' to yeh. They call 'im Dirty Dick in the school."

"Why?"

He drooped and spluttered and waved his hands, "Don't arst me. You'll learn soon enough." I liked him for that, and wanted to say something grateful to him, but I couldn't think of anything. "Come on—let's go the other way, case 'e gets 'old of you again."

Walking round and round the little yard seemed to be the outdoor pastime, and I saw a processional string of boys in couples, arms on each other's shoulders, moving up and down the paths under the low buildings of the school-houses. Others played curious made-up games of a kind not seen in the Poplar Streets—games against the wall with pen-nibs, eccentric amplifications of leap-frog, intricate games against the high grey walls. All the time I was conscious of eyes. Three sides of the yard were enclosed by windows, and at all points there seemed to be masters, monitors and the drill-sergeant. A boy at one end of the grounds could not pick up a stone without a bark from the other end: "Stop that stone-throwing there!"

Within a week I realised that everything that uncle had said about the School was true. It seemed that they couldn't do enough for us. They fed us and clothed us and trained us and exercised us; and every minute of the day they anticipated us and employed machinery to save us the trouble of thinking of things for ourselves. We were like private soldiers, whose whole lives are spent in public. Every moment of our days was known to the officials, and if one of the old men asked, "What has Brown or Smith been doing to-day?" he would have been supplied with a detailed report of Brown's and Smith's bodily activities from eight to eight.   Only in bed did we escape the million-power eye of authority, and then (for there was the master's spy-window) only with head under the clothes.   Free talk with other boys was allowed only in the grounds.   In your house, you might by permission of the master, speak to a chum, but only for one minute; to move from your seat to another boy's seat, without permission, meant instant punishment.   In dining-hall you might speak to your right- and left-hand neighbour only.   At all other times and places talk was forbidden.

No need for any of us to wonder whether there would be dinner.   Meals were there, on the stroke, three times a day—good bread-and-porridge in the morning; meat, potatoes and suet pudding at midday; and bread-and-cocoa at six o'clock.   No need to have wet feet: new boots were always available.   No need to be sensitive of patched or ragged clothes: the repairing-shop was always available, and new suits were given out to all at the same time.   Nothing in the world to worry about.   Everything done for you.   It was, in fact, the sentimental Christian's idea of heaven.

No trouble seemed too great in this endeavour to make us efficient to do the world's work in shop and office.   The ardour and profusion of youth are obstacles against which all systems of efficiency have to struggle, and one would say that to trap it and direct it into labelled grooves were a hopeless essay.   But the three old men of Hardcress did it.

My first term at that School gave me a persistent feeling of chilblains, but with the second I had become a Hardcress boy. I had more sense and less genius than Fosdick; I followed expediency. I caught the tone of the School, the official and the unofficial; the tone proper to the authorities and proper to the boys. In the first few days of talk in the day-room and the ground I perceived that there were certain details of my other life to be elided or embellished. Most of the boys, poor as they were, seemed to have lived in houses, so I suppressed the one room, and gave Uncle Frank a whole house in Gill Street. I took him away from gardening and made him a ship's engineer. Other boys seemed to have relations of some tone, so I looked about for some, and made use of the Big House at Greenwich. I felt that most of the others were lying, but I had to keep my end up; and as we were all lying I judged that it didn't matter.

Through all the shoals of Rules and Regulations the young Cosgrove from Poplar, called Gold Flake because of his yellow hair, was my pilot. He was simple, clean, stupid, and my first term without his thrusting attentions would have been a string of pains and penalties. His father had been a sailor, but he had given his son none of the sailor spirit. Gold Flake would have made an excellent nurse-maid; looking after smaller boys was his hobby, and as new batches entered the Home twice a year, he was never without interest in life. He scattered kindness as the amiable drunkard scatters the contents of his pockets. Every hour of the day, if I were not in sight, he would come scouting after me, lest I stub my toes against the law. He devoted a

Sunday morning to telling me the history of the school, and a Sunday evening to pointing out the monitors and the captain of the football team. He showed me who was to be taken seriously and who should be shouldered; who was All Right and who was . . . like Dirty Dick. He named those masters who were to be feared, and those who were soft. I could hardly make a movement without that prompting voice at my ear. He showed me how to make my bed, how to clean my boots (according to regulations), how to get, decently, into the common bath, how to play the made-up games, and which seats in class were beyond the clear sight of the masters.

We rose at seven o'clock, washed in the lavatory at a long line of basins, and cleaned boots. At a quarter to eight a bell warned us to form up, two deep, for the march to dining-hall. At five minutes to eight another bell signalled us to march from houses. When boys and girls were all in dining-hall, a bell ordered us to sing grace; another bell ordered us to sit and eat; and at twenty minutes past eight a bell ordered us to rise and give thanks; and a final bell sent us marching out to the grounds for fifteen minutes' play. At a quarter to nine a bell ordered us to form-up for chapel, a bell sent us to chapel, and from chapel we marched into classes. In class I found a respite from officialism. The class masters' job was not to mould or to drill us, but to push knowledge into us and quicken our intelligences; and the atmosphere, by comparison, was fluent and keen. At half-past twelve we marched

from classes to houses to wash, and at ten minutes
to one the bell ordered us to fall in as for breakfast, and march to dining-hall. At half-past one
there was military drill in the grounds. Classes
followed until five, when there was Swedish drill in
the schoolroom. At seven o'clock we formed up
and marched to the last meal of the day. From
half-past seven we did "home-work" and from eight
o'clock till bed-time the rest of the day was our own.

On Saturday and Wednesday afternoons we exercised our bodies and felt our life in every limb at
the word of command. We played football or
cricket by orders. We paraded in the field. The
monitors, on the word, chose their elevens and
marched them to their pitches; and on another
word the games began. After the matches, we fell
in again and marched back to the yard.

Only on Sundays were we surrendered for a few
hours to ourselves. Those days which, in Carfax
Street, had been lit with zest and adventure, were
here strait-jackets. Games or any movement other
than walking were forbidden. One mooched and
mooched round the walled grounds or loafed in the
cold day-rooms learning the Collect for the day.
There was the forming-up for the two chapels—
morning and evening—the cold dinner of pork and
bread and the long desultory evening.

Through the drizzle of the daily day the drills
made sheets of red lightning. Round and round
the yard we marched under August suns or January
rain, forming fours, taking open order, dressing by
the right, doing the same set antics twenty times

over until I wanted to yell. Lying full length to the ground, the body supported from it by the arms, and raising and lowering oneself fifteen times on the word of command. I had to bite into the gravel to keep myself from collapsing to the strain on the muscles and the sting of the flints pressing into the hands; and I called all the mysteries of Satan upon the drill-sergeant who strolled among us, picking out for punishment drill those whose stomachs touched the ground.

"Left-right, left-right, left-right. Keep your head up, Fosdick. Keep your hands down, Fosdick. Form fours—left! Double! Left—you fool— left! Haalt!

"If that idiot with the sharp nose doesn't keep his wits about him, there'll be trouble. Odd numbers take two paces to the rear. What is your number, boy?"

"Twelve, sir!"

"Then stand still. And keep your shoulders squared. Now! Form fours—right! As you were! Form fours—right! As you were! Form fours—right! As you were! Form fours—*left!* As you were. Will the boy next to the sharp-nosed fool punch him! Form fours—rr—left! As you were!"

In my dreams I formed fours right and left. I doubled. I took open order. I deployed. I went on marvellous journeys into strange countries; but I could not walk or run; I could only form fours or mark time, bringing the knee sharply up to the level of the stomach, hands down, thumbs close to the seam of the trousers, neck pressed back, chin drawn in.

At first I only wished to kill the sergeant; later, it became an affair of protracted pains and penalties. I would dangle him by a rope from the roof of the chapel until his exhausted arms gave way. I would imprison him in a dungeon and deprive him of water so that the voice that had tormented us would lose its power. I would have him kidnapped and taken to a lonely house and admonish him thus:

"Good-evening, Sergeant. Remember me? No? Just go back to the June afternoon of '97 when you gave the awkward squad three hours' drill. . . . Remember? . . . Well, it's your turn now to jump to the word of command."

In the dormitory at night, many were the torments devised and wished upon him. From what dark corners of what remote world these boys of ten and eleven drew their ideas, one cannot guess. The prize went to the amiable Gold Flake for his plan of . . . but that is not a matter for print.

There were golden moments, though, to break up the grey. The most trifling interruption of routine, the suspension or change of some feature of the schedule was an Occasion, a stimulus. I came to look for Tuesdays and Fridays—history lessons; to Mondays—treacle went with the dumpling; to medical examination—when supper was served at half-past five instead of seven; to Wednesdays— geography lesson—when we "did" Asia, and studied and marked the map of China, and in every town I could imagine the home of Quong Lee; to Saturdays—writing-home days; to the days when well-dressed subscribers from the world outside came down to the hall to watch us feed; and always there was Gold Flake, with whom I could talk about home and the river and the Causeway. To be ill was to make a beautiful escape. Then one went to the village hospital, and matron and nurses were jolly human creatures, who fussed you and chatted with you and brought you illustrated papers to look at, and showed you as much kindness as though they were your aunts. Until you were well; then, down came the curtain of officialism, and tones became cold and manners aloof; ending with the formula: "Now, you boys, wash yourselves and get ready. They're fetching you back to the Home this morning."

From my history lessons and casual reading I began to invest the place with dramatic touches. There was the march in winter from the gas-lit day-room through the windy yard to dining-hall; the journey to one of the central rooms for singing lessons with the girls, through unknown territory at the back of the Home. These points I peopled with scenes from history—encounters, battles, rescues, escapes, the ringing of the hoofs of adventure.

There were brisk mornings when the air held the smell of moist meadows and the hills beyond the walls hinted of great doings and scampers in long grass. There were evenings when distant windows were red with fire-light, and lights twinkled in the valley-town where ordinary children lived in their own homes with freedom of streets and shops; and

these moments lent something of their quality even
to the School grounds. Once in a way we got news
of the other world, when one of the masters
would lend us a newspaper, or tell us, in summer,
what Yorks and Surrey were doing and, in winter,
how the Villa and the Spurs were going. Twice a
year we were taken into the town for a walk.
These walks were at once exciting and abasing;
exciting to be "out," abasing because the boys of
the town looked at us so queerly. I know now that
those streets were shabby streets of shabby utility
shops; but they were then enchanted streets, and
their shops as gracious and shining as the shops of
Bond Street.

Sometimes, in sick moments, I thought of Miss
Cicely and the toys, and wondered what she would
think of me if she saw me now in these clothes,
eating bread-and-porridge off a bare table; and at
the thought I went lower than the worms.

But there was one thing that has left a glow even
on the grey walls of Hardcress. That thing was
Fosdick. Fosdick became my Causeway: my secret
city of refuge. In him and in the idea of him I could
escape from those barracks and their tread-mill life.
He accepted me, almost from the outset, as friend
and worshipper. For Gold Flake, who did so much
for me, I had no feeling, except as he represented
something connected with home. It was the dark-
eyed Fosdick, who did nothing for me, who won
my immediate interest and, later, friendship. Fosdick was colour and rhythm, poetry and goodness.
Being with him was like standing at that little win-

dow peering at a world transfigured from dirt and
nastiness into the things that so allured me; the
beauty that lies behind our dreams for ever, though
the dream dies. He was of heroic stuff, still defiant
after his first attempted escape, still breaking himself upon the crags of Rules and Regulations; for
only by physical adventure could he express the
vague poetry that streaked his blood. But Hardcress had had that type before, and though he did
at last escape, the escape was Hardcress' conquest.
The wilder the adventure the more he was for it,
whether it was climbing a loose gutter-pipe or breaking bounds, or cheeking the masters, or hiding in
the lavatory at drill-time. He never turned from
a fight with a boy stronger than himself; the more
he feared, the more he fought. He had been a
leader of boys in his past and held himself boldly;
but Hardcress had him in the end.

He was a year older and an inch taller than I,
and the worship I gave him he took magnanimously,
as his right. To be with him was bliss. To march
to dining-hall and chapel at his side, to sit next him in
class, to walk round the grounds with him on Sundays, to smile to him at drill—these were the moments of benediction. I wanted to give him wonderful presents, to do beautiful things for him. It was
bitterness for me that we were in different Blocks
and had to part every evening at half-past six.

Mooning round the grounds or under the arches,
he opened his heart to me alone, and told of his
home in Birmingham and his early doings. Glittering memories. Despite his "refined" air, he had

been a Lad, leader of the Blue Button Gang. He
showed me one of the buttons which he had somehow smuggled into the School—a large glass button
of the kind used for women's cloaks—and unfolded
a panorama of shining streets and dark alleys, break-
neck leaps over fences, Red Indian ventures over
railway tracks, mighty battles round the goods
waggons; moonlit nights, bounding pulses and
scampering feet. Once—once—they had been
chased down two streets by a Copper. It was
because of this that he had been "got into" Hardcress; but he wasn't downed yet. The devil was
still moving under his skin and glinting through his
eyes. He was going to Show 'Em. Obedience and
Safety First were not for him. He talked to me
of making them sick of him before he'd been there
long. (He did, but not to his own programme.)
He talked of organising the other boys against the
sergeant, and began to be really sorry for the sergeant.

But he did not know Hardcress then. I got a
hint of their methods with rebels in my first term.
We were marching to dining-hall one evening when,
as we passed near the girls' wing, above the tramp
of our boots, came a high scream—many screams.
I asked the encyclopædic Gold Flake, "What's
that?"

"What you'll git 'fyou don' smarten up. On'y
one o' the gels coppin' it. They don't 'alf make a
row." He dismissed the matter with that, but all
that evening I felt sick. I couldn't eat my cocoa
and bread, and as to leave anything was against

the Rules, I managed to slip my toke to Gold Flake.
All day the girl's cries hung in my ears, and I carried
before my eyes a fancy of the upper room whence
they came that made that upper room a dungeon
of the Tower of London; and the thought made a
weight on my stomach. But Fosdick met the reality.
It was this way.

We were at military drill, and Fosdick missed an
order. I suppose he was dreaming. He told me
often that he filled the emptiness of the drill hour
with wondering what they were doing in Birmingham—whether the Gang had disbanded, or whether
they had found a new leader, and were wiping the
Robsart Yard boys; what his mother had had for
dinner,   and   whether. . . .   Anyway,   half-way
through the drill I saw with a shock that while
others had taken the order to kneel for trunk exer-
cise, Fosdick was still standing up, staring straight
in front of him. I made violent signals to him, but
I was too late.

The sergeant roared his name. "Fosdick! Step
out. . . . Double!"

The sergeant bent to him. "Take that wool out
of your ears."

"Arn't got any in."

"Why didn't you hear the order?"

"I was thinking."

"O—oh? You were thinking, were you? And
who told you to think?"

"I—I was just thinking."

"Oh, indeed? . . . Well, Master Fosdick, this
is your fourth piece of insubordination. First you

try to run away. Then you refuse to obey your
master's orders. Then you fight in the dormitory.
And now you come on parade *thinking*.

"We've had about enough of you, Fosdick. To-
morrow afternoon, when the others are at cricket,
you will turn out for two hours' punishment drill."

"I don't care."

"What? . . . Eh? . . . Ha! . . . That's your
tone, is it? Very well, Fosdick. We shall see, Fosdick. We'll see, Fosdick, if we can't change that
tone of yours. And you, boy—with the sharp nose
—report for punishment drill to-morrow as well.
When I say Eyes Front I don't mean make goggle
eyes at Fosdick."

At Punishment Drill next afternoon Fosdick and
I were two among ten. Under the eye of the sergeant we marched round and round the yards in
single file, and always the sergeant's eye was upon
Fosdick. I trembled for him. I knew somehow
that there would be disaster for him before the end
of the drill.

Round and round we went while the clock tolled
the quarters. I counted the bricks in the wall. I
counted the number of flags in the paving. I picked
out a brick of bright yellow, and used it to give
some point to this endless circulation. Each time
I came round to it I greeted it as a pal. My head
began to be full of bees. My knees grew weak.
To clear my head I followed Fosdick's fashion of
thinking about home. I thought of Carfax Street
—of the river—of the steamers—of tram-rides—
of the Lady's garden—of strawberries and cream

—of "The Barge Aground"—of the music-hall orchestra—of Creegan—of his double-bass. The vamping accompaniment to "Hot Time in the Old Town" ran through and through my ears. I thought of the Causeway and of Derby night and of kippers for tea; and my feet went kip-kip-kippers-for-tea, kip-kip-kippers-for-tea. I took thirty steps on my toes and thirty steps on my heels, alternately, to vary the insane march. I counted the number of paces in each round. I studied the boy in front. I wondered why his ears were white at the tips. I counted the stitches in the seam of his coat until my eyes danced and watered, and I swayed. Fosdick was at the end of the file, behind me. There was no way of flashing him an eye-greeting.

. . . the sergeant! . . . the sergeant! Plod-plod-plod.

I had reached the point when I felt that I had spent my life going always round and round an archway looking for a yellow brick when the voice barked at us: "Double!" We broke into a trot, and for two minutes went like donkeys. "Haalt! Front-turn! Squad will stand at attention for five minutes, hands down, thumbs close to the seam of the trousers, necks pressed back on collars, chins drawn in. One movement from any boy and the whole squad will report for punishment drill next Wednesday."

We stood like posts. Those who were frequent offenders took it easily, but I was new to it, and as for Fosdick, I knew what torture this rigidity must be for his fluent body. My head wouldn't keep still. My eyes hurt. My hands itched, my nose itched. My neck was twitching. After one minute I felt I must either move or fall. There was a bar of iron across my chest. If I could only sit down for ten seconds. I bent my knees to relieve the weight on my thighs and chest. After two minutes I felt that I must step out and tell the sergeant I couldn't do it, and take what dreadful penalty might come. Then, just as I was summoning the courage to step forward, I was saved . . . by Fosdick.

Out of the tense silence of those arches came a noise. As though a bomb had blown the School to pieces. As though the Veil of the Temple had been riven. As though a devil from the pit had laughed in the face of heaven. Fosdick's voice rose in a yell, and said firmly and clearly:

"God damn and blast your bloody punishment drill!"

For ten seconds the silence that followed it made the ears ache. Then the sergeant looked quietly across us, picked out Fosdick, and said, in a tone expressing the calm resentment of one who has received an expected insult: "Stand out, Fosdick."

Fosdick stood out. The other boys glared at him with fury for the double dose he had brought upon them, but I felt sick.

"You're doing well, Fosdick. Very well. You foul-mouthed little guttersnipe. Stand away from the others. Right against that wall. At six o'clock you will see Mr. Cleemput. We've medicine here for poisonous rogues like you."

The other boys took advantage of the moment to look at Fosdick, and I saw that they were no longer angry. He had ceased to be their enemy, and was about to become a victim of something that most of them had escaped from knowing. He was set apart, lifted out of the everyday world. I had a swift dream of rescuing my hero, of arriving with revolvers and shooting right and left and swinging him over my shoulder and escaping with him; but it passed, and I was left numb; and the circular march went on.

At six o'clock that evening Fosdick was taken to Mr. Cleemput. At a quarter to seven he was carried over to his house and put to bed. Other fellows in his house told me about it. When they went up to bed he was moaning; and when they asked him how he felt, he swore. He said, "Oh, Christ, go away. Go and —— yourselves!" And he lay there shouting, ". . . the sergeant! . . . the doctor! . . . the lot of yeh! Oh, Christ, I wish I was dead. Oh, for Cry's sake, *go away!*"

.   .   .   .

In my third year I was moved to the senior block, and moved into a world as strange to me as my first week at Hardcress had been. A cold, dark world of new types, new ideas, new manners, in which all talk moved coldly and darkly upon one theme. My first night in that dormitory was a nightmare; I was no longer among boys, but among creatures of the farmyard. Among the juniors these things were known, but they were not discussed. In the senior school they were of more interest than football; and every night, after the lights had been turned out, from different points of the twelve-bedded room came greasy murmurs that made bedtime a horror. The unclean thing that had noticed me when Gold Flake first had charge of me exercised his privilege as monitor by claiming me as a favourite; but I was unresponsive. I remembered what Gold Flake had half-told me, and besides, there was Fosdick, whose shining heart turned things meaner than itself to mud. Fosdick had pronounced upon these matters, and they could not live where Fosdick lived. So I was coldly received and lived in the Coventry of the "Saints."

Among the seniors I found it the fashion to have a girl from among the girls of the school; and the names of certain girls were bandied freely about the dormitory, with much occult and brutal whispering. Those boys who had sisters in the school were permitted to see them once a month in the central offices, and these boys became messengers, carrying notes from other boys who had picked out, in dining-hall or chapel, some Nice One to possess in fancy. The sisters conveyed these notes to the girls indicated—"The dark one, facing us, fourth from the end"—and on the next visit conveyed answers. Young Gold Flake had a girl, and, as a mark of confidence, showed me one of her letters, nudging me and pointing out the "bits." She was eleven years old. The letter was a cascade of corruption.

But I knew that that was nothing to do with sweethearts. Fosdick had talked to me of girls

and love, and had shown the business to mean
something solemn and lovely. Something like Con-
firmation; only more solemn. I didn't quite
follow this. Fosdick, the adventurer, invested
many ordinary things of life with mystic significance, and though I stood aside, privately smiling,
I always felt that Fosdick had the right of it if
only I could understand.

Of all the girls, the goddess, for the elder boys,
was Jessamine Drubar, who distributed the favour
of her letters as though she were a dealer at Nap.
At least twelve of them were in correspondence
with her. She stood out from the dumpling faces
of the dining-hall. Hardcress hadn't crushed her;
there was an invincible something that it couldn't
reach; something that gleamed in her eyes, which
were far too pure for innocence. She was fourteen,
and she shone—a rhododendron luminous among
green leaves. With her opulent colouring, her dark
curls, and her candid glory in herself, she was
marked for disaster; and it wasn't long before she
got it.

Under the influence of this atmosphere I felt that
I must put myself in the fashion and make claim
to a girl; and I did. I had long noted, idly, the
top girl near the door. I had clear views of
her as she led her procession and, having isolated her, I began to watch for her. Then I began
to think about her; to wonder what sort of girl she
was, and where she came from, and what class she
was in. In about a week I discovered that I had
Got a Girl. I was uplifted. I was in the select

company of the romantic. I belonged. I began to talk casually of My Girl, and was chipped about her, and the chipping was pleasant.

I had now a new world for the stale moments of the day. There was purpose now in entering dining-hall or chapel. There was the thrill of awaiting the entry of the girls, of hearing their steps on the outer stones, of identifying Her step, of picking out from the uniform procession one face that coloured the hall with the stuff of dreams. Though often I could not see her through the ranks, I knew that she was there, and one spot of that hall was for me charged with the magic that seemed always near me but always beyond reach. It was quite different from the feeling I had about Fosdick, though I couldn't tell how it was different.

Steadily I worked her into the pattern of my life. Lessons, chapel, drill, gymnasium, football—all revolved upon her. If I could get myself hurt at football, and appear at table with a scarred face, I would stand well forward, clear of obstruction, in the hope that she would see me and pick me out with awe as a dare-devil. I began to clean my boots a little brighter, and told myself it was for her, though across the gulf that separated the tables she could see no more than head and shoulders. For every thought and action of my life I set her as audience, and began to long for some affair or disaster whereby I could appear before her as brilliant, popular and applauded, like one of the artists at Creegan's music-hall, or as the centre of the world's pity, like Napoleon at St. Helena.

By inquiries among boys with sisters I learned that her name was Iris Marjorie Hay. I learnt that she was twelve years old, and that her nickname was Nosey. (I dismissed the latter abruptly; the sort of thing low minds would say about anybody better than themselves.) With red ink I inscribed I.M.H. on the palm of my hand, as dedication, and during military drill I could look at it and escape.

But nothing further. I dared not smuggle a letter to her; she looked the sort of girl who would be shocked by a letter. I was sure that she was not like those others—Jessamine Drubar, or the girl who wrote Gold Flake's letter. Her face was clear and grave. Her smooth brown hair was held back by a crescent comb, and as she stood upright at her table she made the grey calico frock and the stiff yellow apron things of beauty. Hardcress hid her grace in clown's clothes, and she made them gracious.

No; I dared not write. I lived with her only in thought; walked with her on the hills outside the school; sat next to her in cathedrals; rescued her from sounding perils. In all blank moments I built about her wondrous enterprises. The roof of the dining-hall fell in, and I alone was strong enough to support the beams while the School marched out. Old Mr. Cleemput, staggered at the exploit, offered me whatever I might ask; and I answered: "Let me and Iris Hay always be together, sir," and it was so. Or a live snake got into the chapel, close to her, and I, with the power of mesmerism, transfixed it just as it was moving upon her. There were impossible moments when I got "over there"—across the stretch of floor that separated us from the girls' tables—being sent on a message to one of the girls' matrons. The mere thought of it choked me. To be there, to stand in her presence, to look clearly into that face which I saw only from a distance—I knew that I could never endure it. Such bliss would destroy my rest for ever. I dared not look straight into her face, and as for touching her . . . it was unthinkable. The knowledge of her presence in the School, and the distant sight of her, were enough; and though I never approached her, never heard her voice, I lived in that happiness vouchsafed only to the mind fixed beyond self.

To-day it is as though I sat in a dusty law court listening to recitals of mean things, but seeing through a far window a field, a river, and wild flowers high above the green. Yet I am happier now than I was then; much happier. These things are of another life, fragments of a dream, or the tale of a boy I once knew. The flash of white wings.

But when Fosdick's romance came it lived and moved and rose swiftly to its appointed end, and by it he was to know defeat and darkness. He, who had shared my rapture and discussed it with magnificent solemnity, also Got a Girl; or the girl got him.

Jessamine Drubar, as bold as he, crowned him her king, and finished both his rebellion and his poetry. Her roving eye had spotted him in chapel, and one brother-and-sister day a junior slipped into the senior ground with a screw of paper for the dark boy near the piano, second from the end. He went up in flames of exaltation. I had created romance for myself, but romance had come unbidden to Fosdick, mysteriously, and he accepted it as befitted a hero. We read that letter over and over again, and next morning, though he had never before noticed Jessamine Drubar, he was in love with her; and he went into love with flash and stab. He was possessed. Together, I being the better writer, we drafted a reply to be conveyed to her next month; and through a month of Fosdick's raptures I stood by as equerry, knowing that I would feel as crazy as he felt if a screw of paper had ever come to me from the marvellous hands of Iris Marjorie Hay.

He grew darker of manner. He brooded, and went lonely, as a knight might go in the days before his vigil. And after Jessamine Drubar's reply, two months later, he fretted and fumed. He was the lover of every girl-child's dreams—heroic, forthright, all bounce and bloom. Hardcress had a little dimmed his quality, but this whirlwind of romance brought it up. Out of his broodings he conceived a splendid tribute to his lady. He confided to me the nature of the enterprise, and in a secret despatch he advised Jessamine Drubar of it. The boys' ground gave a clear view of the windows of the girls' dormitory, and in his latest letter he asked where she slept, so that he might pick out the nearest window to her bed, and look at it at nights from his dormitory.

Her bed was under the first window from the angle of the schoolroom and dormitory.

That was enough for Fosdick. On that knowledge the enterprise was laid; and though I protested, begged, argued, wheedled, pointed out the awful nature of the crime and its consequences, used every trick I knew to dissuade him from this crash of folly, he waved me away. Heroics were in the air, and he was outside himself. Even when I said: "Remember that Punishment Drill, and what happened afterwards. This'll be worse'n that if you're caught," he was immovable. His face was set fanatically towards the first window from the corner.

There came a night, and eleven o'clock of that night. When everything was quiet Fosdick left his bed (he told me), half-dressed himself, crawled along the floor on his stomach, below the view of the master's window, and went downstairs. There, he said, he unbolted the House door, and sped, with staccato rushes, through the Big Yard, from point to point, past old Mr. Cleemput's cottage, and so across the main entrance-yard. Then, over the wall into the girls' playground. Then to the corner where schoolroom and dormitory joined at right angles. There he crouched, took off his boots, tested the gutter-pipe, and with fingers and toes worked himself up to the first window. Hygiene demanded that all dormitory windows be open day and night. In two minutes from leaving the ground he was inside.

.   .   .   .

They found him there.

He told me later, in jerks and dashes, how they found him and what they did.

The stern governess, making a last inspection, found him there. He was on his knees by Jessamine Drubar's bed. She was sitting up. His face was resting against her curls. They had one arm round each other. Their hands were clasped.

Jessamine Drubar cried a husky, "Oh!" Then two sharp blows on the face separated them.

.   .   .   .

Next day there was perturbation among the staff, and much whispering and sagacious glances. Fosdick's bed was empty at calling-up time, and he was absent from breakfast. None knew what had happened, and monitors' questions to the master were ignored. It came out, though, and went murmuring through the yards and the class-rooms. Old Fosdick had been found over the girls' side in bed with a girl. Good Lord! No? He had, though. Good Lord! Crumbs! Blimey!

It was a record. Daredevils there had been before, but this . . . He had added a line to that school-history of heroes which is the history of rebels.

All day the story rustled about the school, and groups, constantly broken up by ushers, gathered to debate the frightful visitation that would be his.

To venture three paces outside the walled yard in search of a lost ball, to cock one leg over the boundary wall of the grounds, were crimes that brought punishment. But this—— The enormity of it made gossip difficult: and worse still, a rumour came that sent many boys' faces pale; a rumour that the girl's Block had been searched and Letters Had Been Found.

Among the staff the outrage was viewed with heat. That one of those little wretches should dare —dare, not only to get out of bed, but actually to leave his House at night; and not only leave his House, but cross the grounds; and not only that but—the girls' wing! The mere thought of it brought open eyes and bewildered words. It was a blow at all history and tradition. It was as though a guardsman on parade had spat in the face of the inspecting field-marshal. And at a girl's bed. . . . He was a danger to the School. And the insolence of it! How he could dare think of it, let alone do it. And him having two floggings already. The boy couldn't be right in his head.

But the thing had been done. Despite all precautions and barriers and bolts and penalties, the thing had been done. The flaming swords had been ignored and passed.

The penalty followed swiftly. Fosdick was kept in isolation for two days. Then, at twelve o'clock on Sunday, the whole School was ordered to the main schoolroom. When we were all assembled old Mr. Cleemput appeared, followed by the drill-sergeant, the usher, the doctor and—my friend.

He was made to stand where all could see him for the Beast that he was. There was an Address— an Address full of terrible words that were fastened upon Fosdick.

Then, when the address was done, he became the central figure of a Black Mass; and while I wondered why God didn't strike them dead, for ten minutes, before the eyes of his comrades, they tortured his uncovered body. For ten minutes, under the sunshine that streamed through the open windows, they broke his grace of spirit, until what was left of him collapsed in moans on the floor, and the doctor gave the signal that put an end to it. And at the same hour, from another wing, came noises by which we knew that the mistresses were dealing with Jessamine Drubar.

That night Fosdick was fully a Hardcress boy; of the mould. Captaincy was gone from him. Poetry had been wiped out. His eyes were dull and half closed, as though he had seen some very dreadful thing. He moved at the word of command with the limbs of a puppet. He seemed incapable of thought. All the next day his face was changing colour and his hands shaking.

To all but me he was dumb. To me, under the arches, weeping on my shoulder (yes, Fosdick, or what was left of Fosdick, had fallen to tears), he spoke darkly. "It wasn't so much the flogging, though that was . . . I might a'stood that. But to do it in front of all the School. . . . An' the things he said about us. The things about Her

. . . the filthy things!" He was not swearing now. He made only racking murmurs, the whimper of the trapped rabbit.

Agonised in the presence of agony, I comforted him with arms and low talk, until the dormitory bell rang. "Good-night, Fosdick. See you t'morrer. I wish I could do something."

"Oh, it don't matter."

"I'll see ya first thing t'morrer."

"Yuh. If all's well an' nothin' 'appens."

I stopped. "What ya mean—if all's well?"

"You'll see."

"You ain't—you ain't goin' to—to try to—bunk?"

"Ah!"

"Ooh—*Fosdick!*" I turned back to deal with this dangerous lunatic. "Ooh! You won't git away. An' you'll on'y cop it worse. Ooh, don't Fosdick. Don't!"

"They carn' do much more than they done."

"But how . . ."

"Listen—would you—shall we—you an' me—together?"

"Oo, Fosdick!"

To bunk! I paused on the word and looked about me, scared. It opened enormous avenues of peril and dismay; and if caught——! The vision of Fosdick on the platform slid between me and the idea. My knees went to paste. Dare I? With *that* in front of me?

I knew I dared not.

"But Fosdick—we can't. We'd never git away. We'd be copped, an'—an'—ooh, don't think of it. It's no *good.*"

"You won't come, then?"

"It's no good. We'd never git away. An' after yesterday."

"That's why. You know what they done to— to—Jessamine Drubar?" He whispered the name.

"I heard."

"That's why. See? I don't care fer anything now."

I looked up and down the arches, and in the moment of looking I had again the feeling of being outside this business; of seeing myself always face to face with this problem, this hesitation between personal fear and loyalty to my friend. As though I had walked on to a stage where this thing was being played, an interested intruder, seeing myself loving Fosdick and Fosdick going away. As though never had life held any other puzzle than this. Then Fosdick was speaking, and I was back again at the heart of it, one of those two figures.

"I don't wanta force yeh. You kep' outa trouble so far. An' I don't wanta git you mixed oop in it." He, too, looked up and down the arches, listlessly, as though already withdrawn from me and from Hardcress. "No. I reckon I better go alone. It wouldn't be fair. I'm older'n you. And p'raps after all one's better'n two in a thing like this."

"I would if there was a chance. But there ain't a chance, Fosdick. You know there ain't."

"All right. It don't matter. Goo'-night, mate.
An' if I do get away, I'll let yeh know some'ow,
and when you leave we'll . . ."

"But 'ow're you going to do it? Tell us what
you're going to do."

"No. You best not know. 'Cos if I'm caught,
they'll be asking questions, an' . . ."

A yell came from a window. "Now those boys,
there—into yer Houses!"

I turned towards my house, and Fosdick turned
to his; and I knew that the dull flow of Hardcress
life was broken. By yesterday's doings and the
dark humours of my friend my mind was curdled,
and I could not sleep. I was desperately afraid
for him. I saw farther than he did. My streak
of caution saw always the consequences where he
saw only the act. But this time there was no public
consequence.

He was never seen again.

Two days later came an affair of my own. A
letter came, not in Uncle Frank's scrawl, and the
style was new to me. It read like a book. It said
that Uncle Frank had passed away, while trying
to stop a runaway horse. It said that Mr. Creegan
had taken possession of the room and its contents;
that Mr. Sturt and a few friends had defrayed the
cost of the funeral; that he was selling the furniture, with the exception of the chest of drawers,
which he had removed to his room, and would hold
it and the money received for the rest until what
he called my Release, and that when the time came
he would do what he could to help me.

CHAPTER IV

ESCAPE

I CANNOT remember what I felt about this news. I don't think I was able to realise the fact of death and of my own position: the two shocks, coming together, had numbed me. Anyway, I was given little time for contemplation. Freedom came sooner than I had expected. A smart energetic boy was required for a "living-in" position in a London hotel, and, though my leaving-time was a year distant, I was selected as the most likely lad, and sent out into the world.

In a state of bemused excitement, I was put on the train for London with a letter to the hotel and a written paper of directions how to find it.

When I found it I was disappointed, and at first thought that I had made a mistake. But there was the name all right, on the fanlight over the door, and I was in the right street. It wasn't at all like the hotels I had seen when out with Uncle Frank. Those were huge places, with soldiers in gold lace outside, and lots of carriages driving up to them, and carpets on the steps, and swing doors and red carpets inside, and flowers and ferns on little tables. This was a place no bigger than an ordinary house, and almost dark. Nobody at the door; no carriages about; no long windows showing silver and glass. Although its door was open it looked as though it were shut up. There was a flight of steps leading to the door, and one window on either side of the steps, and below each window a basement window. I went through the door into the little hall, which had a smell that didn't seem to belong to a Temperance Hotel, but recalled the parlour of "The Barge Aground." A brown smell, I called it, and then wondered why I had thought of the word brown. Yet it seemed right. The hall was lit by a gas-jet turned down to a tiny fan that flickered to the smallest movement of the air. From the door-mat I could see four doors and a staircase covered with worn oilcloth; but the rubbing of my boots was the only sound or sign of life in that house, whose silence made a noise in the ears.

For a minute or so I stood still, not knowing whether I should knock or call out. The hall was dark, and the doors looked very private. There was no noise of servants or guests, or the rattle of plates; no bells; no footsteps. And yet it was only half-past seven—too early for everybody to be in bed. A funny hotel altogether. Through the dusk I could see a battered old arm-chair in the corner of the hall, with a great rent in its seat, and two brooms propped against the wall. Then, from somewhere upstairs, came a low whistle. Without a sound one of the doors opened, and a rustling bundle came out of it and waddled upstairs; and there was silence again. I wondered whether there were other hotels like this in London. But that didn't seem possible. The word Hotel meant something Swell. Perhaps this was a lodging-house. But then it was labelled outside as a Hotel. But perhaps that was just Swank. But then, why was it so quiet? And so dark? And so smelly? And why . . .

Then a door opened. A huge man appeared, and in crossing the hall he suddenly turned, saw me, and said, "Wodder you want?"

I handed him my letter. "Oh——come in 'ere."

I went into a small room furnished with a plush sofa, many wooden chairs, and a table with a plush cover. On the table was a box of cigars and three used glasses. He read my letter and looked down at me, chewing the end of a cigar, legs apart. His face had the gross proportions of his body: it was florid and square; and though at first glance I thought he looked stern, at the second I thought he looked hearty——something of the jolly-uncle sort. When I came to know him better, I found that my second guess was correct. He was prosperous and, in his little kingdom, powerful; and he knew it. But he did not display his prosperity or his power. He wore them as he wore his bowler-hat. Prosperity was the natural raiment of Mr. Mylchreest.

He shot three or four gruff questions at me, and dismissed as of no account my claims to know "invoices" and a little shorthand. Apparently he had no use for such things. He hoped I was a Worker. He had no time for slackers. I was to be polite to everybody in the hotel (I wanted to ask him where Everybody was) and to give no back answers, and always to be on the spot when wanted.

If I did that we should get on very well. And I could take my things downstairs and ask Mrs. Jones to show me my room. So, thus abruptly, I began life.

At eleven o'clock I was sent to bed, but I did not sleep. When I had blown out my candle, the room was densely dark, and in this fog I lay awake, listening. All night that hotel was filled with strange, quiet sounds. Feet went slowly up and down its stairs. Doors clicked. Floor-boards creaked. There were long whisperings in the passage where my bedroom was. There was the gurgle of the cistern. My bed was a towzled affair of worn blankets and split mattress, and I couldn't settle in it: it seemed damp and warm. My body was tired, but my brain was kept alert by the padding and muttering outside. I wanted to know all about it. What business could be going on in a hotel at three o'clock in the morning? And, since so many people were engaged in it, why the whispering and creeping? Why were they afraid to make a noise? What were those quiet whistles for? What was that rumbling noise? What was that husky voice saying? Who was that *crawling* down the passage, and making noises like being ill? What was that rustling noise against the door?

All night long these muffled sounds persisted. Talk-talk-talk, pad-pad-pad, slither and slide, and low laughter. A horrible fancy came to me that it was a lunatic asylum, and that the people had got out of their rooms; and even if I could have slept I felt that sleep would be dangerous.

But next night I slept soundly.

.   .   .   .

Caledonian Road has more the air of a bye-street than of a thoroughfare, though it has enjoyed that estate these hundred years. It is meek and melancholy. It has little appetite for life. Its shops and its houses hold the misery of its prison without the prison's strength. In the morning it presents the face of a draggled woman who has been up all night and even the darkness cannot lend grace to its rags and wounds. It is a street of cobwebs; and Scollick's Temperance Hotel was its symbol.

My day there was usually of fourteen hours, but the work was spread thinly, and I flourished on it.

Each morning I got the early tea, cleaned the boots, "did" the brass, swept the passages (which were dusty an hour afterwards), went out for the cook, cleaned the knives, washed the breakfast things, tidied the little room where drinks were served and the fusty back room where breakfast was served—for the few who wanted it—had a kip in my bedroom at noon and a bit of *Starlight Nell, the Female Footpad,* went out for an hour, came back, gossiped in the back room with cook, brought up the bottles for the night porter's store, and generally fiddled away the dead hours of this curious hotel, which only began to stir with the late evening.

In the six months I spent there I learned my way about it, and could talk to people and size them up, and take my part in back-chat. Mr. Mylchreest was a good boss, who effused a smoky cheer. He

gave me a good kip and plenty to eat, and for
pocket-money there were the pennies that customers
gave me for little services. At Hardcress I had
lived every day with a sense of humiliation. In
Mylchreest's hotel I felt nothing of that. Rather,
I expanded. Mylchreest, recognising that I was
an anxious worker, gave me half an eye of interest
that was worth all the zeal of Hardcress. It was
personal. He may have seen in me a new Mylchreest. He kept me in order; urged me, as man
to man, not to smoke yet awhile; showed me that
betting was a mug's game; counselled me to keep
my eyes open. Some characters wilt under constant
attention, and flourish when left alone. I was unconscious now of living; I just grew and was at
ease with my world. I was visited by none of
those moments of inward disturbance, by no hint
of the mocking magic of the Causeway. I was
happy. I thought often of Uncle Frank and
Fosdick and the Causeway and Creegan, but without pain; and though I remembered that Creegan held property of mine I was not interested. I was happy where I was. I grew to
like Mylchreest and to admire his way of getting what he wanted done without giving orders.
I felt that I would like to be that sort of fellow
myself. I ran about for him, gaily, and my comic
songs brought threepences, and occasionally a sixpence, from him. I quickly made friends among
the staff, and especially with the coffee-room girl.
She was known there as Lively Lil, and was in great
favour. To me she was a sort of unusually jolly

big sister, but sometimes she had a serious mood. "Y'know, kid, I sometimes think there's better places for you than this. 'Tain't exackly the place for a boy like you."

"Why not? What's the matter with it?"

"Oh—nothing. I often say the first silly thing that comes into me head."

That was another queer thing about this very queer place. All the people kept telling me that I ought not to be there. I couldn't understand it; but I didn't worry much; it was enough for me that everybody was pleasant to me. I had heard people say that Mylchreest was a Bad Man, but that didn't sound sense to me. The sergeant was a Bad Man, and Mylchreest was nothing like the sergeant. A kind, hearty fellow like Mylchreest couldn't be really bad, and if his place was a bad place, why was I happy there?

.   .   .   .   .   .:   .   .

But after six months of it I was rudely jerked out of Caledonian Road and set upon other ways. One evening, while taking the hour off allowed me three times a day, and wandering round King's Cross, I was restless, and my mood was one of reaching forward. I found myself thinking over the remarks of Lil and of others. So far, I had asked nothing better than this job, expected nothing better. Hardcress had taught me to be modest in my ambition, and to follow the precepts of the Church Catechism. But now I began timidly to look beyond boot-cleaning and tap-polishing. I saw that other lads of my age had money to spend, and wore collars and bowler hats. Their appearance stirred me with a feeling of inferiority. I began to see washing-up and tea-making as something Low. I began to see junior clerks as cool and elegant gentlemen. I wanted to be liké them, to branch out, to "get on." I looked towards the dignity and cleanliness of office work; cuffs and respectability; train journeys to business.

I had had a jolly time with Mylchreest, but I felt with conceited modesty that Lil and the girls were right; I was fit for better things. I couldn't go on for ever in this job. Everywhere at that hour (six o'clock) the streets were filled with neat and bright young men coming gaily (it seemed) from their offices, and I felt that that was where my work lay. Surely with my shorthand and my invoicing I could get a job in one of those thousands of offices? But then I couldn't throw old Mylchreest over. For one thing, I hadn't any money to make a start with; the very suit I was wearing was Mylchreest's. Of course, Mylchreest had no pull over me now, but it wouldn't be decent to give him the chuck after the way he'd behaved. Perhaps I could speak to him about it. I could say, "Please, Guv'nor, I've been thinking, and as there don't seem no chance here to rise up, I'd like to get some job where I could rise. I want to Get On." What would Mylchreest say? Would he fly at me as he flew at the cook when he found her taking home a couple of chops? Or would he chuck me down the steps by the neck, as he chucked that fellow

who called him "an old ———" Or would he say,
"Of course, me boy, I quite understand. I'll give
you a good reference and speak to one or two
friends of mine?"

Mylchreest did none of these things. The occasion never arose.

For into this mood of mine rolled, that evening,
Mr. Creegan.

I was standing outside St. Pancras, hands in
pockets, eyes searchlighting, when a hand touched
my shoulder with a sharp pat. In the moment's
panic I wriggled under the touch, and turned to
run; but as I turned I looked up and saw first the
baize-covered double bass of Mr. Creegan and behind it his swarthy face. My mouth opened, and
I said, "Oh!" He twisted me round, and said,
gruffly, "It is you, then? Thought I wasn't mistaken." He seemed to accept this dramatic encounter as nothing unusual. To me the smallest
break from day-to-day happenings was matter for
wide surprise, but Creegan was a man of breeding.
He would have taken the Last Trump as a matter
of course. He patted me again on the shoulder,
and I said, stupidly, "It's Mr. Creegan."

He said, "Well, well . . . Quite given you up.
Didn't know you'd left that place or anything about
you. . . . H'm. . . . Well, this is an occasion;
you'd better come and tell me all about it." He
smiled and pointed to a tea-shop across the road,
"Come over there."

Stirred by the encounter I followed him, and
we sat at a stained marble table and drank coffee,

and talked.   Creegan, it appeared, had left the
hall by the river because his friend, Phillips, the
drummer, was sick of it; and they had joined with
a touring opera company carrying "full chorus and
augmented orchestra."   He and Phillips were part
of the extra strength and went with the company.
They were going all over England.   I expressed
envy.   This meeting with him recalled the music-
hall and the music and the surge of his instrument.
It seemed a grand thing to be Creegan.   I wished
I were a musician or an actor, to be able to go all
over England and see different places and people;
but he dismissed the glamour with an irritated
hand, and called for my story.

I told it, from Fosdick's death onward, including the half-hour in the grounds, and he listened
with interjections: "Well, well. . . . Queer. . . .
Really?"   But when he heard where I was working he looked up sharply.

"A *what* in Caledonian Road?"

"A hotel."

"Hotel?   Caledonian Road?   Indeed.   And
you've been there all these months, eh?   Why
didn't you write to me?"

"Why, I—I never thought of it."

"Oh?   Is this—er—hotel busy?"

"Fairly.   We get plenty when there's games on."

"Games?"

" 'M.   Sometimes, of an evening, they play cards
and that."

"Oh, I see."   He leaned back and stared at me.
I seemed to puzzle him, but I think he knew little

about boys, or he would have known that there is an age and class that mixes esoteric knowledge with guilelessness, blocks of premature wisdom with blanks where essential understanding should be. At last he got up and said, "Well, I'm leaving London to-morrow. Beginning of the tour. I'll be glad to be relieved of your property. You'd better come along to Poplar and collect it, sir."

"All right, Mr. Creegan. I'll just pop in, and ask 'em if they'd mind——"

He took me by the arm. "Any property of yours in that place?"

"Er—no. Only a few magazines Miss Fortescue give me."

"Miss . . .? Never mind. You don't go back to that place any more. Understand? You come right along to Poplar with me, young man." He pushed me out of the door. "Here—get on this 'bus."

"But they'll be wondering . . ."

"Let them wonder. Get on this 'bus."

There was always something compelling about Creegan. I don't know why I obeyed him, but I did. I got on the 'bus, and he followed, dragging his instrument after him, and the 'bus bell clanged and we were off eastward.

I breathed and blew. That was that. The very change I had wanted had been made. The business had been taken out of my hands, and here I was, finished, it seemed, with Caledonian Road, and going with Creegan to what I did not know, but anyway, to something new. It certainly seemed shabby to leave Lil and Mylchreest like that, but I had made an effort to refuse and it had been brushed aside, and I didn't think that even Mylchreest could have stood up against Creegan when he commanded. I was powerless, recognising, a stronger voice than Mylchreest's, and also recognising, faintly, that I was doing what I wanted to do.

In about an hour and a half, after many changes, I came again to the familiar streets of Poplar, and the familiar smells and noise, and my mind was a battle of dreams and actual sensations. The ordinary streets, pleasant as they were to see again, had little to say to me; my thread of interest in them was thin and long—five years long—and since leaving them I had seen things and done things and suffered things. I had moved, and I had now little enthusiasm in faded associations. But there was one street, across the way, where I would go first thing to-morrow.

I awoke next morning in a back room of a house in Gill Street, where Creegan lodged, but I could not go immediately to the Causeway. Creegan made it a day of business. We sat together while he handed over Uncle Frank's trifles and settled my future for me. He first dragged a small box from under his bed, unpacked it, and littered the table with its contents. There were Uncle Frank's watch and chain, Uncle Frank's rent-book, his silver tie-pin, his tobacco pouch with embossed initials, the signboard of "The Galloping Horses," a bound volume of *The Practical Gardener*, a

Diamond Jubilee medal, a silver medal from a Surrey Horticultural Society, my school certificate for Regular and Punctual Attendance, and a bundle of papers.

We stood and looked at them, and at sight of them I felt for the first time the fact of my loss. From this regalia rose a cloud of cheerful days and nights, of growls and chuckles and ribald comment; and instantaneous vignettes of the grey figure at the fireside, in the garden, in the parlour of the "Barge Aground," and the last memory of his plodding through the narrow door of the Hard-cress school. My eyes went hot. I turned the things over and over. Creegan went to the window and hummed.

After a minute or so he spoke briskly. "Well, now, that's that. What you've to do now, sir, is to look to the future. Any plans? I suppose not, or you wouldn't have been in that place."

I told him that I had been thinking of trying to Get On and find something better.

"Ha! Well. Have to think of something. Certainly you couldn't have stayed in that—that—Hole."

"But why not? They were awfully kind to me. All of 'em."

"Kind? *Kind?* I daresay they were. But kindness isn't the only thing in the world."

"Isn't it? I think if people are kind . . ."

"You've got a lot to learn, young man. Ready to stay in a place like that because people were *kind* to you!"

"But why not? Why . . ."

"Oh, God, boy, can't you See? A little sense to balance your feeling is what you need."

Under his eyes I began to be ashamed of having liked Mylchreest and Lil. I felt as I felt when Uncle Frank found that I hadn't washed my neck. I wanted to say: "Well, I'm no better than they were." But I didn't. I just looked at Creegan, and wished that I could be like him, who lived in one room in a dirty street and wore shabby clothes, and yet carried himself with the air of people who lived in big houses and had servants. Still, I wasn't that sort; I was just an urchin; and say what you like, Mylchreest and Lil had been friends. I had "got on" with them, and it seemed decidedly dirty to bolt from them without shaking hands and saying, "Thank you." What would they think of me? Set me down as one who was out for what he could get. Yet still, under Creegan's eyes, I felt ashamed of them, and ever since then a word or a look has often crushed my foolish enthusiasms, and set me wanting to be something better than I had the capacity for being. Three years later, when I went back to Caledonian Road, I found the hotel had become a private house, and Mylchreest and his staff had vanished.

He tapped the table. "No plans, then. What would you *like* to do?"

"I don't know. I think I'd like"—I stumbled at the daring ambition—"I'd like to be in an orchestra like you."

Again he waved the fancy away. "Lord, boy,

keep off that. That's no life for a young man. Anyway, you don't know any instrument. You didn't make much shape at the violin, the few lessons you had, and unless you love it and can't keep away from it, you'd do better selling papers."

"But you——"

"Never mind about me. We're talking about you. What *can* you do?"

"I know shorthand—the first book. And I can do invoices."

"Ha! Well, shorthand's not much good, I believe, unless you're expert. Might help you to a start, though. Think you'd like office work?"

"Oo, yes. I'd like to work in the City. Not half."

"Well, if you think that's all right. And it seems to be the only thing you're fit for. At present, at any rate. . . . Main thing is to start you somewhere right away. Look here—we shall be out for about two months, I expect, and I leave to-night. Now I know a man in the City—man with several interests. He might put you in the way of something. I'll write a note to him, and you can take it up to-morrow morning. But for the Lord's sake, don't let him know where you've been working. I'll tell him about the school, and just leave it that you've been with friends since then.

"Another thing. Your uncle's furniture that I sold. It fetched four pounds. That will help you to make a start. Clean collars are important, sir. And clean shirts and sound boots. Fit yourself

out with this money, but be careful of it. Don't
fling it about.

"Another thing. If you get work in the City,
Poplar will be too far away. Cost you too much
every day for fares, and too far to walk both ways.
There's a woman I used to lodge with, just the
other side of London Bridge, when I was playing
at The Star. Mrs. Flanagan, Bussell's Grove,
Bermondsey. If she can't put you up she'll know
somebody who can. And she's cheap. You can
sleep here to-night and have breakfast in the morning. I'll settle with the woman downstairs about
that. But first thing to-morrow fix yourself up at
Bermondsey, and deliver the note I'll give you to
Lime Street. If he can't do anything for you, just
live as cheaply as you can, and go to the Public
Library and study the advertisements in the news-
papers there. You'll find them under the heading
'Situations Vacant.' Understand? I'm sorry I
can't do more for you, young man, but as I say
I'm off to-morrow. I expect you'll be all right,
though."

"Oo, you bet I will, Mr. Creegan. I know me
way about now."

"I daresay. But if I were you I should forget
anything you learnt at Caledonian Road. Start
afresh. Evening classes at the Board Schools are
very useful things. If you get into a mess of any
sort, or want advice on anything there's Sturt at
'The Barge Aground.' Not brilliant, but he's got
sense, and, what you attach so much importance to

—he's kind. You can write to me and let me know
how you get on. Go to the Public Library and
look at the *Era* List of touring companies there, telling you where each company is that week. Look
for the Ucelli Opera Company—see what town
we're at and write to me at the theatre of that
town. Mark the envelope care of the company.
Understand?"

"Oo, yes, Mr. Creegan. I'll certainly write to
you. And I reckon I'll be all right. I've been on
me own some time now."

" 'M. Well—there's your box of things, and
there's your four pounds. And now I'll give you
that letter for Lime Street, and a note to Mrs.
Flanagan at Bussell's Court."

At seven o'clock that evening he started for Victoria, and I went with him as far as the church.
In the few minutes of waiting for a 'bus, he gave
me directions for finding Lime Street and Bussell's
Court, and some afterthoughts of counsel; then, as
the 'bus came up, he jerked his instrument under
his arm, nodded, turned towards the 'bus, turned
back, and said, over his shoulder: "Well, good-
bye, young man. And do, for God's sake, sound
your aitches, and don't say Not Half and You Bet,
and don't speak through your nose or one side of
the mouth. Or you'll never get on. Good-bye."
He waved his free hand, mounted the 'bus, and my
last sight of him was the scroll of his double-bass
against the skyline.

He left me crimson.

Spoke through my nose.

Dropped my aitches.

Out of the side of my mouth.

Nobody had told me about it before, but Mr. Creegan, the true gentleman, had noticed it at once. Probably was disgusted with me. I was no better, after all, than those yobs skylarking up and down the churchyard. Not fit to mix with people like Creegan. Now I thought about it, there was a difference between Creegan's way of speaking and Mylchreest's way and the way of the Hardcress people. I felt suddenly ragged and inept. I had thought that I was doing well at Caledonian Road; now I should have to start all over again and learn how to talk.

Then, as I stood thinking about myself, which I had not done these six months, a new wave of heat came over me—the heat of the memory that I hadn't said a word of thanks to Creegan for all the things he had done—for looking after uncle's things, and the money, and bringing me from Caledonian Road, and putting me up for two nights and giving me breakfast and dinner, and those letters and—— What must he be thinking of me? Truly I was a pretty specimen. But perhaps if I had thanked him he would have been wild. People were so Funny. It was a queer world.

In this mood of ache and shame I turned slowly away from the church and had reached the Causeway before I had any remembrance of meaning to go there.

It was twilight—one of those early spring evenings when the light seems to open out and reveal new aspects of old things; when the streets widen, and roofs and figures stand out in the fixed detail of the stereoscope. The sky was clear and cold, charged with the last white gleam of the day. The fried-fish shop gave out a clipped square of running gold. The lights of Chinatown made beads against the bricks. The walls of the docks, the funnels of the boats, the filigree scaffolding, carven against the sky, seemed to stand within arm's reach. Down the wide stretch of West India Dock Road, the yellow men and posturing girls lingered as though waiting for something to happen. From Charley Brown's came the cry of a concertina, and on the steps of the Asiatics' Home, a black man, singing to the evening star, gave breath to the still-life moments between light and dark.

It was just as I had left it five years ago, and in turning into it, those five years, and all that belonged to them, slipped away from me. The old excitement came back. The shops, the signs, the quiet, shadowy figures, the harsh voice singing; here was something was that always strange, yet more familiar than the things of daily life. I had assumed at Caledonian Road that when I went back to it I should go clothed in experience, a knowing fellow; but directly I turned the corner that clothing was taken from me, and I felt again as I had felt when standing at Quong Lee's window. Change counted for nothing here; it knew neither change nor growth; and as its people were, so would they always be. Of all my memories one only came to me as I walked towards the shop—

standing in the yard with Fosdick very much afraid. And the misery of that memory wiped out the shame of Creegan's farewell. It was no use for me to try to stand on my own feet or hope to be self-sufficient. I wasn't a Fosdick or a Creegan, or even like those careless fellows in the churchyard. I could see myself. I was a kid, and should always be a kid. What we are at ten years old, we always are. These years are years of change; then we are formed; and though, after that, in colour, style, and gait, we develop, we do not change.

I felt it, and a minute later I knew it; for, passing Quong Lee's window, I hesitated before going into the shop, thinking that he would not recognise me. Nothing had changed. His window was dressed just as I had left it, and he was as I had left him, sitting on the stool, looking out to the street. I paused at the window to prepare some simple words by which I could make myself known to him, and as I paused he lifted a finger and beckoned. Though I was fifteen years old, two inches taller and much fatter of face, he recognised me in the moment of pausing. I was still the Kid.

But once in his shop I didn't care. I gave myself up to its serenity. I had come home, and nothing of the world outside that street could worry me. I forgot who I was or what I was about. I forgot that I had no home, no work, and four golden sovereigns. I forgot that to-morrow I was to set about life by myself; to find work, to find a room to sleep in, to find my own food and clothes; and to think about aitches and talking through the nose. In Quong Lee's shop To-morrow seemed always very far away. I forgot everything and felt that I should stay there for ever and that everything would be sweet and good.

I stayed with him two hours, trying to tell him about things in words of one syllable. A little of it he understood, and answered with "Huh!" and an occasional smile. Then, when we had sat some time in silence, he said, "Tchah?" I remembered that word, and nodded briskly; and he took me through the shop to the back room, where I had never been before, and began to make tea.

I followed him with a tickle in the throat and the usual prickling about the head that accompanies all my emotional moments. By that introduction to his private room and by the offering of tea, I knew that I was not only accepted again and that we resumed where we broke off (I had half-feared that he would not want me) but that I was promoted in his friendship.

The room was a mixture of East and West, except its smell, which was wholly East; the very cobwebs seemed to hold the odour of pickled eggs. It had English sofa and kitchen chairs. On the walls hung strips of yellow paper with written mottoes and an almanack from a Poplar grocer with coloured portraits of Edward and Alexandra. The floor was bare, but the walls, to a height of four feet, were covered with dark carpet. There was a deal table littered with crockery, a set of Chinese chessmen and a dirty pack of Chinese cards. In the corner stood three or four pipes, a little lamp, and a wicker basket. Some banners were suspended from the electric light cord. On the mantel-shelf were a joss, two terrible vases of the sort exchanged for trading-stamps, a plush photograph frame containing a newspaper picture of a Chinese, whom I later knew to be Li Hung Chang, and, balancing him, in a violent gilt frame, Lord Roberts. On a gas-ring by the fireplace a kettle was simmering.

I was in his private room, by his own invitation; and as we sat and drank tea I suffered that feeling of excited content that follows some difficult achievement. He had remembered me and waited for me. He had celebrated my return by this special favour. He was coming nearer to me, and every moment was laden with a precious unrest. I knew that I should always love him. His face and his head and his hands and his voice, the very chairs and tables of his room, were for me alight with peculiar charm. But even while surrendering to this charm I puzzled myself with wondering why. Why was I there? Why did I love him? Why did he take this trouble about me? What was the secret beauty that he and his shop held for me?

I did not know. It was many years before I did know, and then the secret, like all great secrets, disclosed itself as something that I had always known and that everybody knows; something as clear and simple as the sunshine.

Chapter V

CITY

FOR all who daily cross London Bridge at nine in the morning and six in the evening—your prayers. There they go, like flies on a window-pane, witlessly back and forth, up and down; the crawlers. Once those men were lads, upright, like the office boys who walk among them, going to the treadmill while the morning sun climbed up the sky, and the traffic rang and flowed, and the Thames swept out to the Nore; and there they are now, bowed and dulled with discipline and foolish work, until they have come to believe that they are useful, and to look upon the City with pride as the centre of life.

. . . .

I found Bussell's Grove without much trouble, and I found Mrs. Flanagan, an irritable woman with a ferret face and a faint echo of Creegan's accent; an accent that I heard all round me. I was in the Irish quarter, and I found it many points lower than Carfax Street or Caledonian Road. It was, indeed, down and out, condemned even then as unfit for habitation; but here, as elsewhere, the condemnation was pious only, and the hovels remained and were occupied. It ran alongside the enormous archways of the two London Bridge railways, and day and night its houses rumbled and trembled. Hot sparks from the engines fell into their windows; moisture dripped from the tracks down their walls; and the air had a thick taste of tanning-sheds and pickle factories. At first sight of it I didn't like it, but later I was to see it shining as a part of myself and of beauty touched and lost.

"What? Who?" said Mrs. Flanagan. "Creegan? Don't know the name. Eh? Oh . . . yes, I fancy I do recklec now. Yes, I might let you 'ave a room. I dessay I could. But I'm just doing me scullery up now. 'Ow much can you pay?"

"I don't know. I want something cheap."

"Oh?" She wiped her hands on a coarse apron, with an air of flurry. She looked me over. I had a feeling that I had come at the wrong time; that Mrs. Flanagan didn't want me; that it was very saucy to expect people to let you a bedroom off the doorstep, so to speak; that I looked like a· thief; that I was certainly a cadger.

"Well, depends what you call cheap. You could 'ave the back bedroom for four shillin's a week. I suppose you're respectable?" Still with an air of having more serious business in hand.

"Oo, yes. Mr. Creegan's known me a long time."

"Huh!" She sniffed. "Look very young to be on your own. Ain't done nothin', 'ave you?"

"Course not. Only I'm just getting work in the City, and I want to be near, so's to save fares. I useter live at Poplar."

Mrs. Flanagan sniffed. "Oh, well, bring yer traps in then. I shall want a week in advance."

"Oo, that's all right." I dropped my little tin box in the passage, and produced one of Mr. Creegan's sovereigns. Mrs. Flanagan looked at it.

"Well, I ain't got change fer that. 'Owdya come by it?"

I explained. "Oh? I see." She swung her hand horizontally across her nose. "Well, you can leave yer box 'ere, an' pop out an' get change. There's a Post Office down Bermondsey Street. They'll change it there. I shan't be able to do yer meals—'cept breakfast; an' then I can't be bothered with cooking things."

"Oo, that's all right."

"I could give ya tea an' bren-butter in the mornings, fourpence a day."

"That'd be all right. Thank you."

When I had changed my sovereign, and satisfied her with the deposit, she asked no more questions, but told me I could go up; and I carried my box to the little hole at the top of the stairs, where was a single bed, a wash-stand and basin, and a rickety chest of drawers.

"You'll find yer own candles an' firin'."

"Oo, yes, that'll be all right."

"I ain't got a second key just now, but I'm always in durin' the week. I'll git ya one later on."

I came out from the interview bewildered. I had not yet adjusted myself to the sudden yank from the friendly routine of Caledonian Road into a world of new values and new reactions. The first excitement of the occasion was passing, and I began to be chafed by doubts and dismays.

I arrived at Lime Street, an alley leading from Fenchurch Street, in a mood that was something between fright and irritation. The office to which my letter directed me was on the third floor of an ugly block of chambers, full of dust and fog and the bicker of typewriters. The door opened on a counter, which preserved a bounding line of intercourse between callers and office. Four clerks sat at a high desk, with vast ledgers before them. They worked with the manner of men of affairs, scrutinising papers, shuffling them, and consulting files. They bent over their desks, eyes tense, brows pleated. Clearly they were at the heart of Business: Men of position. They pinched their chins. They stroked their hair. They muttered to themselves. The greyest of them, wearing a celluloid collar, with tie riding grotesquely on the top edge, a coat frayed at the sleeves, and shiny trousers, went to the telephone, and said he wanted the Head of the Firm, and when he got the Head of the Firm, he said he Couldn't Have That. He wasn't going to pay two hundred pounds for rubbish, and if there wasn't an improvement in the next lot he'd place the order elsewhere. It wasn't Business, and he didn't do things that way. I was surprised that nobody laughed. But perhaps it wasn't meant to be funny; perhaps it was all part of Business that clerks should talk as though they were the company. I looked forward distantly to the day when

I should be able to tell the Head of some firm that I Couldn't Have That.

I stood there for a minute before anybody took notice of me. I was wondering if I dared cough or shuffle my feet, when a middle-aged man with a sour moustache turned to me wearily. The gesture said: "Well, if you won't go, I suppose I must attend to you."

"What do you want?"

"I got a letter, sir, for Mr. Pollock, sir."

"Well, put it down, boy. Put it down."

"I want an answer, sir."

"Well, give it to me, then."

He came to the counter, took it from me, looked at it, looked hard at me, turned it over, and said:

" 'M. Who from?"

"Eh?"

"Who *from?*"

"Mr. Creegan, sir."

"Don't know the name."

" 'E's a friend of Mr. Pollock's, sir. 'E told me to bring it and see Mr. Pollock about a situation, sir."

"Oh?"

He had another look at the envelope, and another look at me; then threw it on the counter and went back to his work.

"Will it be taken in, sir?"

He stared at me as though he had just seen me, and turned again to his desk. "I've no doubt it will, when Mr. Pollock is disengaged. Sit down and wait."

I sat down on a wooden bench and twiddled my cap in my fingers. I studied the almanack of a coal-mining journal until the phrases of its advertisements ceased to have any meaning. Explosives, detonators, pumps, batteries, safety lamps, picks, chains—dull, mechanical things. The advertisements gave pictures of all sorts of tools that looked cold and hard, and these and the office seemed in some way associated. The journal called itself the *Colliery Guardian*. Silly name. Why did a colliery want a guardian? I studied the back of a ledger turned towards me. It was labelled Consignments. What were Consignments? I studied the shelves round the walls, which held rows and rows of fat, dusty books, labelled Letter Book, and rows and rows of fat, dusty cases labelled with the names of coal companies. Everything was very still and quiet and dusty. I had heard that business was always rush and tear; but nobody came in and out; nobody talked, nobody dashed about. Nobody took any notice of me or of anybody else. The only sound was that of pens and the turning over of leaves. I began to think of Lil and to wonder how Caledonian Road was getting on without me.

After three-quarters of an hour of this, I decided to speak, and after framing my sentence, and waiting to catch somebody's eye, and preparing to speak, and postponing it, I got out a little quaver. "Er—as 'e—er—as Mr. Pollock—is 'e disengaged yet?"

No reply. The four faces were bent over their papers. Perhaps I hadn't spoken loud enough. I

coughed, and "Is Mr. Pollock disengaged yet?"
The man with the sour moustache looked round.

"In a hurry, aren't you? Think Mr. Pollock
has nothing to do but see boys who want jobs?
Have a little patience."

I wilted and blushed and sat down again.

A few minutes later a girl carrying a note-book
came from an inner room. The sour man nodded
towards the counter. "Letter there. You might
take it in."

The girl snatched the letter from the counter and
disappeared with it. I read the meaningless coal
advertisements over again, hoping to soothe my
mind for the coming interview with an Influential
Man, and sat for another ten minutes, ignored.
Then a distant bell rang, the sour man went into
the inner room, and came out jerking his head at me.

"Come through—you."

I followed him into the mysterious inner room, as
dusty and littered as the outer room, but with one
flat desk in the centre, and a rug. I stood on the
rug, looking at an old, small, pasty man, who was
writing. Then the old man looked up, stared at
me, and said, "Did you bring this?" holding up
the letter.

"Yes, sir."

"Oh. Sit down. This chair. So you want to be
a clerk, young man—eh?"

"Yes, sir."

"Well, we can find a place here for a smart, energetic boy to attend to the post, copy the letters,
answer the telephone, deliver messages and be gen-

erally useful. Your wages will be ten shillings a
week. Your hours will be nine till seven. Nine,
remember, not a quarter past."

"Oo, yes, sir."

"You'll come on a week's trial. You'll start next
Monday at nine o'clock. Understand?"

"Oo, yes, sir. Thank you, sir."

"Very well, then. Tell Mr. Collins, in the outer
office, that you're engaged. And don't keep saying
'Oo' every time you speak. You're not a pigeon."

. . . .

Next Monday, fearful of being late, I left Bermondsey at eight o'clock, and made one of that
march of marionettes over London Bridge. Now I
was beginning life in earnest, and though I was still
sensible of doubt, the stimulus of adventure over-
rode it. My shirt and celluloid collar were new.
My trousers had lain all night under the mattress.
My boots were as bright as Mrs. Flanagan's nearly
bald brushes would make them. I walked among
the City clerks as one of them. I had got a start
in the City. I was not Going to Work; I was Going
to Business. I had prospects of getting on. I
rather pitied the poor chaps who had to go to Work
as errand boys or apprentices to trade. If I worked
hard and carefully Mr. Pollock would take notice
of me and would raise me step by step until I became a partner in the firm. I had only to work
hard and the world was mine.

But I was no sooner in the City than I wanted to
get out. Within a week I discovered that the prospects were illusory and that office life was loathsome.

Fortune had handed me the packet I had asked for, and behold, it was empty. The City was hard and ugly; the work was as interesting as turning a handle; and I found the clerks as detestable as they must have found me.

I was shown immediately that I was not a personality, but a specimen of the Boy class—an implement for their service—and to the vanity of morbid youth that was jarring. Nobody called me facetious names or punched me in the ribs; I was the Boy. I had expected to be taken as one of the staff, and trained in the traditions of the firm; instead, I was treated as a hired outsider. After the bluff geniality of Caledonian Road, this frigid atmosphere was disconcerting. It seemed that they didn't want me to get on. They looked through me as though I wasn't there; took papers and messages from my hands as though I were a tray. I was ordered about—not cheerily, as at Mylchreest's but snappily or coldly, as from high to low.

"Boy, get me the black ruler."

"Your hand's just on it—there."

"I said 'Pass me the Ruler.' None of your impudence. And don't frown."

Why were respectable people so bad-tempered, and the people at Mylchreest's so jolly? It didn't seem right.

They quickly made me see that my manners and accent were alien to a business office. They forced Creegan's advice upon me every day, and every day I winced. At Caledonian Road I had had a taste of liberty and ease. That job made no call for shames or pretences; I could be myself at my worst and was accepted as fit. But here I was enclosed by rules and standards and inhibitions. They told me not to say "Oo." They told me to speak up and not mumble. They told me not to get excited. They told me not to stamp when I walked. They told me not to look so tragical. I saw that I was a creature utterly coarse, but whenever I made labour to catch their manners and voices I only achieved a simper. Soon I gave it up. What did it matter? What was the good of trying? I was the office-boy, and it would be impertinence for the office-boy to try to talk like them. Two of the younger clerks were public-school, and it became hateful to me to hear their talk. The tone was so self-satisfied, so sure of itself. They seemed to have no doubts of their rightness; they were there, set, and their passivity could outshine my brightest action. However I might copy the accent, it would never come rightly from me. They were poised; I was wobbly. They were easy; I was jumpy. They were suave; I was all prickles. To the trivial occasion I brought intense surprise; they had the air of adventurers familiar with earthquakes. They had a background of neat villas at Putney and parents and servants; I was an outcast, with the smell of Bermondsey and charity about me. No inward grace could supply their outward manner. I had to prove myself; they hadn't.

All my attempts at talk were snubbed; and I was made to see that my eagerness to acquire the spirit of the office was presumption. I was not really interested in the business of coal-mines, but even my zealous endeavours to work up some sort of interest and so give greater satisfaction were snubbed.   An office-boy is paid to Do, I was told, not to think, and when I asked, "Why do we do this?" and "What's the difference between Silkstone and Brights?" and "How many collieries does the company own?" I was told to get on with my work and not to bother my head with what didn't concern me.

But I did bother my head.   I did try hard, in a blundering way, to increase my Efficiency—there were then no Postal Courses by which you could rise from office-boy to chief accountant in six months.   I read all the current correspondence, learnt the names and addresses of the firm's cus- tomers, and spent empty minutes among the old files, trying to light up the dreary business of address- ing envelopes by dramatising the dead names of the correspondents into personalities, visualising the Godfrey of Godfrey, Hobbs & Co., or the Sells of Charrington Sells, Dale & Co.   By this means I was able to save the invoice clerk from a row by pointing out that he had invoiced the last lot to the Imshi Line at a lower price than was quoted— I had seen the contract.   And the clerk asked me what I meant by poking my nose into the firm's private papers.   When I said that I could work better if I knew what the work was about, the clerk said, "What?   D'you think the heads of a busi- ness are going to spend their time letting a parcel of boys into their affairs?   What next!"

My last effort was another act of grace. While copying the letters one afternoon I noted that the traveller was to give himself the pleasure of calling upon Messrs. Knowles Brothers at eleven o'clock to-morrow. At twenty to eleven, the next day, the traveller shuffled into the office. His brow was tight. His eyes were heavy and wavering. He put his feet down with a little too much care, and instead of throwing his gloves on to my table, he put them down deliberately, and then missed the table. He fiddled about the office, picking things up and putting them down. I noted these things, and deduced, by knowledge gathered from office talk, that the traveller had been Up West. At ten minutes to eleven I went to him.

"Please, sir, you haven't forgotten that appointment with Knowles Brothers?"

"Eh? What? What?"

"That appointment at eleven o'clock. Knowles Brothers."

"Er. Oh! I—er—yes, of course. I know all about that." He turned hastily to the door; then turned back. "But how do you come to know my business?"

"I read the letter, sir."

"What? Read the letter? Who gave you instructions to read letters? Your business is to copy them, not read them. I'll talk to you when I come back."

I gave it up then, and adjusted myself as a shuttle, and made the office a dusty background for the adventure of London. Chiefly, through those four years, I was conscious of hunger and loneliness, and these things resolved themselves into the one fact of poverty. I was hungry and I was lonely because I was poor, and as I wandered and brooded among rich streets, or worked, silent and ignored, in the office, I saw poverty as a hideous shame.

I belonged to the Poor—the Poor, who were always presented as comic and gawky in a world whose standards were discretion and ease. The Poor, who had to answer insolent questions that never were addressed to the Rich. The Poor, who were written about and talked about and admonished, as though they were animals whose ways were not fully understood; interesting specimens for study, to be patted and coerced like dogs, their curious doings and sayings giving light material for lecture platforms. The Poor, who, as one of the elegant young clerks said, always smelt poor. The Poor, whose children were bundled and herded into Christian Homes. The Poor whose sorrows and joys were always public. The Poor who, when charged in the police-court, were not given a seat in the dock, but were addressed, even when married women, as Brown or Jones, and whose remarks were printed with (Laughter) if they pronounced a word wrongly. Nobody talked that way about the Rich or the aristocratic. These were often condemned, but always with respect in the condemnation. The Poor were often approved, but always with patronage in the approval, as in the gentleman's benign approval of professional sportsmen. When Dukes said silly things these things were examined as

Points of View. When a poor woman said a silly thing, the magistrate capped it with a flippancy, and it was handed out for public amusement. If a poor man got drunk on Bank Holiday, it was "Father Has His Fling." If a titled youth got drunk on Boat Race Night, and kicked over old men's baked-potao cans and knocked women down, it was "Lord Henry Slummocks' Daring Escapade."

I was poor, and in the self-pity of adolescence I despised myself, and the standards by which I judged myself, while feeling that in a world of other values I would rank decently. But in this world I was despised, and for me there seemed then but one way out—downward—among the yobs and van-boys. But that, now that I had touched respectability, was unthinkable. So I went on being a soulless organism—the Boy, successor to many boys—and life was one long hunger, and the half-empty stomach re-acted in mental laceration.

Every mid-day was a tantalising dance of savoury odours. My lunch was tea and cake at a tea-shop, and always some tactless brute would sit at my table and order stewed steak and carrots and potatoes and apple-tart, until the sight of it made my teeth weep, and I had to go out. But I had my pride. I had tasted respectability, and desperately as I sniffed at the rich smells of Harris' Sausage Restaurant, and gloated on the onions and the pork chops sizzling in the window, I would still take my crumbs at Lyons'. Better a tea and bun, dignified, than a fat meal bought at the counter and eaten at bare tables among van boys and warehousemen.

It wasn't until my second year that I gave up yearnings towards dignity, and accepted Lockhart and Pearce and Plenty as the fit places for me.

Slowly my ambitions drooped, and I fell into the crawling way of life, comatose. In my room at home, in the evening, I fed myself on violent foods: faggots, black puddings, penny tins of bloater paste, cheese eaten with bread thickly laid with mustard, or with condensed milk at twopence a tin; (a penny tin of mustard lasted me for a month, and took the place of butter) and in the mornings I was hot and petulant and pale, and reached the office with buzzing head, stinging eyes, limp knees, and flushes of heat through arms and back. That walk from Bermondsey to Lime Street was daily a forced march, and often I would forego the piece of cake at lunch, and have only coffee, in order to ride over the Bridge. Yet, though night after night, for four years, I went hungry to bed, actively hungry, I never dreamt of food. But I did dream often of encounters with Quong Lee.

I grew pesky and abnormally sensitive. To the clerks in the office I must have been an odious little beast. I fancied insults where none were meant. I had large hates. In all comeliness I saw Swank. In every carriage I saw a fat brute. Life was a string of envy, hatred and malice. Where they came from I don't know; it must have been either the black puddings or the mustard. I couldn't settle to anything. I drifted. Sometimes I would tell myself that I would go to Caledonian Road and see Lil, and then I wouldn't go, and then at night I would wish I had; and sometimes I would go out in the evening, and wish I had stayed at home and gone to bed, and sometimes I would stay at home and then wish I had gone out.

I began to hate myself. Only once or twice did a gleam of grace come to me and set things in proportion. Then I would say: "You beast! You've got ten shillings a week and a bed to sleep in and a roof over your head. What have you got to whine about? This is life, and you're in the thick of it. There's thousands worse off than you." But I was sixteen, and sixteen is so deeply concerned with itself that it seldom sees itself.

Days of my youth, say the forgetful; happy days! That is one of the many precious lies that grown-ups like to tell themselves. I had little happiness then, partly because I was young, and partly because I had no friends, no money, bad food and no hope. As for those who wish they were young again, I suspect them. There was just one good thing I had then which belongs to all youth, however miserable. Though utterly joyless, I had a tremendous *capacity* for joy.

. . . .

In isolated moments this joy came, and when it came I seized it. Behind all my distress shone the great adventure of London, and against the hourly fret of hunger and shabby clothes and broken boots were set some splendid evenings. If my City life was a fog it was shot with random flashes of beauty. The wonder of life! The magic of people! The fun of living in Bermondsey, and having shops to look at and streets to walk in, and sunshine in the mornings, and the thunder of traffic, and the long lines of evening lamps. The blessedness of bread-and-mustard when you were hungry; the delight of a bedroom when you were tired.

At seven o'clock I was free of the streets, and there night by night I wandered, letting London soak into me and resigning myself to my circumstances. I could see no way of getting on or getting out; I had no abilities for the City, and had lost all desire to attain them. For anything else I was useless, and it looked like ten shillings a week for ever. I didn't believe that it *would* go on for ever; I felt that something would have to happen; but at that time I could see nothing but the chemist's shop or the gas-ring in Mrs. Flanagan's kitchen. Many a time, under the dark cloud of my age, I lingered on the bridges and brooded, but London saved me. Lonely as I was, it was a romantic lone-liness, for there was all London to be lonely in. Sometimes of an evening I dashed threepence on a cup of tea and a piece of lunch-cake in an A.B.C. shop, away from my daily groove, and sat at my ease, regardless of the clock, and looked out upon the phantasmal streets, violet in the September dusk, or ebony and gold at winter, and the flash of faces from nowhere into nowhere, and the surge of their commerce. Once or twice, when I got a tip from a caller, I had buttered toast, and those occasions were high festivals. Afterwards I wandered wherever my feet led me among queer streets and people, and suffered moments of rapture and of morbid gloom.

I saw all London at all hours of evening and night, and when I think of London I think always of lamps and spectral figures. Until I was twenty-four I knew nothing of London's mornings outside the City. I did not see Hyde Park at eleven o'clock or Piccadilly Circus at mid-day or the Strand or Oxford Street at afternoon tea-time. I knew them only at night, but every night was an adventure. On pay-days I took 'bus-rides (on top, just behind the driver) and rode through London, and got off wherever my twopence left me, and roamed right or left, and felt the awfulness of Westminster Bridge Road or Notting Dale, and their side-streets thick with all the wonder and dismay of life's pilgrimage; and the dark rumour of Cromwell Road, and the grandeur of the Kensington hotels through whose lacy windows I saw magnificent people having Late Dinner. I peeped in at stately restaurants and clubs, hovering and slinking, conscious of my impudence and fearful that the commissionaire would push me out of the way. I stood outside theatres and watched the arrival of the broughams with their sleek and silken parties. It was a world of elegance and coolness, of music and brilliant people talking brilliantly: a world to which I had no claim, by merit or indulgence, but the world where I longed to be. With the City in prospect, I had dreamed wildly of some day rising to a head-clerkship at three pounds a week, but now that I knew the City

in fact, I saw that that was beyond my achievement.
Even a pound a week seemed outside my reach;
and never, even as a moment's dream, did it come
to me that I might some day sit at those tables or
ride in those cabs or enter those glittering vestibules
as one entitled to enter them.

I wonder what happened to those places between
then and the time I did reach them?   What Alad-
din has been at work to dim their magnificence?
Where are those splendid hotels of Kensington?
Where are those cool, cultured people whom I
watched going into theatres?   Where are those
brilliant minds that I saw exchanging wit at the
Embankments windows of the Savoy?   Where are
those radiant women and august waiters and golden
lamps and peacock carpets?   What imp of the bottle has turned Gatti's, in the Strand, from a palace
of gold and blue, fit only for princes and princesses,
into an ordinary restaurant where bank clerks and
people like myself now lunch or dine?

At first I took these rambles as an escape from
the City and from hunger, but soon the streets got
hold of me, and I turned to them, not as to a nar-
cotic, but as to a stimulant.   I went out deliberately every night to find excitement.   I loved the
great highways and the lights and the noise, and
the meditative squares; the gleams of light and the
rich shadows, and the mighty spirit that lived in
all of them; but mostly I was drawn by the long,
dark side-streets that led to far countries or to
secret encampments of alien and outlaw.   Spitalfields was as foreign to Bermondsey as the West

Indies, Camberwell Green as Siberia. The men of
Islington were not as the men I worked among, and
the ways of life of Clerkenwell were not the ways of
Bermondsey. I went peeping through doors and
windows upon strange and alluring worlds. The
meandering streets or the recesses of the alleys held
the secrets of Walpurgis. Nothing could happen in
the Bermondsey streets; I dismissed them as known
and empty; but anything might happen in these
streets abroad. I charged each one with the occasion of romantic encounter. One might open a door
and stumble upon a murder. One might walk up
an alley, and a face at a window might beckon one
to the beautiful adventure. The most foolish dream
might come to life there among the bizarre beings
who peopled them; the most pleasant tale of young
love, the quaintest tales of gnomes, the nightmare
tale of legend.

I carried away each night little parcels of pictures.
The haze of a fried-fish bar. The tinkle of an organ
hidden in a back street. A lamp in an alley giving
just enough light to make darkness horrible.
The reek and murk of a public-house. The massed
lights of factories hung, as it were, from the sky.
The gleam and gush of drapers' windows. Voices
mourning or crying from unseen points. Street-
corner groupings carven out of shadow. Strange
life moving behind curtained windows or half-open
doors. Darkness settled upon the city in a hundred
hues: the leaden darkness of the Thames, the sable
darkness of arches, blue spires and the shoulders
of great buildings looming against deeper blue, the

clotted horror of fog; each darkness shading from the sky into its separate mood.

I followed these streets wherever their aimless curves and crowded corners led me; and every night some fresh aspect was revealed, some suave mingling of gleam and gloom, some wayward arrangement of light. Things and places that by day were uncomely were re-born in night-beauty; and the meanest yard, the dreariest street became as awful as the topmost peaks of the Mountains of the Moon. A narrow street by day was a narrow street, one of a regiment, wanting colour and distinction; but with the coming of the night it made revelation. Its lamp-posts, by day pieces of iron, were then living watchers; and under their light the street was changed. Touched by the mystery of darkness and lamp, it became itself, took new lines, new form and spirit. It was not even the twin of its daytime self, but a changeling of the night, with something of that goblin spell that hovers about the changeling. A warehouse wall at night was a monster. Ludicrous chimney-pots held the challenge of the gargoyles of the Middle Ages, and railway arches were creatures of grace and strength hollowed out of the manifold darknesses. Villiers Street was an expression of the hour of escape; the diminishing lights of the Embankment carried the rhythm of great rivers; and every square was charged with the thoughtfulness of night.

London became a living thing, and I walked round and round it, trying to read its tale, and brushing shoulders with wonder. I met Frenchmen

in Soho; Italians in Clerkenwell; Roumanians in
Spitalfields; Arabs in Canning Town; Swedes in
Shadwell; Germans in Charlotte Street; Russians
in Stepney. I went alone through the crowding
bricks, and alone through a masque of faces—faces
in millions—faces sad, gay, empty, morose, evil;
faces ugly and beautiful; faces of the pavement;
faces that floated in 'bus and tram, and faces that
peered down darkly from upper windows. I wanted
to fit every face with its story. I wanted to stop
these wandering creatures, and ask them where they
lived and what they were doing, and what it was
that made them sad or happy or cruel. I wanted
to tell Quong Lee all about it.

Where other lads, more comfortably placed,
turned for respite from their routine to music-halls,
or billiards, or the parks, I turned to the streets and
drugged myself with them, and walked for miles in
muzzy exaltation and went home hot and dazed.
I threw my world aside, and entered into the
imagined lives of these people, and invented stirring
episodes, figuring myself as a being of parts with
opportunities for display. I passed young men with
whom I imagined jolly friendships; girls about
whom I built romances. I had miraculous adventures in Bethnal Green and the back streets of Islington; desperate rescues in Maida Vale; dark hours
under the whispering windows of Shadwell. Certain
actual encounters I did have with queer women of
Marylebone; twisted creatures of the alleys; queer
old men. They saluted and sometimes followed me.
They said Good-night, or said that it was Warm or

Wet, and asked where I was off to. Twice I was invited to dinner "just round the corner," and once to a music-hall. I didn't accept, because I always thought they had mistaken me for some young man they knew. But it happened so often, and in different parts of London, and there was something so similar about all the men, that I had to abandon the idea that it was some secret brotherhood of the kind I had read about in *Tit-Bits*, and recognise that the game was what it was.

Two years I spent thus; doing my daily work without thought, and going nightly to bed without hope. Then there was a rustle and a stir, and, though my outward life remained unchanged, except to become more detestable, I awoke from within.

I discovered literature.

CHAPTER VI

DISCOVERY

I CANNOT trace the processes of that discovery. It seems that one week I was reading *Tit-Bits*, and next week I was sitting in a tea-shop, lunching on coffee and cake, and reading a copy of a paper left on the seat by an earlier customer. It was called *T.P.'s Weekly*. There was no gradual awakening. I was conscious of an immediate opening-out and suddenly found myself confronted with the blaze and dazzle of literature and music. Why I devoured that paper I don't know. It dealt with matters that were wholly strange to me, and yet I felt that I could find my way about in it. I knew nothing of that upper world of spirits that lived with culture and recreated what they knew for the joy of men; yet I was attracted by that paper, and every Friday thence I lunched on coffee only and bought it.

The great exploration began. I joined the Public Library at Bermondsey, and the assistant-librarian, a middle-aged creature with a face as dry as his alpaca jacket, took an interest in my plunge. He told me of *The Bookman* and *The Book Monthly*, and drew me on to the poets. I wasn't sure about those poets. I had always looked upon poetry as matter for laughter. In my world poets were figures of fun—timid, crazy things with long hair and effeminate hands, who went about looking at the moon. One could speak seriously of Dan Leno, but poetry implied derision which was expressed in unseemly parodies of "The Village Blacksmith," and "Come into the Garden, Maud." Poetry meant "The Wreck of the Hesperus," "The May Queen," and "Casabianca." Of Keats, Shelley and Browning I had not heard.

The librarian started me with Keats. Difficult stuff. All about people whose names I couldn't pronounce: Lamia, Hyperion, Endymion. Most of it bored me, but here and there I felt that there was Something About It. Shelley was worse. What he was raving about I really didn't know. Byron was a bit better, and bits of Browning had Something About Them. But I must confess that I did not quickly find my way about the realms of gold. I stumbled among these poets; and though an odd line from this one or that sent shivers down my neck, I was mainly perplexed. The biographical prefaces held me more than the texts; and I soon found that poets weren't the ninnies I had imagined them to be. They were interesting people, who lived interesting lives and suffered beautifully. Even when I couldn't understand their work, I was lifted and swayed by it; there was a surge in Byron and in some of Browning like that in Creegan's double-bass. Anyway, I was done with *Tit-Bits* and the comics. I began to swank, and to decide that I would be intellectual, and walk above the herd; be like Chatterton and Mangan—a dark, pathetic figure. Clearly that was where I belonged; and I began to wrestle with poetry and to read everything I could find about the poets. I began to walk over London Bridge to the beat of single lines: "In Xanadu did Kubla Khan"—but what he did I couldn't discover—"When looking on the happy Autumn fields"—"O lyric love, half angel and half bird."

One book led insensibly to another. I discovered new poets and new authors each week. I began to look into book-shops, and yearn towards possessing my own books instead of the greasy, pig-bound library copies. Then I discovered the *Canterbury Poets*, at ninepence, and the *World's Classics* at a shilling; and I sacrificed three lunches and saved up a month's tips, and bought Edgar Allan Poe. Being seventeen I turned naturally to those poets who had been miserable—Poe, Chatterton, Mangan, Burns, Otway—and if I couldn't read their poetry I read their lives. London was now touched with a new magic—the magic of noble association; and though I couldn't travel with Ariel I could feel the brush of his wings. The hard lines of Poultry became softened because Hood had been born there, and Waterloo Bridge was charged with passion and terror. Oxford Street was no more a busy main street; it was steeped in darkling clouds, not of London, but of bizarre countries of the fancy; and at every corner fluttered the imperial purple of the opium eater. (Him I could understand, and I carried him about with me for weeks.) The horrid terra-cotta of the Prudential Building assumed grace as covering the site of Chatterton's last lodging. Tower Hill was lit with Otway, Bankside with Shakespeare and Greene, and the Borough High Street with the Canterbury Pilgrims. Even my own court, Bussell's Grove, took something of the spell. I dramatised it. Perhaps Chatterton or Savage had lived in just such a place as this. It was no longer a slum under the arches, but a corner of Spain where beautiful faces lingered in doorways. I saw the end house as waiting for the right tale to claim it and unfold itself there, a tale of youth and love and midnight. From the window of my room I looked across a shingle of red and grey roofs to the upper structure of the Tower Bridge, and this, too, began to live. The smell of hops and the reek of the tanneries, the grumble of the trains and the clamour of the river traffic, no longer disturbed me. Bankside was not so very far away, and the voices from tug and barge were crying in the accents that were heard by the Bankside folk three hundred years ago.

I had hot moments in tea-shops over my evening tea-and-cake, and there are certain branches of Lyons and the A.B.C. which for me have something of the quality of that shop in the Causeway. In a Cheapside shop on an April night I first read "Love in the Valley." In another, on a December night, I first read "The Fall of the House of Usher." In another, on a hot evening of June, I sat until closing-time reading "The Urn Burial." In yet another I read "In Memoriam" at one sitting. Those shops to-day effuse beauty with the odours of tea and toast, and lunch-cake is more than something that can be bought at a penny a slice.

Hot with the hunter's passion, I began to chase everything labelled "standard." Criticism was beyond me; the hungry man has no time for the fastidiousness of the epicure. I was hypnotised by the word Poet. A poem by Keats (some trifle never meant for print) was a poem by Keats. Pope and Cowper and Kirke White and Mrs. Hemans and Samuel Rogers were Poets. That was enough. I heard of a great novel called *Vanity Fair*. I tried three chapers and left it. I heard of a classic work called Boswell's *Johnson*. I read a few pages, and took it back to the Library. I heard of George Borrow, and found him dull and ungrammatical. I tried *The Vicar of Wakefield* and was bored. But in the mood of intellectual swagger induced by my plunge into great waters I hid these failures. At the office I began to show off, and to carry "standard" poets with me, and leave them about, and at last they began to notice me, though the notice was edged with deserved ridicule. They could not understand why a boy of my sort should want to fill his head with That Stuff. I see now that they were justified; they were my employers; but I couldn't see it then.

"These rubbishy books lying about. No wonder you're so slack. Making your head silly with all this reading. Why don't you study something that will Get You On?"

I answered with a superior smile, and continued to swank. I read books that bored and books that jangled, and told the clerks how wonderful they were. I read those pompous weeklies that seem to be written by God in collaboration with Lord Curzon, and came to regard normal people as oysters. I read Walter Pater and Matthew Arnold and Ibsen and Bernard Shaw and Maeterlinck. It is doubtful if I fully knew how much they bored me. The names held glamour, and seventeen is not an age for self-honesty and sharp likes and dislikes. I knew I was doing right in reading them; I knew that I was lifting myself above the office herd; and I deceived myself into thinking that I liked them. But the strain was too great for a half-empty stomach, and I soon returned to the black magic of Edgar Allan Poe and de Quincey, and the headlong urge of Byron. I was at home with colour and flame, but the quartz of Carlyle didn't go down with bread and mustard: the figs and nuts of Emerson were useless to me. The tepid lustre of Matthew Arnold, the marble tiles of Pater, the cold-water homilies of Ruskin left me unsatisfied. I was particularly snappish about Emerson and Ruskin. I felt that people who wrote polished sentences about the spiritual dignity of poverty should try it for a month—in Bermondsey.

But I continued to read them, and soon my mind became a lumber-room. Philosophy, poetry, romance, truth and lies jostled one another and fought. I read every new book in the light of its predecessor. I made no attempt to range or relate them, but accepted them all, changing my ideas of life to the tune of each new author. I went about London aflame with loves and hates; hate of the City, of the office, of the jargon of commerce, of dull people, and love of London and poetry and the world of intellect and fancy, where people Did Things; and Oh, my God! how I despised, in the mad pride of intellectuality, the tattered folk I had to work among. To me the meanest red-nose comedian in a third-rate music-hall stood in achievement far above the biggest buyer and seller. But I was young then. I thought I was unique. As I grew older I learned that the desire for beauty is not the gift of intellectuals or divines. Everywhere it manifests itself. Every working woman in the slums who puts a coloured almanack on the wall, every clerk who potters in his garden, is satisfying the yearning for beauty. The girl who saves up for a feathered hat of clashing colours is striving for beauty as she sees it. The working-man who spoils his cheap furniture by painting it with flowers is striving for beauty. This instinct has nothing to do with culture; it is an inward force. Even the boor who guffaws at the sight of a beautiful picture or a poetic moment in a play has recognised beauty, and his guffaw is his abashed tribute.

Slowly, and unknown to myself, my voice and accent changed. I was just as awkward, just as uncouth, but by constant rehearsal of my favourite passages, I achieved control of the letter "h," learned to give words their full value, and dropped certain locutions of the "not 'alf" sort. But still I was depressed by loneliness. There was nobody with whom I could talk of these things, except the

librarian, and he didn't encourage personal acquaintance; only thrust new books into my hands and
finger-pointed new paths of reading. Nobody in
the office had the smallest interest in these matters,
or in life. Nothing outside their own daily day
interested them. But though I affected to scorn
them, they could still crush me with a word or a
look. They answered my new eagerness with dis-
dain. At first I had been merely the Boy, but when
I began to turn up with *A Critical History of the
Renaissance* and *An Interpretation of Browning,*
they began to grin, and I heard them speak of me
as "half potty." When I told them that I had
been to the Causeway in Limehouse the night before they stared at me as though I were some freak.

"Nice place for a walk. Been to see one of your
aristocratic friends?"

"No. I haven't. I know a Chinaman down
there, though."

"Know a Chinaman? You!"

"Yes. I often go down there. It's fine down by
the river at night."

"H'm. P'raps you feel at home there. You
look half a Chink sometimes with that flat hair and
those eyes of yours. You're more like an old man
than a kid. Why don't you be like other boys and
go and play football? Mooching about by yourself.
And in the East End, too. Still, if that's your
taste. . . ."

"I like it. The walls. And the lights shining
down. And the funnels against the sky, and
the . . ."

"Don't keep wagging your hand like that. You're not Lord Rosebury."

So I drew more and more into myself, and grew sensitive of being looked at in the streets. There must have been something funny about me, because other boys grinned at me, and girls giggled and said "Oo-er!" Men found something funny in me too. I overheard things on London Bridge.

"Look at that nipper in front. Thinks he's the Lord Mayor already."

"Ah, but that's the sort that gets on, though." And the boys would say, "Gorstrewth—look at that little bounder in his free-and-ninepenny!"

But I had my own world. New sensations and discoveries awaited me with the turn of every week. There was the joy of watching sixpence grow to sevenpence, then eightpence, then ninepence, and a Canterbury Poet within reach; and then yielding to the flesh, and letting the whole ninepence go in one blazing burst of sausages, potatoes and onions. From literature I moved, by the guidance of *T.P.'s Weekly*, to pictures and music. Here again I posed. I went to the National Gallery, and felt profound (as I had been told to) before the Dutch and Flemish masters. They were indeed wonderful. Oh, yes, they were. But when I came to Turner and Constable I didn't give them phrases. I just looked and looked, and my mental state was "Oo!" With music it was the same. I read something about Promenade Concerts and the Opera. Promenade Concerts, obviously, were concerts where you walked about instead of sitting, but what "the opera" was I didn't know. I had heard of comic opera, but that was vulgar stuff. Was there only one opera? I went to the Reference Library, and made investigation, and found that there were quite a lot of operas, and that different operas were played every night from May to July; and that opera was just like a play only everything was sung instead of being spoken.

By missing three teas and carrying a parcel for Mr. Pollock, I was able to sample a Promenade Concert, and discovered, first, that you couldn't promenade, and second that Beethoven and Bach and Haydn were great composers. Undoubtedly they were great. I had read that they were great, and I felt, while listening, that there was Something About Them. But Rossini, William Tell overture, Wagner, Prelude to Act 3, Lohengrin, Brahms' Hungarian Dances, 1812, Raymond, Berlioz Hungarian March—were another matter, and they shook my belief that "The Lost Chord" and "Ora Pro Nobis" were the majestic expression in music.

Oo!

These brought positive pleasure; the others only the pleasure of attending something serious, and being different from the people who lined up at music-halls. There was the long wait at the door, listening to the music-talk about me. (I felt that I was in the world of grace and refinement where I had longed to me; among clean people with sweet manners and brilliant minds.) Would I ever know enough about music to be able to talk like that? The opening of the doors. The stampede at the

pay-desk. The sheep-like rush downstairs. The
scramble for a seat near the orchestra. The red-
shaded lamps. The soft carpet. The cigarette
smoke. The solemnity of everybody. The gladi-
torial entry of the musicians. The tuning-up—little
flourishes of melody from the strings, soft blares
from the brass, teasing runs on the wood-wind.
The immense number of them; enough to make
thirty Creegan orchestras. Four double-basses.
Eight 'cellos. I stared at this stupendous army of
instruments. I was seeing things to-night; the larg-
est orchestra in the world, surely. I wanted to go
out and tell people about it. I was sure that nobody
in the City or Bermondsey knew about this orchestra
and these concerts. It seemed impossible that——
A mild wave of clapping: the leader had entered.
Then a Hush. The entrance of the shaggy-haired
magician who was to control this mighty thing. The
applause; the solemn bows. At last, perfect silence.
The raised bâton. The moment of suspense. And
then—ah!—the grand plunge into the Tannhauser
March. . . .

But the Italians at the opera! There was no
pose here. They took me down my own streets.
I made my first venture one Saturday evening, following a month of hard saving and close attendance
upon Pollock. The opera was called *La Bo-
hème*, all about poets and artists and their love-
affairs, and for me it held the dignity of tragedy.
There were singers whom I had seen described in
the papers as the greatest singers in the world—
Caruso, Melba, Scotti, Journet.

That was a night of "Oos." You see, I was un-
prepared for anything like this. I had heard no
singing except street-corner or music-hall singing;
and coming suddenly upon the new thing, I was
almost drunk. I had never dreamed that there
were such voices in the world. Oo—to be able to
sing like that! To be able to write music like that!
I sat tight in my cramped seat, hands on knees,
fingers clenched, while a stupendous voice welled
out of the dark, filling the house and ringing round
the gallery. A voice that laughed and wept, and
rose above trumpet and drum, and now was like a
little bell, and now rippled and sparkled and surged;
a voice that made me think of crimson velvet.

Coo-oo!

I felt that with that voice I was in the presence
of something even more wonderful than poetry.
Through the intervals I sat rigid and dazed, but
when at last the curtain fell I came out reeling, and
stood for half an hour near Waterloo Bridge, my
ears full of the voice of Caruso and the phrases of
the opera. I wondered whether Caruso had ever
been poor, and whether he had been an office-boy
and what it must feel like to be a singer and have
friends wherever you went. But no—that creature
might have been a gipsy, but never a creature of the
squalid makeshifts of the back streets. He might
have been hard up, but never meanly poor. I had
read about famous people who were said to have
been poor, and I had found that the word "poor"
meant whatever you wanted it to mean. People living in their own houses in the suburbs and having

three meals a day were said to be poor. Authors were said to have "struggled" on two pounds a week. Great painters whose fathers kept shops were spoken of as born among the poor; but I had known people who kept shops in Bermondsey, and they had plenty of money and sent their children to the Higher Grade School. Creegan always called himself poor, but Creegan had a bank-account and a cheque-book. I didn't believe that anybody who got on had ever been really poor. No matter how clever you were, before you could get a chance of getting out, you had to look respectable, and how could you get a decent suit out of ten shillings a week? No—none of those wonderful singers had been like me: their faces hadn't got the "poor" look. They had been born among musical people, and had gone right into it.

I wondered at which of those big hotels Caruso was staying, and what his daily life was like, and how many servants and carriages he had, and what he would have for supper, and what he felt about Things, and . . . then in a spasm of irritation at my own idiocy, I kicked the bridge and went home to Bussell's Grove.

Ten years later I told him about that night, and in a little wine-shop at Beausoleil we shared a bottle over it, and drank to each other and to Covent Garden.

.   .   .   .

My inner life was now all music. I went to the opera three times that year (I cultivated Mr. Pollock who liked scrapes and bows) and I lived on melodies, worked on melodies, walked home to melodies. Instead of lines of poetry I carried tunes about with me, festal tunes. I placed Puccini and Mascagni as radiant creatures living far above my own world in a fairy world of sound. Bach? Beethoven? Yes, but with my small stature I could hardly see them. They lived in clouds, but these others had their feet on the earth. I saw all creative work as the spirit of God speaking through common men, and I even found the spirit of God in a derided Intermezzo. But with delight came a wild desire to do something like that myself. I wanted to make something. I wanted to tell people what I thought and what I knew. I wanted to tell them about Quong Lee and his shop. I remembered my violin lessons, and tried to write music for the violin, and found that all my phrases were bits of opera. I tried to make verses about Quong Lee on the model of Byron and Chatterton; and lit the fire with them. I wrote poetical addresses to my poets inside the covers of their works, to all except one of them. This sort of thing: "O Keats, that died while yet the harp was trembling. . . ." "O Shelley, when the waters covered thee. . . ." "O Wordsworth. . . ." "O Byron. . . ." "O Chatterton. . . ." I gave each of them ten or fourteen lines. All but Burns. Burns stumped me, because he was writing in a foreign language; and if by chance you find on a second-hand stall a copy of the Songs of Burns in the *Canterbury Poets,* with two words written on the fly-leaf, "O Burns," that's my copy of Burns.

I tried to draw Quong Lee's shop-window, and
found that I couldn't even copy an advertisement
figure; and I felt sick with myself. I was good for
nothing. The office was all I was fit for. Should
I ever get out of the City? Should I ever get among
people who were leading real lives and doing real
things? Should I ever get a chance to do something?
It seemed hopeless. Anyway, what was it that I
wanted to do? I didn't know. I only knew that
my whole being was itching to get something out.

Then, one night, after a long visit to Quong Lee,
I walked all the way home, and, walking home, I
saw, quite suddenly, what it was inside me that was
struggling to get out. That shop. I hurried home
then, and when I got home I routed out all the bits
of paper I could find, and started to write. In three
nights I finished the thing; and at the office, after
the staff was gone, I punched it out, slowly, on the
office typewriter. I sent it to *T.P.'s Weekly*. It
came back, but the printed slip bore half a dozen
written words. That was enough for me: I knew
then what it was that I wanted to do; and I began
to write stories and essays and send them out. For
several months they came back; but upon one glorious evening I found a letter on my bed, and the letter said that the Editor had pleasure in enclosing
cheque for one guinea in payment for the copyright
of my story appearing in the current issue of his
paper.

I was an author!

The world went warm and opened out. At last
I could do something; and every night thereafter

I sat and wrote till midnight; and though I wrote stories, essays and descriptive articles, the spirit behind everything I wrote was the spirit of that shop.

For the next ten months whatever I wrote came back; but I continued writing in that mixed mood of delight and disgust known to every striver. There were weeks when I couldn't write; when nothing came; and I felt then that never again would I be able to write a paragraph. When I couldn't get at the office stationery I wrote on used envelopes or on fly-leaves torn from my few books. Thousands of words I wrote and destroyed. Always there was the blank between the conception and pencil and paper; always the self-assurance that I never *could* and the foolish persistence in trying; and always the printed rejection slips seemed to say so much more than "Not good enough." They seemed to say, "Thou fool!"

Then I began to study the papers; and when I was seventeen I sold three articles in one year, and made thirty-three shillings; and on top of that the office gave me my first rise. The junior clerk was promoted, and I was given the junior's work to do, in addition to my own, at fifteen shillings a week. I began to see that life was moving. For five weeks I put the extra money aside, and at the fifth week I went to the big outfitter's in Newington Causeway, and came away with a ready-made grey suit at twenty-two-and-sixpence. I went in as a slommock. I came out a dandy. When I had cast off the baggy, frayed trousers and the stained, ragged coat that

had served me for more than two years' daily wear,
and settled myself inside the shining greys (a bit
tight under the arms and across the chest) I had
again the Hardcress emotion about clothes, but
reversed. I felt as though I had had a full and
perfect meal. Energy came to me, and I crept out
of my shell. The very feel of the clothes filled me
with the holiday spirit; I could have walked for
miles that Saturday afternoon. I was respectable.
I could look at myself in shop-windows without
shame. My bowler hat was certainly a bit battered,
and the boots were badly turned over, but in general
appearance, I was All Right. And I had fifteen
shillings coming in every week.

I began to take things seriously and to write in
every spare moment that I could snatch—at home
or under the blotting-pad at the office. I worked
without guidance or plan—now striving to make
something beautiful, now striving to do anything
that would get me out of my present reek and stain,
away from the nastiness of wet boots, bad food, and
stupid people. I had no determination to succeed
and no hope. I just went on writing. I didn't
hitch my waggon to a star, because it was such a
little waggon; but I did solemnly copy out certain
passages from my reading, and solemnly pin them
over my fireplace. This sort of thing—from Wagner:

"*I believe in God, Mozart, and Beethoven, and
in their disciples and apostles. I believe in the
Holy Ghost and the truth of art. I believe that*

*this art proceeds from God, and dwells in the
hearts of all enlightened men."*

And this from Ibsen:

*"Is it not an inexpressibly great gift of fortune
to write? And how far-reaching its effects!"*

And this from an American novelist:

*"I never truckled. I never took off the hat
to fashion, and held it out for pennies. I told
them the truth as I saw it; I knew it for the
truth then and I know it for the truth now."*

And this from Emerson:

*"Doubt not, O poet, but persist. Say, 'It is in
me and shall out.' Stand there, balked and dumb,
stuttering and stammering, stand and strive, until
at last rage draw out of thee that dream-power
which every night shows thee is thine own.'"*

I held that only those men who had given to the
world the crystallisation of their visions of beauty
were of use in the world; and that all others were
dust. I could not see that we can only give what
we have. Like most serious lads of my age, I was
the unconscious prig. Partly, I think, this attitude
was shaped by my loneliness. There was only
Quong Lee, and he was only a city of refuge from
certain moods. There seemed no hope of meeting
anybody like myself and making friends. Were
there no young fellows of seventeen and of my own

class who cared for life and poetry and music and
All That? There *were* poor, intelligent people in
London: I had heard them talking in the gallery
outside Covent Garden; but none of them were of
my age or of my own class. They were mostly
middle-aged, and they talked with rather cultured
voices, and seemed to know all about everything.
Once or twice those who were alone had spoken to
me, but it never got any farther. With the finish
of the show it ended, and I couldn't tell them I
would like to see them again. That, I felt, would
have sounded Queer; and, anyway, they probably
had friends of their own at home and wouldn't want
to know me. How did one get to know people?
Supposing there was somebody else in London who
was a junior clerk in the City, and loved Byron and
de Quincey and Poe and Caruso and Wagner, and
the streets and everything that happened, and ate
at good pull-ups and lived in a court—how could I
get to know him? There were lots of people one
passed regularly in the streets, year after year, but
unless something extraordinary happened they would
never take you as a friend. I was bursting with
friendship then; I would have been a friend for life
to anybody who would have talked to me about
Things. But nobody did.

And it has always been the same, except with
Quong Lee. Always I have been prodigal of
friendship, only to find other people discreet and a
little ruffled by my crudity. Later, when I did
make acquaintances, I always wanted to be a friend,
and I was always repulsed or neglected. Not con-

sciously, I think; only the other party failed in eagerness. It was always I who had to write and suggest meetings; I who had to call for them or wait where I was likely to meet them. Always I was sitting on their doorsteps; never they on mine.

But at twenty I did find a friend.

.   .   .   .

Although twenty in years, in appearance and in spirit I was sixteen; and, living in clouds of poetry and music, I had been incurious about women and girls. But suddenly, it seemed, I began to look up from my books, and a detached corner of myself noted that I was becoming sensible to the beauty of young faces, and agreeably conscious of their presence in 'bus or tram. I tried to dismiss the matter, feeling that it was profanity. I had been living in fields and cathedrals, and now I had to face every boy's struggle with this new thing. Why did these matters obtrude upon one's reaching-up to what was rare and noble? I wondered whether everybody who was "good" and who made beautiful things had this same struggle, or whether goodness was natural, like genius. I had not then the wisdom to know that it is these moments that balance men and keep them human. The mighty genius may live on peaks, but the mass of us cannot breathe their air. Our instincts are of meaner hue, though some of us have a mind above our instincts: too big for our boots and not big enough for the next size; hence we struggle until we know that our place is among the crowd, to live with them, laugh with them, suffer with them and be one with them.

Chapter VII

GRACIE

AT twenty I met Gracie Scott, who was fourteen. For weeks I had been building stories
around a little girl in a grey coat who, every morning, was just ahead of me as I turned out of St.
Thomas Street by the Borough Market, and always,
like myself, alone. She reminded me of Iris Marjorie Hay, whom I foolishly figured in my mind as
stationary at school-age, forgetting that she was
now my own age, a grown woman and perhaps a
mother. I began to make her appearance a moment
of the morning trudge; to look for the grey coat
and the red tam-o'-shanter and the black curls; and
if I were late and missed her, I was conscious of a
blank. Soon I was starting earlier, that I might
meet her face to face as she came along the Borough
High Street; and every morning I followed her faith-
fully over the bridge to King William Street. Sometimes she would stop to stare at a shop-window,
and whenever she stopped I wanted to go up to her.
I thought of forms of introduction, of accidentally
treading on her foot, of asking her if she had
dropped a handkerchief; all the usual hoggish
tricks of the street gallant. I even thought of
slipping a note into her half-open hand as she stood
at the windows: "Please Miss Unknown, may I

speak to you one morning?" But I could not thus pounce upon her maiden delicacy; it would shock and hurt her, and she would think horrid things of me.

I wondered in what strange, dark home she lived, to what lost corner of South London she belonged; and pictured the mysterious kitchen and tea-table where she sat at evening amid romantic creatures disguised as Cockneys. I wondered whether she had father and mother; whether they were kind to her or were blind to her beauty and treated her as part of every day. I wondered whether she lived in lodgings or a house; what she would have for tea; what she did in the evenings; what time she went to bed. I longed to follow her to her home, and I thought how wonderful it would be to sit round the fire with her, and see her with her coat and hat off, and meet the people who made her circle.

She was not beautiful, but she was at that age when all girls are pretty, quivering at the tip-toe of growth. Sheer beauty would have awed me: I knew my place and dared not aspire to it. But her presence warmed me and thrilled me. Our feet were on the same earth, and the street-lamps lit her eyes and organ-tunes were in her step. She had short black curls and a wistful mouth. A cast in one eye gave a touch of salt to her serious face. She was little and neat, a finished statuette, with the candour of childhood and a hint of woman-wisdom.

As she went slowly along the Borough every morning, she had a trick of turning her head from

side to side, wearily; and these flashes of an untold
story filled me with dismay because I might not
go and comfort her. As I could not do that, I
made it a business to follow her, morning and evening; to be at hand if ever she were accosted; awaiting her at Newcomen Street and King William
Street, and amusing myself with the fancy that I
was her accredited protector, and that my daily
escort was a trust in which default meant penalties
for her.

Slippery roads, indifferent scavengers and careless
drivers saved me from the club-footed effrontery of
a forced introduction. I blessed them, for if the
road hadn't been slippery, and the scavenger hadn't
neglected to scatter sand, the horse wouldn't have
fallen down, and if the horse hadn't fallen down——
A horse down is always an occasion for a crowd and
in England it's only in a crowd that strangers may
speak to each other without offence.

It was like this.

October evening, seven o'clock; the Borough
misty, the mist sparking and gushing with lamps
and shop-flares, and reeking with the odour of tea
and bloaters from the Good-Pull-Ups. Along the
East side went, faintly, a little figure in a grey coat,
and a few yards behind her an inept figure hidden
in a bowler hat and a shiny overcoat. Then, at
Union Street, there was a slither of hoofs—shouts—
jerks—a rattle of harness—and the horse was down.
She stopped. Slowly I drew near; slowly I reached
her; slowly I came and stood beside her on the kerb,
nearer than I had ever been to her. I trembled.

I felt that tingling at the back of the head and that tremour in the stomach which with me is the indication—corresponding to the "heart" of the poets —of intense emotion. For some moments we stood thus, watching this affair of oath and struggle; then she turned.

She turned and looked straight at me, with the timid impudence of the London sparrow, and even as I looked away and tried to appear as though I were waiting for a 'bus she spoke.

She spoke to me.

She said: "They didn't ought to let 'em drive 'em on these greasy roads, did they?"

I said: "N-no. No. It's—it's dangerous." My voice was husky. I cleared my throat and hot-pokered my mind for other things to say. "Er— mind he doesn't kick this way when he's getting up. You might get hurt."

"Ooh, I'm all right, thank you. . . . You work in the City, don't you?"

"Yes; Lime Street."

"Ooh. Quite near me. I see you nearly every morning going up."

"Do you? I believe I've seen you once or twice."

"Have you reely?"

"Yes. I—I believe—I remember now. I've noticed you on the Bridge. You go down Cannon Street, don't you?"

" 'M. I work at Scollard's, the tailors. I take the work out."

"Yes. I didn't notice you standing here when I stopped."

"No? No more didn't I you neither. D'you get overtime when you work late? We don't."

"Nor do we. However long we stay."

"What a shame! They just give us tea-money at our place. Fourpence. That's all."

"We don't even get that."

And there I stuck. It was exciting to be so near to her, in the thick of the evening, and to have her talking to me. To me; not to anybody else in the crowd, but only to me. Talking freely, too, just as though we were friends, though she couldn't have guessed how old I was. With every sentence I was fearful that she would go or that both of us would dry up. Still, now that we had spoken I would be able to see her and speak to her on the way to work; perhaps walk up with her every morning. I had got to know her, and would be able to learn all about her, and tell her all the wonderful things I knew— London and the Causeway and Byron and Poe and Caruso and Wagner and All That.

She lingered until the horse was up. Then: "Well, I'll be off." She didn't move, though; and I made a sudden grab at the situation. "They got him up pretty quick—eh? I say—may I walk down the road with you? I live just near here—Bussell's Grove."

"Ooh, do you? I know it. I don't mind." She looked up at me and flashed a smile that brought sudden intimacy. In that moment of lingering we had made one leap across the stepping-stones of conversation and gradual acquaintance, and were arrived at mutual acceptance. I felt that I had always known her. "But I'm going to walk fast."

"Why? Do you have to be home early?"

"No. But I want my tea. I have to get my tea meself. There won't be nobody at home. My stepmother goes out every night."

A stepmother. I hated that stepmother. "What a shame. I say"—I felt a spark in my throat—"I say"—my knees wobbled—"I say—I was going to have my tea out to-night, over there." I pointed to The Workmen's Friend, hazy with warmth and light. "I wonder whether—as we both seen each other so often—I wonder if you'd come with me. Only across the road, and have tea with me?"

She looked down the street and up at the roofs. "Ooh . . . I don't know."

"Would your stepmother mind, d'you think?"

"Ooh—she don't matter. She don't care what I do. But I don't know——" She swayed on one leg, kicking the kerb, and looking away from me.

"I wish you would. I haven't many friends."

"Ain't you? No more havn't I."

"And as you've seen me so often . . . I'd have spoken to you before, only——"

"Only what?"

"I don't know."

"You *are* a silly."

"Do come. Please. You must come."

"I don't know. . . ."

"Come on."

She looked at me, wavered, and smiled; and although I knew nothing of the girl or her character,

I felt that we should be friends and that she liked me and wanted to be friends. With that I put out a hand, took gently the sleeve of her grey coat in two fingers, and with infinite care led her through the traffic. In the Workmen's Friend I slipped her into a little pew, and sat at her side, seeing for the first time at leisure the soft face and dusky hair and the queer and mischievous right eye. So we sat, heads turned to each other, taking stock of each other. She looked long and gravely at me; then giggled and clasped her hands.

"What's the joke?"

"Oo . . . I dunno. I was just wondering what made me come with you."

When our meal was brought—tea, bread and butter and bloaters—I discovered why she was in a hurry to be home, and I looked away while she ate. I was hungry, too, but the occasion had blunted my appetite, and she had eaten five slices of bread and butter before I had eaten two. I ordered toast, thankful that it was Friday. With the toast she began to talk, holding the toast to her mouth, smiling at me over it, and biting and nodding with swift turns of the head and frisking of curls.

"I like this. I never had tea out before. I always take my dinner with me and have tea at home. This toast is lovely. What's your name?"

I gave it. "And what's yours?"

"Gracie Scott."

"I like that name. Whereabouts d'you live?"

"Rayment Gardens. Just off Trinity Square. We got two rooms there."

"Is there only you—no brothers or sisters?"

"No. Only me and her. My father's dead."

"I see. I've only got one room. Just a bed-room. In Bussell's Grove."

"You live all alone then?"

"Yes."

"Ain't you got nobody?"

"No. I'm all on me own."

She looked at me, as though being on my own lent me a new and romantic interest. We talked and ate and talked again; in short thrusts at first; then easily and at length. I knew by her abrupt smiles that she was with me in this affair, and I tingled again. I had found a girl. Not a "little girl" of the sort the clerks talked about, who was usually a woman over twenty and taller than them-selves, but a real little girl. Women I had never looked at: they were women; big and obvious and self-sufficient; all Lils or Cooks, who patronised you. Gracie Scott's morning grace for me shamed and shadowed the deliberate dignity and confidence of women; and then her mind seemed nearer to mine. Though I was seven years older, I found that in innocence and experience we were about level. She knew nothing of the "And Thats," per-haps, but I felt that she was of my own cast, and in her company I was at once easy and delighted.

While we ate I showed her Uncle Frank's watch and how it was wound up, and the Diamond Jubilee Medal. I showed her a blue pencil and a sheet of our office paper. And I told her of my job in the office, and how I hated it, and wanted to do something serious; and how it was Invoice Week, and that day I had addressed a hundred and forty envelopes; and I told her that I had Written Things, and had had them accepted and printed; and she smiled at the Gay Romancer, until I told her that I had a story at home printed in a paper with my name and address to it at the top, as the author of the best story sent in that week. She stared then, and seemed worried. But she soon recovered, and told me of her daily job, with sketches of the people to whom she took the work in Aldgate and Stepney; but of her home and her stepmother she said little. Only—"I never want to go home, except for tea. Nothing to go home *for*. Only you can't mooch about when you're tired."

After an hour we got up to go, hot with tea and the long talk. I called for the shot, and suddenly, as the drab of a waitress took the money, romance received a shock. She looked at us closely and queerly. She looked through half-closed eyes at Gracie, and then at me, and then back to Gracie. By that look I knew that she had seen through my apparent boyishness and had guessed my real age; and as we went out to the misty Borough, I heard her speaking to somebody at the back: "Wonder what he's up to—eh?"

We went together down Great Dover Street, mostly silent, but now and then spurting half-sentences at each other. In a side street I told her that I liked her and wanted to see her every day, and she laughed, and knocked my arm, and said I was a silly. Once or twice I was concerned about her time, but she was careless. "It don't matter. She won't be home yet. She's never home till ten or eleven."

It was ten before we parted. We stood in a warehouse doorway and talked, without knowing why, in murmurs.

"What do you do on Sundays? Could you come for a walk with me?"

"I dunno. I don't do nothing Sundays. I just stay in. But I don't like walking about the streets. I get enough o' that all the week."

I did some mental arithmetic. "Perhaps we could go for a 'bus-ride?"

"I like 'bus-rides. But not Sundays. It's so dull. Everything shut up."

"Well—I . . ." My head went hot again. Mrs. Flanagan was out all day Sundays, an extra hand at a public-house at Peckham Rye, and the other lodger, an elderly woman, went to her married daughter's. I was always alone in the house. Was it possible that I might have company? "I—I'm all alone Sundays at my place. They're out all day. D'you think it'd be—I mean——" She looked at me without expression. I stumbled; tried to think of another ending to the sentence, and couldn't.

"Think it'd be what?"

"Why—er—I was going to say—if you could— if it would be . . ."

"Go on."

"If you could come round and sit and—and— perhaps make the tea? Eh? I'm all alone and I

get the hump sometimes. I wonder if it'd be . . .
But perhaps you wouldn't——"

I left her to pick up the sentence, wishing that I
hadn't said it, sure that she would think I was up
to something, and expecting her to turn and run.
I felt that I had killed the whole affair. If I hadn't
suggested that, we could have gone on meeting every
day; now, perhaps, she'd never speak to me again.
But she didn't run. She gave me another of her
long looks, as though X-raying my character; then
an abrupt smile. "I think I'd like to. I dunno if
I ought to, but. . . . What time?"

She'd like to! "Oh—would you? I'd be jolly
glad. Er—well, any time *you* like. Half-past
two?"

"I couldn't be as early as that. Half-past three,
I might."

"That'd be all right. I'll come and meet you.
Top of Newcomen Street—eh? Half-past three."

"'M. I'll be there. Half-past three."

My nerves were still tingling at the audacity of
this invitation to a little girl picked up in the streets;
and now that the tension was eased by her calm
acceptance I couldn't think of anything else to say.
For a minute or more we leant side by side against
the warehouse door, looking at each other in the
dark. Then she moved, and I went with her towards Great Dover Street. There she stopped
me. "I go down that turning—over there."

"May I . . . ?"

"No. Better not. People might see you and
say things. Good-night."

"Good-night. Sunday. Half-past three. Don't forget."

I walked home through a world lit up. I had a friend at last. A romantic and adventurous friend of my own colour. So began six months of delight. The longer I knew her the more I came to love her. I did not think her the most beautiful girl in the world; in newspaper shops I had seen picture post-cards of Phyllis Dare at fifteen; but her grace and her smiles brought a lilt and a sway to the streets of Bermondsey. Two years ago I took a taxi from Streatham to Queen Victoria Street, and instead of being driven over Blackfriars Bridge, I was driven up the Borough to London Bridge. The season was November, and evening, and the Workmen's Friend was still there, unaltered save that electric bulbs glared in place of the softer incandescent. I saw it unexpectedly before I had time to turn my face away.

On Sunday at a quarter past three I was at the corner of Newcomen Street. There are few sadder spots than the Borough on Sundays. Denied its week-day traffic it looks wan and bald. London Bridge makes a despondent curve. The air is filled with the drone of bells. The closed shops and offices have the air of creatures of valiant front turning indecent backs upon the unfamiliar. Men and boys walk or lounge, wearing Sunday clothes as fetters. Winkles and shrimps are cried over the roofs. Concertinas and harmoniums wheeze, and songless voices make song, and through it all goes the lamplighter laying a trail of stars. But this dusty corner was linked in my mind with the gambols of the Bear Garden, the laughter of the Globe Theatre, the grace of poets, and the caracolling of the Canterbury Pilgrims; and though it wavered ignobly between the gravity of the business man and the gusto of the market porter, that wavering seemed in accord with a place whose glory is departed; and the sad odour of vegetables seemed to dramatise its mood.

Then, swimming to me out of the dark green light of October afternoon, came Gracie; and it was touched again with all the poetry of past adventure. As I stood waiting for her, I wanted to run and catch her, but when she stopped fully before me, I received her respectably with, "Hullo! You've got here then?"

"Yes, I got here. Where'bouts is your place?"

"Not far. Down this way."

We went without talk down Newcomen Street and Snow's Fields. I saw that she was excited by this affair; that she was conscious of doing something daring, almost wrong, and that she knew that I knew. I tried to think of something to say to carry it off, but nothing came; and in the ten minutes of walking to Bussell's Grove the only exchange we made was a giggle.

I opened the door, led the way upstairs to the tiny room where a tall man must have stooped to get into bed; and then we were alone in the house, alone in the world, and still more awkward. At the door she paused, pulled off her hat, and stood looking about her. I discovered then that a girl in her outdoor coat, without hat, reveals a new and piquant personality. I saw for the first time fully her pale brow, and the dark curls streaming over the collar of her coat, and the brown, capricious eye; and for the first time in my life my hands touched a girl's hands. I put my arm on her shoulder. I looked with her at my room as though seeing it after long absence.

"So this is your room?"

"Yes. Such as it is. Come right in."

"Wish I had a room all to meself."

"Sorry I haven't got a fire. But this is only my bedroom. I have tea in her kitchen and go down there any time I want a warm. You better keep your overcoat on. Shall I take your hat? Sit down."

She handed me the hat and stood swaying. I hung it up with mine, and shut the door, and for some moments we said nothing, but stood looking about, smiling when we looked at each other, and, on my side, feeling at a loss and annoyed at being at a loss.

"Isn't much to see out 'of the window. Only roofs and the top of the Tower Bridge. But it's quiet. Sit down.

"Those are my books over there.

"That's my uncle—that photo.

"I cut that picture out of a paper. It's Keats. He was a great poet. And that one's Beethoven. He was a great composer. Sit down.

"Those are programmes over there. Promenade

Concerts. I keep all the programmes. They tell you all about the music. Do you like music?"

"Some. Not the bands in the park. But I like nice music. . . . What did you have for dinner?"

"I went out to the South London Road. Sausages and mashed, and baked apple dumpling. Sit down."

"Oo! We only had——"

"What?"

"Oh, just our usual. What's that on there?"

"That? Oh, my uncle's writing case. I don't use it much, though. Sit down."

"I like your room."

"Not so dusty. Not what I'd like, though. I'd like two rooms separate, with nice pictures and a bookcase and—everything—you know—Nice."

She laughed. "You don't want much."

"Some day I may have it. You never know. You cold? Come over here and sit down."

I sat down on the edge of the chair-bed. For a moment she didn't move, but stood looking down at the empty grate, a mignon figure, only as high as the low mantelshelf. Her hands hung idle, her hair fell in two bunches, and her lilac-sprigged frock danced through her opened jacket as she waved a grey leg back and forth. I wished to goodness she would sit down and said again sharply:

"Come and sit here."

She looked up then, the piquant right eye correcting the gravity of the left, and came slowly towards me and stood still. "What d'you do Sundays generally?"

"Stay in mostly and read. Or write."

"That true what you said about writing stories and having them printed in magazines?"

"Yes—I'll show it you if you like, and you'll see my name and address at the top."

"Oo! You must be clever. You fond of reading?"

"Fond of reading? Why, I—I couldn't get on without books. Not having any friends, you see."

"You read all those?"

"Yes—two or three times over."

"Cuh!" Suddenly and inconsequently she looked from the books to me and said, "I like you. You're different from the fellows down our street."

"And I like you. It wasn't true what I said about only noticing you once or twice. I've been watching you for weeks and following you home from work."

The amazing child said quietly: "Yes, I know. I wondered why you didn't speak. You always looked as though you wanted to." She came closer and abruptly sat down; and there we sat together and the long ruminative Sunday afternoon flowed past us until the room was blotted out by shadow and the window was a green square. We talked now, without stumbling, about ourselves and our work and Life and Things. My world-hate and mufflings of reserve fell away. Besides a friend I had found a living piece of beauty to make my room bright with her presence and to give poetry personal application. I had a living book to read; and from then onward I ceased to study my books while there was life to be studied. I wanted to write

something for her—something fine. But at six
o'clock I remembered that I was host and kicked
myself.

"Why, Gracie—I'm going to call you Gracie—
you must be wanting your tea. I forgot all about
it."

"Did you? So did I. But I am a bit hungry."

"I'll go down and see what's in the kitchen. Come
with me—eh? There's nobody else here."

We went down together, and Gracie filled the
kettle at the sink and put it on the gas-ring, while
I found bread and butter and some mixed jam in a
broken tea-cup. "Shall we have it here or upstairs?"

"I like your room best."

We carried the meal upstairs, I with the enamel
teapot and two cups, and Gracie with the food; and
I lit the candle, and we had tea at the chest of
drawers. When Gracie had finished her sixth slice
of bread and butter and jam, I knew what her dinner had been, and was angry with the world, and
wanted to get money to take her out for glorious
feasts and buy her a thick coat and warm her with
little comforts and a necklace of Good Times.
That home of hers. That Stepmother. While we
ate I swung up and down with elation and distress—
the desire to succour her and the consciousness of
my own futility.

Then we talked and talked for another two hours.
You see, I hadn't really talked to anybody for five
years. I hadn't had a conversation since leaving
Caledonian Road; that was why I had taken this

dreadful step of bringing a young girl to my room. Hunger and thirst are painful things, but to be deprived of human companionship and talk is a torture which men, especially young men, will do anything to ease. Some years later, in a bar, a youth thrust himself upon me, and talked and talked in a cascade of sentences that had no connecting links. I answered him. I assumed that he was drunk, and took his points as amiably as I could. He noted my expression; and with his first words of correction I understood his case. "It's all right, mate. I ain't drunk. And I ain't arstin' yeh fer money. I just come out. Eighteen months I done. 'Ard. I ain't arstin' you fer anything. On'y—I just got to talk to someone or go up the loop. Eighteen months. 'Ope I ain't borin' yeh, but yeh dunno what it is not talkin' fer eighteen months."

That was my case with Gracie, and once I was started I felt that I should never stop. I had all my recent adventures among books and the opera to talk about; all my love of London; all my views and opinions and resentments. In the middle of the cascade she gurgled.

"What is it?"

"Seems funny, don't it, me sitting here with you? Older than me and clever. Wonder what She'd think? D'you think it was wrong of me—coming here?"

"No. If it was, it's my fault."

"They always told me awful things about men speaking to girls of my age in the street. But I

could see you was different some'ow. Not that
sort."

"Good Lord, no!"

"Oh, I knew it. Anyway, I like being here. And
I can't see anything wrong in it, can you? Course
I know what She'd say. But let her. What'd you
do if you had lots of money?"

"Do? Why, first I'd spend a lot. Just to see
what it felt like. I'd have a month of just spending.
Buying anything just for the fun of it. Then I'd
have a little house instead of one room—a six-room
house in a nice street, with a bath-room and a
front sitting-room where I could go after Sunday
dinner. And I'd have a fire all day in the back
room and the front room. And I'd have a proper
writing-desk. And I'd buy books—dozens of books
—not shilling ones, but real books. And pictures.
Good ones. And I'd go to concerts whenever I
wanted to. Book my seat and walk in without
waiting. And I'd have three pairs of boots and a
clean shirt and collar every day. And I'd find out
all the people who've been kind to me and set them
up. And I'd hire a carriage and drive round to the
office and tell 'em what I thought of 'em. And I'd
try to learn the violin again, so's I could play good
music. And I'd have all day to write in. And I'd
take you out of Southwark, and have a housekeeper
to look after you, and I'd take you to theatres, and
I'd take you to late dinner at one of the French
cafés in Soho, and . . ."

A distant bell chimed the quarters. Gracie

jumped up. "Coo-er! That nine o'clock striking? I'll have to be off."

We came back to earth and Bermondsey. I got up slowly. "I wish you didn't have to."

"So do I. It's been awfully nice. Still—I'll see you to-morrow—eh? I must run now."

We parted at St. George's Church. "Good-bye. Don't come any further." Then, in a bright whisper, "To-morrow morning!"

"Yes. I'll be here. Half-past eight."

Then the tam-o'-shanter was lost in the Sunday evening crowd and she was gone. For some seconds the streets were blank, and the hours stretched long and empty. Then I turned to those wonderful words, "See you to-morrow," and the streets were warm again. We would walk to work together to-morrow; and we would walk home to-morrow evening and talk and talk, and perhaps have tea together. And the day after that—and after that—and that. No more would the London Bridge journey be a trudge; it would be a holiday ramble whose anticipation would tint every night with the colour of to-morrow. Instead of moving on a chain of days that came round like a tread-mill, the week would unfold itself in seven adventures.

I went home by roundabout ways, stepping as lightly as Gracie, and humming bits of opera. My room was no more a top-back-room of dust and blear. It meant something; it was alive. Beauty had breathed upon it. That hour before I went to bed was an expansion of the moment in Quong

Lee's shop. I seemed to have awakened from
sleep; to know and to understand; and to see that
room cut off, as by a window, part of the eternal.

.   .   .   .

Thereafter followed months of morning meetings
and evening partings. The flutter of a grey coat
now touched the Borough into a street of elfland
and quickened its aged streets with the steps of
Springtide. It was no coat such as are sold in
shops. It assumed character; and every street
where it moved became that harlequin highway
known to all who have picked up those talismans
that life drops on stony pavements, and have
stepped aside into countries of fable.

We had met in a gush of youth. She was all
eagerness and wonder; I was aflame with poetry
and music. Odious fancies ceased to trouble me:
smoke and miasma could not live in the keen air
of her youth and of our friendship. The world
became clean, and every morning, when I turned
my eyes to the window and thought of her, life
flowed into me with the cool feeling of fresh linen
to the skin. All the ardour and affection that had
been choked back during my years of loneliness,
until it had turned upon me and soured me, was
now released upon this child. She was my precious
charge, and to her—well, I don't know what I was
to her.

Whether I pleased her or bored her by my
babble of books and London and poetry, I don't
know. I know that I played teacher to her, and
tried to lead her among books. I was drunk with

the *Canterbury Poets,* and, with the generosity of
the drunkard, I loaded her with poetry, and she
listened gravely and wonderingly, not guessing, I
think, that mine was the position of the teacher
who is one lesson ahead of his scholars. At first,
as I had been, she was a little apprehensive of
"dryness," and then perplexed; but slowly she
began to share my excitement. She listened in-
tently to my volcanics when I tried to show her the
beauty of the streets, and how poetry could make
all common things sweet; and soon we were both
raving. There were stumblings, of course; poetry
was not plain speech; but after a week or two she
became as dreamy as I was drunk. I had divined
from the first something of seriousness in her,
some spot of delicacy that could be moved by fine
things while it could not yet understand them; and
we became fellow-pilgrims. Where I found my
feet with Byron she found hers with "The Idylls
of the King."

Every morning we met at St. George's Church,
and every evening at the King William statue; and
all the way down the Borough we talked. In the
evening I sometimes took her for rambles to the
West End; and once or twice a 'bus ride and tea
in a Strand A.B.C. shop, where we could sit upstairs in the window and watch the traffic of the
pleasure-world, and feel fleetingly that we were of
it, and that there was no City and no Bermondsey.
There were two shining evenings at the Prome-
nades, and one night at the opera.

But always she preferred my room. We were

alone there, for one thing, and she felt easier in Bermondsey than elsewhere. There were no rich, smart girls there to make you feel mean, and no shops and hotels and restaurants to remind you how poor you were. Walking through those big streets was no pleasure to her, and she never understood why I liked them. You were a stranger, and didn't belong there; but in Bermondsey there was nothing to jar you; you were all as good as one another. So every Sunday afternoon was spent in my room, and there we sat on the low bed together, in that state of light coma that goes with semi-starvation; or she would flutter round the room chirping about Tennyson or *The Mill on the Floss*.

My chief pain was that I could feed her with poetry, but only once here and there—on pay-days —could I feed her with a large meal. Her week's money she had to hand to her stepmother, and out cf it she received ninepence a week for pocket-money. Her dinner was bloater-paste sandwiches; her tea and breakfast were bread and butter. Only on Sundays did she get a hot dinner, and that was never certain; it depended on stepmother's mood and state. Of the mysteries of her home she would not speak. I wanted to know why the stepmother was always "out"; whether she did any work; if so, why didn't they have better meals; whether Gracie hadn't any aunts she could go to; why they had two rooms when one would have been cheaper? But Gracie put up a barrier, and said it wasn't worth talking about, and let's talk about something else. She was quite all right as she was, she said;

and she'd rather have things as they were, because the old woman left her alone, and she could do pretty well what she liked, so long as the old woman didn't find out. Not that it wasn't horrid at times. It was; and some day, when she was old enough to do it, she'd look out for a better job and go off on her own and live somewhere else.

But at present she could put up with it. There was Tennyson and my room and our meetings and all sorts of things. "Ain't it funny, the way poetry makes you sort a feel Good? You know. Makes you think of nice things. Like I felt the time we went to the country once, with the Church Holiday Fund, and woke up the first morning and looked outa the winder. I can't explain it, but you know. . . ."

The fount of wisdom and experience opened. "Of course, Gracie. But that's because you're good yourself. You only get good feelings from things if you're good yourself. It's got to be inside you. Nasty people can never really love poetry."

"'M. I see. Like when you've done something mean you don't feel fit to look at people—eh?"

"Yes. Same when you hear music. When I've been to the opera . . ."

"What's the opera?"

"I'll tell you in a minute. And I'll take you there one night if I can get some money. I sent two things to *Ally Sloper* yesterday. Well, when I've been there, and heard Caruso and Melba, I feel clean all through. I hate coming home to

Bermondsey and going to the City next day. Know
what I mean—it's like a bath, and you don't want
to get near anything that's going to dirty you."

"I know. That's just what I feel, only I can't
say it like you."

"And knowing you's just the same."

" 'M. It can't be nasty, can it, like people'd say
it was if they knew—our being here together."

Our visit to Queen's Hall was as thrilling for me
as for her, for though I had been before this was
a new excitement—to listen to music with Gracie
at my side. My other visits seemed tame in retro-
spect. During the hour of waiting at the shilling
door, I displayed it and explained it, proudly, as
though it were my Promenade Concert. For her
it was revelation; but by my reading I had become
aware that much of the music that had stirred me
was considered inferior; and promptly I found it
so, and waited tolerantly during its performance
for the Brandenburg Concerto, which I loathed.
But Gracie was happily unconscious that brows
were being lifted in select circles against her joy in
"Poet and Peasant," "Zampa," and "Coppèlia."

She was silent when we came out.

"Well?"

"Eh?"

"How d'you like it?"

She sighed. "I dunno how to put it. It's just
—I never heard anything like it before. I feel all
—you know—all tied up."

"I know. When you get home, you'll have to
read those notes on the Programme. Tells you all

about the composers and helps you to understand the music better."

"I don't think I want to understand it. I like it as it is."

"Ah, but——" The walk home to the Borough was paved with slabs from Groves' *Dictionary of Music.* "And if you think that was wonderful, you wait till you come to the opera. In the Spring."

And one Saturday in the Spring I made her a present of Covent Garden. "The opera's called *Madame Butterfly*—Japanese. But it was written by an Italian, and it'll be sung in Italian. Man named Puccini. You'll hear all the greatest singers in the world. Caruso, and Scotti, and Madame Destinn. And . . ."

We were at the gallery door at six o'clock, and stood for two hours, and I illuminated opera for her, but in whispers, lest I might be wrong and arouse the ridicule of the learned people about us. I suppose we were a noticeable couple—the pale child in short frock, grey stockings darned with black, and cracked shoes; and the thin-faced youth in the twenty-two-and-sixpenny suit, now frayed and shapeless. Certainly we were noticed.

"Look at those two children there. Brother and sister, I suppose. I wonder what they know about opera. Hope they haven't mistaken it for Drury Lane."

"Shouldn't think so. They know what they're up to. Look at their faces. They're the new sort of enthusiast that's growing up in the working-class districts."

I went hot and hated those voices behind me. Just because we were poor and young, people thought they could laugh at us and talk about us as specimens. I bet I knew as much about opera. . . . Then a stir moved down the line, and heads were turned as a hansom came along Floral Street. In it sat a stout, coarsely dressed man wearing a straw hat at the back of his head, and smoking a cigar. There was a rush to the roadway. As the crowd came forward, the man lifted the straw hat, nodded, and—*winked* at them.

"Caruso!"

"Look, Gracie—there he is. Look. That's Caruso. Did you see him?"

"Yes. I see him quite clear. He looks quite ordinary, don't he? Only a bit foreign."

"Lots of big people look ordinary. You wait till you hear him sing."

Then the doors opened, and we were in, sitting close to each other, arm in arm. And at last the lights were down, the first bars were played, and the curtain was up. Gracie crushed my fingers in hers, and sat, head forward, eyes blank. Pinkerton entered. I whispered, "That's Him." She nodded. Sharpless entered. "That's Scotti." She nodded. As the first act went on she squeezed my hand tighter and tighter, and I knew that she was having what I had had only a few months before. Even when the curtain fell she did not relax; only turned her squinty eye to me, shook her curls, and shivered. When the last call was taken we got up, and she breathed deeply as though coming to the sur-

face after a plunge, twisted her fingers, and smiled.
I was satisfied.   My opera was a success, and
Gracie was of the believers.   All the way home she
bubbled.   "O-o-oh, isn't it lovely?   I shall dream
about it all night.   I never thought it'd be anything like what it was."

We parted at St. George's Church, both stirred
up.   "See you to-morrow—Newcomen Street, half-
past three?"

"Yes.   I'll be there.   Here," she handed me the
programme.   "I better not have this.   She might
see it, and find out who I been with."

"I see.   Righto.   To-morrow, then?"

"I'll be there.   Toodle-oo!   It was *lovely!*"

.   .   .   .

But she wasn't there.

I waited till four.   Half-past four.   Five.   I
walked down to St. George's Church and back.   I
wandered here and there.   I fidgeted.   I thought
of Rayment Gardens, but I remembered that she
had never told me her number, and I daren't inquire
there for her.   Could she be ill?   Had she caught
a cold last night?   No—she was all right when we
parted.   It must be that her stepmother was ill,
and she had had to stay at home.   But even then
she could have got out for ten minutes to tell me.
At six o'clock I went home, apprehensively, looking
all about the court and the opposite street-corners
for some sight of her.   But she did not appear.   I
went upstairs and came down again.   I put the
kettle on, and made some tea, and cut myself a

slice of bread and butter. I ate it in the kitchen; I could not carry it up to that empty room. I itched for to-morrow morning and an explanation. I felt that I must go at once to Rayment Gardens and hang about on the chance of seeing her.

But at seven o'clock there was a knock at the street-door. I went quickly to it, opened it, and saw nobody. Then, at the far end of the alley, I heard a cough, and I recognised the tone of that cough as though she had spoken. I went out and there she was, standing against the wall, peeping behind her at the street.

"Gracie—what's the——"

"Sh! Can't come in. Meet me Tower Bridge half-past eight."

"But——"

"Can't stop."

I saw a flash of frock and two grey legs in the dusk, and she was gone. I stood irresolute, in the court, debating whether I should run after her or follow her instructions. What could be up? Clearly something very serious, or she wouldn't have come like that or talked like that. Had I done anything to upset her? No—it wouldn't be that; she wasn't the sort to be upset by little things. Had she found somebody else—somebody more her own age? I walked upstairs and downstairs, and in and out of the kitchen, until the house sickened me; and at a quarter to eight I went out to kill time in the streets. Everything seemed to stand still. I tried to think of last night, but it had a bitter taste to it. I tried to think of verses, and they wouldn't come. I tried to observe what was going on in the streets, but my mind wouldn't register; wouldn't move from half-past eight and Gracie.

I was at the Bermondsey end of Tower Bridge well on time, and at last I saw her coming from Gainsford Street. She saw me, beckoned to me, and I went across to her, and she led me under an archway. I noted that she was paler than usual and out of breath.

"What's up, Gracie? What's it all about?"

"I-can't-see-you-no-more." The words came out in a splutter.

"Eh?" Something went cold inside me.

"I-can't-come-to-you-no-more. She's heard about it. She's been at me all day. She's found out where I go Sundays. Somebody what knows her lives in the next court to yours, and see me and you at your window from the back yard.

"She dared me to see you again. Says if I do she'll——" She stopped short. She peered over my shoulder. "Look out! Run!"

I turned. I had a sight of a shrewish figure, bearing upon us with the roll of the sailor. I saw a face of the hue of red cabbage, a shot-silk coat, a feathered hat nodding with temper, and an umbrella carried at the support-arms position. Then she was at us, driving us under the archway, and I felt as though we were assaulted by a bad smell. This was what Gracie had to live with; Gracie, who was kind and young and reaching up to beauty.

"Caught ya, me beauty, 'ave I? So you're the dirty beast that's after my gel, are ya?"

As we fell back she followed us, and looked me up and down. I looked back at her, and made what must have been an idiot gesture. "I don't know what you mean. Gracie and I just met, and——"

"Oh, yerce. You and yer Just Met. I know ya. Likely, ain't it?" She chanted the words. "Pickin' up kids of 'er age, and takin' 'em to yer room. I know ya. So now!" She paused. Then, satisfied that she had made her effect, she proceeded more coldly. "Well, what ya going to do about it?"

"Do about it? I don't understand."

"Come on, now. I'm not a fool. What about it?"

"Eh?"

"Don't 'Eh' at me. What *about* it? What ya going to *do?*"

"I don't know what you mean? What should I do?"

I blinked. I looked at Gracie. Gracie was shrinking against the wall, looking at her feet. I looked back at the woman. She came closer to me. The feathers fluttered in my face. "Come on. No muckin' about. What's it worth? Unless you'd like me to——"

"Worth? I don't know what you're talking about."

"Oh, don't ya, Mister Innocent. Grrr . . . going about with my kid, and then expect to git orf fer nothing. She's worth something better'n yew. I'll see to that. Yes, me lady, you march off to Aldgate to-night. See? Mrs. Rosenbloom'll look after you. She'll *City* you. No wonder you bin kep working late. Now then—you—'ow much?"

I saw it then, and I said "Oh!" explosively, and stood like a fool. My head was churning with inexpressible things. I wanted to say something cold and terrible that would put me in command of the situation, but all that came out was, "You—you—you old Beast!"

Then there were two screams in my ear. One said, "Run—run!" The other said, "What? What?" I saw the umbrella raised in the air. I ducked. In ducking I hit my head against the wall. I felt a stinging blow on my cheek and another on the back of my neck. I heard Gracie cry out again. I saw her leap at her stepmother and wrestle with the umbrella. Then the twilight of the archway went dark, the stars came out, torrents of water fell all round me, the concrete at my feet rose up to my eyes, and I passed into a world of dance, and was there for some years.

When, three minutes later, the storm ceased, and I escaped, I found myself lying under the archway, alone. My head was aching. Blood was trickling down my lips. One eye felt like a cabbage. With the instinct of the wounded I clambered to my feet, and found that my right knee was cut. I took out my handkerchief and wiped my face; and at the

sight of the blood I remembered the umbrella, the
occasion, and Gracie. I loped out of the archway,
and looked up and down the street. Which way?
How long had I been there? I could see to the far
end of the street, and there was no sign of them.
Perhaps the Tower Bridge Road end. I
reached it at an awkward trot, and dodged from
side to side, peering through 'buses and the Sunday
evening crowd. No sign. Then, over by the
Bridge, I saw in the mixed light of sky and lamp,
the dim shapes of a woman and a girl. It might
be . . . I stumbled through the traffic, and across
the road; and half way across I could make out
a tam-o'-shanter. I did not ask myself what I was
going to do. I was going after Gracie—that was
all. My mind was shrunken and had room for
nothing else; I hardly knew how I had got there,
or what day it was, and was only vaguely aware
that people were turning and staring at me. I was
in a nightmare country of ache and buzz and fog,
and the only sane thing in it was Gracie. I could
see now that the woman had got her arm, and was
leading her towards the Bridge. A 'bus blocked
my way. I dodged round it, came out on the far
side, and ran. As I ran I saw that they had passed
on to the Bridge. I called "Gracie! Gracie!" and
heard giggles around me. She seemed to hear
something, and looked back. The woman jerked
her forward. I blundered against a man. The
man shouldered me into the gutter. I slipped; got
up; and ran, and had almost reached the Bridge

when a shrill whistle and a hoot came from the river; and following it a bell rang from the Bridge house. Two people, coming off, barred my way. I broke through them, head first, stumbled, and met the gate full tilt as it clanged against me, barring all traffic.

CHAPTER VIII

DOSS

I WENT on the Monday evening, after that Sunday, to Rayment Gardens, but I never saw Gracie again. From discreet inquiries I learnt that the woman and the girl had vanished. Went off last night without saying a word to anybody. Just packed their things and went. Not that they had much of their own to carry, but what a way to go off. There must have been something behind it. She'd always been a bit of a rum 'un, that woman. People didn't go off like that unless there was something up. Perhaps I knew what it was? Perhaps I could . . .

That evening and many evenings after I spent on or near the Tower Bridge, or near Minories and Aldgate High Street. Every night I went home dispirited, and next evening I set out again in faint hope of finding her; though what I could do if I did find her I didn't know. I had caught the name Rosenbloom, and I went through the Ghetto, looking up and down the narrow streets and at the names over the shops, and standing in the thick of the crowd by Butcher Row, or among the boys and toughs outside the Three Nuns Hotel.

But I never saw her again.

A fortnight later, the mixed mood of apathy and

fume that had come upon me with thought of what
was happening to her, and of my own futility, ended
my City career.   There was a foggy morning, a
carping head clerk, a fractious junior, and a black
ruler close to my hand.   The ruler went from me
to the clerk's head; missed it, and went through a
ground-glass panel into the Board Room.

It began with a mistake in my ledger, which I
did not admit.   This led to "words."

"You charity boys!   Pity they didn't bring you
up to a trade instead of sending you into an office.
Think you know everything and you don't know
nothing."

"I know grammar, anyway."

"What?"

"I said I know grammar."

"You know—what?"   He was angry now.
"What you mean—talking like that?   You—you
little guttersnipe, you——"

"Oh, blast you, you old fool!"

Biff!

And then crack and crash and alarm; and clerks
coming from the other offices to look at a bewildered head clerk and a pale, defiant youth.   Within
half an hour the youth was out in Lime Street, with
fifteen shillings, no job, no reference, but with a
feeling of escape.   I was glad, very glad to be rid
of them; and I do not doubt that the feeling was
warmly returned.

Then came the demoralisation of idleness.   I
went to pieces.   At first I started out every morning to the Free Library to study the columns

headed "Sits. Vac."; and then to sit in the Library writing self-confident letters of application, stating age, experience and salary required; or plodding here and there from office to office to make personal appearance. I read tantalising advertisements which told me to "Become an Advertisement-Writer—Earn Five Pounds a Week. Start a Mail Order Business. Be your Own Master and Make Pounds in your Spare Time. Let me make you a Brilliant Pianist." I sat hours in cold waiting-rooms, with other out-of-works—men, boys, old men, and girls. I tramped miles and miles north and south, wherever there was a chance of a job. I stole rides on 'buses and trams, by the old trick of going to the top and sitting in the front seat, where the conductor came last, and then asking for a point in the opposite direction, and apologising, and getting off slowly. Properly worked, one could cover half a mile with each attempt. When I began the search I began with clean boots and collar; but I quickly got careless. I let myself go, and every morning I awoke with the feeling that I might as well stay where I was: there seemed no reason for getting up. The afternoon wore itself out somehow, and the evenings I often killed by a long spell of wondering how I should kill it. I began to get numb. Beyond the fifteen shillings I had nothing, and bread and mustard was the only meal I dare take. I sold my poets and my volumes of the Scott Library—twelve of them—for two shillings; and then I had nothing else to sell. I tried to write, but my brain wouldn't work. The days passed in one long stupor, and I would often stop in a street wondering what street I was in and how I had got there.

The stupor was broken by Mrs. Flanagan. At the end of the first week I was conscious that she was eyeing me; and when at the end of the second week I could only promise her the rent next week, she said she knew that something had happened, and what was I going to do about it. I told her I had lost my job, and was looking for another, and was sure to get something in a day or so. She sniffed. She knew that sort of hope; she had seen a lot of it.

At the end of the third week I was utterly done, and she spoke out.

"You'll have to go then." I looked round at my "things"—my tin box and papers, and wondered what I could do with them since I had nowhere to take them. She followed my look and answered the question. "Y'can't take that, y'know. You owe two weeks, y'know. That won't near cover it, o' course, but y'can't take it."

After some feeble arguments on my side, for there were Uncle Frank's treasures in that box, she was kind enough to say that she didn't want to be hard: she'd keep the things, and wouldn't do anything with them for six weeks, so that I could have a chance of paying up and collecting them. But I must get out at once, so that she could have a chance of letting.

I got out, and found myself in the Borough High

Street with one penny, no idea of what to do or
where to go, and the rain pelting down.

I do not remember how that day passed. I remember only a nightmare of streets and a multi-
tude of people. I remember spending my penny
somewhere near Smithfield, on two small rolls. I
remember the dusk and the lights of the tea-shops
and restaurants, and the throb of the traffic in my
ears, and the strange lightness of my body and the
elastic spring of the pavements as I walked. I
remember, somewhere, a great archway, channelled
by wind; and the hard stones; and dreams about
Miss Cicely; and an awakening to a world of drays,
carts and lorries, which made thunder in the arches.
And I remember the moment of madness that possessed me at sight of a coffee-stall. But no more.

The next day I remember more clearly.

All through that second day I walked and walked
because I couldn't stand still. Yesterday's rain
persisted, and I went through it, head down, shoulders hunched, my legs moving mechanically. The
rain soaked through my cap to my head, and then
to my collar, and then down my neck. Where I
went I do not know. Men and women, passing or
overtaking, brushed and jostled me. I ignored
them, and let them shove. I wasn't a man; I was
an organism with two legs. The shop-windows
made rainbow beauty all round me; they seemed to
pick me out in spot-lights and jeer me with their
smart grin of prosperity. I forgot that I was walking or why I was walking. I had eaten my last bit

of roll the afternoon before, and my stomach was empty, and my mind was filled with little hungers and hates. I lived the whole of that day through the senses of smell and touch—the smell of food to the nose and the touch of wet clothes to the skin. By mid-day I was in that state that men call "wet through"—a state which, if achieved, is endurable. But it never is achieved: wet clothes present themselves only at knees, elbows, neck, shoulders and feet; other parts remain exasperatingly dry.

The smell of food was my chief torment. It lured me. I could not hold my thoughts from it. I thought of a vast dish of eggs-and-bacon, sizzling. I thought of steak puddings, steaming. Of boiled beef and dumplings and carrots, bubbling. Of the taste of new bread. Of the odour of sausages and onions. Of roast pork and stuffing. Of the flirtatious scent of fried potatoes. Of brown mutton chops. Of toad-in-the-hole.

These dishes passed before me and made the gutter gay. I saw their colouring. I caught their fragrance. The vision and the phantom smells made me silly. I found myself humming grand opera.

I began to notice that people looked at me, and drew away from my misery of wetness. I was an affront to their respectability.

(Eggs and bacon! Sausage and mashed!)

I hated the people. They were going to dinner or coming from dinner, and in the evening they would go home. I hated them for having homes and dinners. I thought of sleek arm-chairs, which

let you sink into them and lapped you. I thought
of the great beds in the windows of the furniture
stores. I wondered what it would be like to flop
into one of them and roll between a dozen blankets.
Some of the people looked at me as though I had
hurt them. If I had been dry and presentable, and
playing an organ, they would have given me coppers. But nobody gave me anything except offended
looks. I found myself watching certain people as
they came along, and thinking: "Now, suppose this
woman pulled out her purse and said, 'Here, my
boy, you look wretched. Here's two shillings.'
What would I do with that two shillings?"

(Steak-and-kidney pudding! Pork and crackling!)

I began to think that they were pitying me; and
that was the last irritation—worse than the smell
of food. Blast their pity!

(Bloaters and kippers! Sausages and onions!)

I hated them all. I hated those who passed me
indifferently, and those who looked at me. Somewhere, on my tramp, a company of girls were entering a large block of buildings, and I began to think
of them and their soft arms and bright faces. They
looked good enough to eat; and my mind asked me
stupidly—"Which would you rather have—a steak
pudding or go home with that golden-haired one?"
As I passed them they giggled at the drowned-dog
spectacle I made. Grr! I was conscious of two
passions—to get food and escape pity. Food was
to be had. There it was—within arm's reach—in
the windows of the cook-shops and tea-shops:

cooked food, ready to eat. To get it, though, I had to throw a stone and break a window; and that meant effort—even greater effort than brushing the rain from my face. But pity—so long as I remained in the streets under people's eyes, I could not escape pity.

I fell to dreaming of beauty. I felt myself lolling on the rich cushions of somebody's carriage, a beautiful girl at my side; or dining in a velvet room, or sitting in drawing-rooms; lifted up, from the welter of noise and wet where I floundered, into Nirvana.

(Eggs and bacon! Pork and gravy!)

I went plodding on, wishing for the dark and for some place where I might hide, when I found myself in a thoroughfare that seemed endless—a stretch of warehouses, goods' yards, gas-works, broken cottages, and mean shops. It was then about three o'clock, and the light was slate and the rain still falling. There were dejected tram-cars and 'buses, wet trollies, and shining policemen; and against their dreariness came the babble of voices and glasses from the public-houses. Then I heard the jingle of an organ, playing the "Hiawatha" cake-walk, and as I plodded towards it I reached the entry of a court. There, in the court itself, I saw the organ, and around it I saw a group of ragged girls, kicking up black mud to its Bacchic rhythm. The cobweb daylight that entered the court from above illuminated only the faces and tangled hair of the dancers, and feet and bodies could be hardly seen. For the first time that day

I halted, and stood and watched them. Now they went slowly, in mock tragedy, and now they went furiously, and now they screamed. One came near me, and thrust a screaming face at me. I giggled; and, in my weak and dazed condition, I felt ready to plunge into the mud and roll in it with them. As the dance and the cries of the crowd grew more furious, a window on the first floor was thrown up, and into the grey light came a lean, pale face: a face with eyes wide and lips parted in a chuckle; an ugly spectacle meeting my own ugliness. And suddenly, as I leaned, exhausted, against a post, came one of the moments of my life. In that moment I was again conscious of time arrested and of the feeling that I was looking upon a picture as old as the world; and that those tattered children, that gloating face and myself were and had been part of it. And into the thick of my desolation came a glow of exaltation. I was aware of strength and clearness. I felt capable of anything. The most difficult achievement seemed possible to me. I longed then and there for pencil and paper that I might try again to write the tale of Quong Lee's window and of this court.

Then the moment was gone. I came back to earth and to my condition, and all I saw was a muddy court and a pack of dirty children dancing round an organ.

Sick, and weaker than before, I plodded on. My knees were sagging, and I was walking from the loins. Outside a public library a few of my kind, simple souls, were studying the "situations" pages of the papers which were pasted on boards. I laughed. I had played that game out.

(Steak-and-kidney pudding! Irish Stew!)

Damn all!

I slouched on and on, and at the end of this apparently endless road I met the sailor. He was standing with his back against a shop, and looked as wet as I was. As I drew near him, our eyes met, and he said, "Wotcher, chum!" I stopped. I don't know why I stopped, but I did, and, having stopped, couldn't make any words to return his greeting. He grinned, and said facetiously, "Bin out in the rain?" I nodded and sniffed. "Like me. Where y'orf to?"

I said "Nowhere."

He had a long look at me. "On the bum?"

The phrase was new to me, but I guessed its meaning, and said, "Ur."

"Same 'ere. I'm just waitin' till they open."

I drew under the shop to get what cover it afforded, and asked, "Till what open?"

"The Shelters, ya fool. Six o'clock."

"The Shelters?" I said. Then I remembered. "D'you think I could get in?"

He grinned again. "Best ticket for them places is what ya look like. And on what you look like now you'd jump in. Is things like that wiv ya?"

I nodded. "I got no job, and I was turned out of my room yesterday morning."

"I see. Well, you better throw in wi' me, chum. The best place is over the river."

"Matter of fact," I said, "I don't quite know where I am."

"No? Well, that's what anybody'd say to look at ya. This is Ole Kent Road. Place I'm thinkin' of is near Brick Lane. Beffnal Green, y'know. 'Bout an hour's walk from here, over the Tower. I was just havin' a mike, so's I could time it fer a quick walk. If I can git through t'night, I got something coming. Know Digger Morrison's place in Bell Yard?"

I had heard of it, in "The Barge Aground," as a boxing nursery.

"I got a chance there t'morrer night. Novices. I'm goina turn up. I useter be pretty good as a kid, and if ya git through all right ya git five bob and p'raps a chance o' being taken up by one o' the sports. Dunno if I'll be any good; I ain't bin feedin' prop'ly lately. I 'ad two yers at sea, y'know but two yers is enough fer me. No more o' that, fer me. . . . Well, I'm pushin' orf. If yer care to come, I'll show yer the tricks."

He was a lad of bright eyes and shapeless face: a lad who had the air of neither challenging the world nor being beaten by it, but accepting it. He was short and well built, and might have passed for thirty, but was, he told me, eighteen. He looked as though no privations or distress could injure his robust body or disturb his serious grin. He was there and couldn't be moved, and as I walked with him I was thankful for the chance that had brought us together.

The doss-house was in a narrow street near Brick

Lane, and only a few yards from a police-station.
By some occult law, these things go always together.
Wherever you find a police-court, Sessions House,
gaol, or station, in the streets thereabouts, you will
surely find the gathering-place for the rogues and
derelicts of the district. What psychic force it is
that draws them to place head and shoulders within
the enemy's grasp, I cannot tell; I only know, by
experience and observation, the fact.

As we reached the kip, he dug me in the ribs.
"Good! Only ten there so fur. We'll be all right,
I reckon."

We took our places at the end of the queue, and
I rested my sodden shoulder against the wall, and
passed into a half-sleep. The rain came down
more sharply now, and beat about our feet and
legs. Through it buzzed and burbled the bitterly
facetious talk of the crowd.

"Well, mate?"

" 'Ullo, Cock-eye. What's yer good noos?"

Cock-eye answered in a voice that had the sound
of jangled bells. "Work f'r all, and six bleedun
meals a day."

"Wot y'ave fer dinner, Cock-eye?"

"Oysters and turbot and pheasant and cigars!"

" 'Ow much longer 'fore they open this bloody
place—eh?"

" 'Owder we know, Grousey? Ring fer the
stooard, shall I, and tell 'im orf!"

"Wunner what it feels like t'be dry—eh?"

"Oh, shuttup!"

"They say there's soup t'night, 'stead o' cocoa!"

"Soup!" The word passed down the queue and aroused me. At once I smelt it, saw it through my closed eyes, felt it in my throat, warm and caressing. Basins of it floated in the air. My pal spoke to the man in front.

"We got a chance all right, ain't we, to-night?"

"I dunno. . . . I wish I was a dog. I wish to Christ I was a dog. If I was a———"

There was a stir, a rush. The sailor punched me. "Stir up, chum." The queue moved forward, marking time in spasms. Two by two those in front went in. Three more steps and we would be in too. From an opposite corner a man came shuffling. I heard his squelching, and noted the glint in his eye. As he approached us he made towards the end of the queue; then turned and shot past to the door. Two men shouted. The unforgiveable sin had been committed.

"Hi—'ere! Take yer turn! Blast 'im—make 'im take 'is turn. There's on'y room for———"

The men seemed seized with panic. Their basins of soup and the blankets were vanishing into this creature with the squelchy boots. They wailed, and the sailor answered:

"Whassup? Some one dishin'. 'Ere—just lemme———"

He swung round upon the squelchy one, but under the threat and the chorus of commination, the offender turned and slunk to the back of the queue, gibing. And now we reached the oblong of light, and we were inside. In that light and warmth I felt the limit of exhaustion. Another step, I felt, would have killed me. Then slowly my heart began to take nourishment. I fed my eyes and my nose. The rumour was truth; there were soup and great crusts of bread. The incandescent gas-lamps had a friendly glow. The stove stood at the end of the room like a fat host, welcoming us. The floor was bare and dirty with many wet boots. The smell of many years' food floated up the walls, and made the air thick, but I snuffed it up. Away at the door we heard the dreadful words, "Full up for to-night!" and a rumble of voices too low and too full to express clearly fury or resignation. I looked at my pal and laughed. We were inside, anyhow, with the glory of food to come, and the paradise of a dry bed to follow. I began to know that I had limbs, and that they were stiff and sore.

Then I began to use my eyes. We were a well-mixed lot, alike only in wetness. We were not a company, but an assembly of units. There was no mingling, no gossip. Each one stood apart, en-closed within himself, hiding his sorrow like a sick dog. There was a navvy in corduroys, strapped at the knees. There was the sailor in jersey and ragged trousers. There was myself, the best-dressed and the wettest of the lot. There was the palpable tramp, grey-haired, red-faced and snuffly. There was a creature with a rattish face, all winks and cringes. There were men without shirts and men without socks, dirty men and clean men. And one brutal joke of a man with black face (streaked where the rain had caught it) sodden tail-coat, red-striped trousers, a collar once six inches high, now as limp as the trousers, and a cloth cap with a drooping cock's feather in it. His shoulders were decorated with the sort of blue monkeys sold as favours on Boat Race Days. Three whelk-shells were strung round his neck, and across the middle of his back, tied with string, he wore a gridiron holding a bloater made of painted cardboard. All were silent, and most were downcast; but this man, standing alone, serious and proud, was utter misery.

Authority spoke. "Them that's wet, forward to the drying-room. Hang up yer clothes till they're dry. Then dress and come back."

"Come on, chum." The sailor pushed me forward with violent friendliness, and pushed me into the drying-room.

Ah! The joy of getting out of those saturated clothes. The joy of putting on dry clothes. The walking back to the great stove. The bliss of warmth. The sensual delight of the red coals. I could have knelt down and kissed them, and, from the looks on the faces of the others, they felt the same. But we only stood there, stretching out hands, in the attitude of a votary, until the hot soup was thrust upon us. Another joy! The feel of the basin to my hands. The smell of its steam under my nose. The large flavour of onion. The exquisite taste of bread. The joy of it nearly choked me.

Then Authority called upon us to sing a hymn, and I joined with the crowd. I would have done

anything for them after that soup. I could not
blast these people. I would have sung the book
through if they had asked me. I was dry and
warm. Then to bed. The dormitory had a
"smell" to it, but it didn't matter; it was better
than the smell of those arches. The bed was a
hard-stuff pallet, but I found it uncommonly soft.
It was some time before I could fit myself to its
yielding surface; but slowly I relaxed my limbs,
then stretched them. Ah! I rolled on it, snug-
gling into my dry clothes and making noises. I
wallowed. From all round the room came noises
echoing mine—grunts, hiccups, splutters, ughs and
ahs. Authority spoke again. "All out at half-past
five." Nobody answered, and for myself I waved
the threat into fairyland, and settled in deeper content. To-morrow was to-morrow. To-night was
now.

From the farther bed a voice began a song:

"Why should 'e wiv all 'is riches,
    Go wiv 'er what is so pore;
Castin' shaime on 'er relations,
    Makin' 'er into——"

Authority looked in. "Now then, there. Order,
there. Order, if yeh don't mind. Else outside yeh
go. See?"

"All right, guv'nor. I was on'y sayin' me
prayers."

Authority withdrew. Another voice started.
"You can keep yer women. *I* don' want 'em.
Never did. I like me drop o' good stuff, when I

got the rhino, but Uncle Joe don't want no women. No matter 'ow tasty they are. On'y one woman in the world I ever wanted to sleep with."

"Oh—an' who's that?"

"Gaby Dess-lee!"

Somebody threw a boot; there were murmurs and expostulations. "Fer Gorsake 'old yer row, cancher." Then more splutters, grunts, and a snore. The sailor made a magnificent clearance of his throat. "Goo'-night, chum!"

That night I dreamed of Miss Cicely in the garden, and of Fosdick and Quong Lee and clerks and black rulers and Gaby Deslys all dancing in a court off Old Kent Road.

.   .   .   .

The morning began as the night had ended— with snorts, grunts, coughs and splutters. I awoke light in body and mind, as comfortable as I have ever been. I was right down now, and I felt at ease. I was at home with my sailor chum and these other men. Among them, things were what they were. There were no hesitancies, no reticence, no standards. I wondered why on earth I had muddled my head with poetry and essays and music, and worried myself with such matters as speaking well and minding my manners, when there were such good fellows as the sailor, who would take me as I was without sneer or question, just as Quong Lee had——

At this point I stopped and said aloud, "You fool!"

"Meaning me?" said the sailor.

"No. Me. Been wandering about for two days,
and all the time I could have got a place to sleep
in and something to eat. All the time. I only just
thought of it. I got a pal."

"Where? Anywhere near?"

"Yes. In the Causeway."

"What—a Chink?"

"Yes. I could have gone there all the time."

"Huh! I thought you looked a bit scatty. . . .
Well, I suppose you'll be going orf there. I'm
going out to get a bit of grub."

"But how're you going to buy it? I thought you
said you was out."

"Buy it, ya fool? What ya talkin' about? I
ain't gointa buy it. Gointa knock it orf. Easy as
pie to knock off a few things—at the stalls down
the Lane."

"Look here," I said. "Don't do that. If you
hadn't picked me up yesterday I'd a-bin out all
night, I expect. Come down to the Causeway with
me. We'll get something there."

"Straight? That all right? I guess I will, then,
I don' wanta muck about too much t'day, 'cos of
t'night. D'you chew?"

"Chew?"

"Yes, ya fool." He pulled out a plug of tobacco.

"Oh, I see. No, I don't."

"Huh! Well, I could a-offered ya one if ya did."

At half-past five we were out in the street, and
the streets were dry and the sky was clear. We
headed for the Causeway; and the rest of that day
and night are a blur.

I remember that we were received by Quong Lee;
that I made a difficult explanation of my condition;
that he fed us both in the back room on dried fish
and tea and rice. I remember that amid the scents
of manioc and betel-nut, and in the presence of
that calm, acceptant face, my troubles slipped away,
and I was soothed and healed. I remember, too, a
feeling that there was something different about
the shop. It was not a disturbing feeling, but it was
there, and I puzzled myself to locate it. Quong
Lee was as before, but I knew that something had
changed. I could feel it in the air. At night I discovered what it was.

All day we lounged in or near the shop, sometimes taking a stroll down to the river, and sometimes standing outside. As the evening came on
the sailor grew nervous and irritable, and at half-
past seven he went off to Bell Yard, and I sat with
Quong Lee in the back, and tried to tell him about
Gracie. But he didn't understand. He understood
that I was troubled about a girl, but the cause had
no meaning for him; and at last I gave it up, and sat
absorbing the serenity that he gave out.

At half-past nine the sailor came back. More
truly, made a triumphal return. He was lit up.
I was standing on the step of the shop, listening to
the guitar and the sad songs from the shuttered
lodging-house opposite, when I saw him come charg-
ing down the Causeway. With hands in pockets,
he strutted. When he reached the shop he stood
in front of me, put his hands up, did some shadow-
boxing, and hit me playfully in the chest, but hard

enough to send me staggering into the shop. Then
he became grave, and spoke casually. He had done
it. Done it in three rounds. Giving half a stone,
too. Three rounds. "And that ain't all, mate.
Look 'ere!" He held out half a sovereign. "One
o' the sports gimme that. An' that ain't all, neether.
'E's gointa give me another show. 'E fancies me.
An' if I shape all right 'e's gointa take me up an' put
me in trainin'. Now look 'ere—you're the only pal
I got round about 'ere. Me an' you's gotta do something wi' this."

"With what?"

"This. We gotta 'ave a night on this. If 'e
takes me up I shan't 'ave a chance of a night again.
Come on."

"A Night?"

"Yes, a night. Come on. I know a good boozer
just across the road. Let's go there. Come
on. . . . Oh, come *on*, yeh misery! We *gotta* make
a night of this."

We did. Before I could say anything he grabbed
my arm and pulled me out into the Causeway. There
was no hilarity about him. We set forth on that
"night" not as to festival but as to a solemn rite.

.   .   .   .

Five minutes later I found myself in a bar that
I had last entered, and saw faces that I had last
seen, ten years ago. I found myself in the saloon of
"The Barge Aground." Ten years! Yet they had
made little difference. It seemed as though I had
left it but yesterday, and I was greeted by the company in the same casual spirit. Mr. Sturt alone

seemed to have any capacity for surprise at the return of the ten-years-absent.

For some moments after we had entered he stared at me; then he spoke. "If yeh don't mind my asking, young man, what might your name be?" I told him, and added that I remembered him, and would like to thank him for what he had done years ago about Uncle Frank, and. . . . But he stopped me with "Gawd's truth? Well, now! Well, I'm damned. D'you know, I thought it was you directly you come in. The funny way you twist yer nose—just like you used to when you was a kid. 'Ow many yers is it since you used to sit 'ere an' eat 'eart-cakes—eh? Gawd—time does fly, don't it? What'll y'have?"

I said I was with a friend. "Oh, that's all right. Perhaps yer friend'll join us. This is with me. Ten years—eh? Sad about pore ole Uncle Frank, wasn't it? I can see 'im now, sittin' in the Wheel-'ouse, talkin' about when he kept the 'Gallopin' 'Orses.' I felt I'd lost a real friend when 'e went. I did reely. What'll y'ave?"

I couldn't fence the question again, and I couldn't for the moment answer. He took me so much as man-to-man that I didn't like to confess that I'd never been in a bar since my heart-cake days, and didn't know my way about. What did one have in bars? What was the right thing to ask for? Then I remembered a phrase of Uncle Frank's, and brought it out as casually as I could. "Oh, half of the usual."

Mr. Sturt smacked his hands. "That's the style. Glad you don't drink spirits. No good to anybody under fifty. But this stuff won't 'urt yeh. What's yer pal 'aving?"

The sailor joined me with half of the usual, and then he stood a round; and then Mr. Sturt suggested going through to the Wheelhouse, where I should find one or two old friends, and there I found Mr. Fremantle and the station housekeeper; and they stood a round; and I made the discovery that "strong drink" made me like other people—alert and un-self-conscious. By that time the sailor was tired of sitting in one place and said, "What about the 'Blue Posts.' " We all went to the "Blue Posts."

The rest of the night was a smudge. I remember the "Blue Posts" and the "Commercial," and Charley Brown's, and "The Star of the East" and the "White Horse." That is, I remember being in those places. I remember the sailor telling everybody in every bar, very quietly, that he had knocked out—I forget the name he began with, but later it was changed to Pedlar Palmer, Charley Mitchell, Ben Jordan, and Jem Mace. Then, at the last place, the sailor picked up a girl. There was talk about where to go, and the girl said: "I know a place down the Causeway. Ole Quong Lee's. Let's go there." The name came dimly to me, and it was some time before I connected the remark with the difference that I had noted in the atmosphere of the shop. It didn't matter, anyway. Nothing mattered.

We went back to Quong Lee's, and went upstairs; at least, I found myself upstairs, in a dusty room half-lit by an oil lamp and strewn with mattresses.

At first I saw only a cloud of smoke and smelt its sickliness. Then I saw shapeless bundles, smoking, and a few drinking out of cups and glasses. There were murmurs, exclamations; and a woman was babbling and rambling about love. A young girl was sitting on the floor, lying backwards across the legs of a sleepy nigger. He was playing with her.

It was all very queer, and I tried to puzzle it out, but my head was a beehive. I found myself, in flashes of waking, wondering what had happened to Quong Lee? Why had he started this sort of thing? Or had he been doing it all the time? Or were we somewhere else and not in Quong Lee's shop? But no—it was Quong Lee's, because, though I could not see him, I was conscious of his presence somewhere in the room. I remember a vague desire *not* to see him; and then, after squatting there some minutes, I suffered a change of attitude towards him. He was going down: that was clear; and I was not shocked or grieved. I was already down—and drunk; and Quong Lee was coming closer to me. That thought, piercing the muzzy thrill of intoxication, brought me satisfaction. I felt that I now knew all about him and his shop and the Causeway, and its puzzle. And I did know—then. I knew all manner of strange things. I knew what everybody in that room was thinking and feeling. I understood Quong Lee. I knew the sensations of the little girl and of the nigger. I knew the heart of the crying woman. I knew what the sailor felt about his victory. I knew what Quong Lee felt about me. I had grasped it at last. But next morning. . . .

At some point during the night I woke up to wonder what I was doing there among those people. Some far-away memories of Keats and Matthew Arnold came to me. Why was I there? Why was I alive? . . . Why does a mouse when it. . . . Why was I drunk? . . . Why did that girl's face keep floating out of the shadow? "And open, jasmine-muffled lattices. And the full moon and the pale evening star." "Mother of the dews, dark eye-lashed twilight. . . ." Couldn't remember any more. Never mind. I was down; and I felt as though I were sitting in a very agreeable hell. It was all ugly and wicked, and Quong Lee was ugly and wicked, and I was ugly and wicked, too, and ready, as I had been in Old Kent Road, to plunge and be a beast.

Somewhere towards daylight the fight began. The sailor began to bawl a song:

> "Oh, we'll ask old Lee to tea,
> And we'll ask old Lee to tea,
> And if 'e won't come,
> We'll ask his son,
> And all the fam-er-lee,
> We'll all be merry. . . ."

Somebody didn't like it and swore. There was a lot of noise. The room began to be full of people moving, like a roundabout.

Next thing I was out in the air, and somebody was propping me against the wall; and I saw the sailor fighting, and I cheered him on. Then the wall ran away from me.

I woke up next morning in Quong Lee's back room, and after a hazy interlude I gathered that the sailor was in the hands of the police, and that I had been pulled indoors.

Although I knew I could do nothing for him, I felt that I ought to be present, and at ten o'clock I managed to crawl to the court. I reached there just in time to catch his eye as he was being fined twenty shillings or fourteen days for drunkenness, obstruction and obscene language. Knowing that he had spent his ten shillings, I felt that I ought to be sorry for him, but I could only be angry with him and angry with myself. Then I saw that he was grinning.

"That's all right, guv'nor. I'll do the fourteen. Do it on me head. Fourteen days'll just about put me right." He turned to me with, "So long, mate. Keep smiling," and was taken below. I stepped down and as the public door was some distance away, and I should have to pass through a group of people—the mere thought of the effort appalled me—I sat down in one of the public seats and heard the other cases, which buzzed round my ears like voices in a dream. They were the usual overnight cases of drunkenness and assault, but at one point there came a pause; then a stir. A tough youth next to me sent his elbow into my ribs and whispered, "This is the big 'un." Through the door by which I had entered came an inspector, a wardress, and a shabby, tired woman. Her face was drawn and grey. She shuffled. From her neck to her worn-down boots she was enclosed in a heavy plush coat.

Grey towzled hair hung in wisps under a red hat
trimmed with a saucy blue feather. She seemed
to be a hat and coat propelled by a human body:
she entered the dock with the gait of a sleep-walker.

"Maisie Cudmore, sir."

"Manslaughter charge, I think?"

A figure rose from the solicitor's table. "No,
sir. I am instructed to charge with murder." There
were movements in court and murmurs. Those
around me craned forward with open mouths and
the empty looks of a baby at first sight of a novel
object. The principals seemed to have no eye for
effect, but the audience charged everything with
drama. The boy next me examined the prisoner
from head to foot, as she stood exposed in the open-
railed dock, from the flaming hat to the broken
boots; and in my dazed state I too felt that this was
no woman, but a symbol. The very boots held something of the sinister; they had lived with horror.
The hat was already a relic. The plush coat was
an exhibit.

But the woman was neither horrible nor fearful.
She stood scratching her ear, and her face held that
expression that one sees on Cross-Channel passen-
gers when, on the crest of a casual attitude, comes
the sickening apprehension that you're going to
break down. Something in her scheme of things had
gone wrong. A curtain had dropped, cutting her
life in two; and of the next act she knew nothing.
Her life was no more her own, and the little pucker
over her eyes expressed a futile struggle to understand it all. The sergeant who had given evidence

in our cases and one or two solicitation cases entered
the box, and passed, without apparent change, from
the trivial to the tragic. But to the audience he
was a very different figure. If he had chanted his
evidence, he could not have held them more tensely.
The boy nudged me again, and whispered, "He
lives next door to us." He said it to others about
him, and they looked at him as at one who lived in
neighbourhood with greatness. The woman went
on scratching her ear.

"Are you calling any witnesses?"

"Only three witnesses to-day, sir."

Conquering the fascination of that silly hat, I
looked away and fixed my eyes on something
straight before me—the back of a man's head. I
wanted to shut my eyes, but if I shut my eyes I
seemed to rise in the air. So I stared at the back
in front of me, and as I stared until my eyes were
two burning coals, I was conscious of looking at
something familiar. For some moments I fumbled
with it. Then it came to me. However markedly
a man's face may change, the back of his head remains always the same. Had I seen this man's
face only I would not have known him, but the
back of his head. . . . For four years I had stood
behind that head at drill in the grounds of Hardcress.

Gold Flake.

The dribbling, scurrying Gold Flake in a thick
brown ulster, with pomaded hair and dazzling collar. While I was still trying to feel something about
this encounter, a voice called "Frederick Cosgrove!"

and he got up and went into the box, and was sworn.

"At a quarter to eleven last night I was leaving the Acme Music Hall, and Burton, the chief electrician, was following behind me. I saw a woman standing outside the stage door. I was just getting into a cab when I heard a shout and a cry, and I looked round and saw the woman—the prisoner—with a knife in her hand and Burton lying on the ground. I caught hold of the woman and took the knife away from her, and called for help. The door-keeper and the cabby picked Burton up, and then this officer came along and. . . ."

At this point the officer near the door made a clearance through the crowd for a pressman, and, seeing a straight path, I got up and somehow blundered out.

Chapter IX

THE HALLS

WHEN I got through the hall and on to the outer steps I stood debating muzzily what I should do. Should I go back to Quong Lee, or should I go down to the river and stroll about and clear my head? Should I go this way or that way? Not that it mattered, but in the inverted state succeeding an affair like last night's, trifles become affairs of importance and serious occasions become trivial. I could come to no decision, but stood there I don't know how long, staring across the street and turning the matter over in my mind. Then a voice said "Hi!" I turned. Gold Flake, or Cosgrove, a slim and full-grown figure, in appearance old enough to be my father, strode towards me, looked down, and said: "Think we've met before. You was at school at Hardcress, wasn't you? You're. . . ."

"Yes. And I know you. You're Cosgrove."

"That's me. Blimey, you haven't altered a bit. Not a bit. I'd a-known you anywhere. What you doing here, and how's the world using you? Eh? I just been giving evidence in a murder case here. Chap at the hall here, outed by his wife, just because he didn't go straight home. Nice chap, too. Don't you never get married, boy. . . . Well, I *am* glad to see y'again. How're things?"

I hesitated. I wanted to keep my end up, but the sight of this radiant creature disarmed me. His magnificent ulster, his creased trousers, his spats, his blinding boots, his carelessly elegant hat, and his malacca cane shouted of a prosperity that I could not hope to match, even by lies. This, on top of my physical discomfort and the knowledge of my state, made me abject. I blurted out: "Rotten. Out of a job. No money. Out of everything."

"Oh? Like that—eh? What you been doing at the court?"

"Pal of mine was brought here."

"Brought here? What for?"

"Er—I had a bit of a—a doing last night. With a chap I picked up, and—— He got pinched here."

He thrust his head down at me. "Naughty boy!" and grinned the old vacuous ear-and-mouth grin. "Well, I'm glad to run across you again. But sorry to hear you're all messed up. Here— let's go and have a drink and talk it over—eh?"

"A drink? Oh, Lord, I——"

"*I* know, young 'un, *I* know. You come with me. I'll put you right." He grabbed my shoulder and took charge of me as he had done at Hardcress. "I know what you want. Come on!" I was too weak to resist if I had wanted to; but I didn't: I was in a state when I would have gone anywhere with anybody. I had a sudden sense of comfort and security in meeting this solid creature in the midst of my shifts and misfortunes. I felt as I had felt on my first day at the school, and I let him

lead me across the road, and into a bar. He pushed
the door open with his foot, strode in as though he
owned the place, forced a way through the crowd at
the bar, and said: "Bass for me, and listen—I
want a gin-and-soda, with a dash of angostura and
a slice of lemon. That's the idea. There y'are,
boy. Just what the doctor ordered. Get outside
that."

I obeyed and drank a large mouthful of it. He
spread one arm magnificently on the counter, and
waved the other and spluttered over me. "So
you're on the beach, eh? Sorry. Wonder what
we can do about it. I'm on the halls, y'know."

"On the what?" Although he had spoken of
leaving the Acme Theatre late at night, and was
loud with dress, I hadn't given a thought to what he
was doing there; no more thought than he had given
to being witness in a murder case.

"The halls. Music-halls."

"What—in the orchestra, or——"

"Orchestra, no! Comedian. Look 'ere—see
that bill." He pointed to a framed bill hanging on
the wall—the Acme bill for the week. "There I
am—in the middle. I'm playing down here all this
week. See?" I saw his name in the body of the
bill, in red type, with a smaller line in blue, "Freddie
Cosgrove—One of Nature's Nibs." I looked at
him. Was I still in last night, or was this really
Cosgrove—the witless, thrusting Cosgrove? Yes,
it was Cosgrove all right. I knew it was, but the
jump from one to the other was so wide that I could
not conceive how it had been made. I wondered

whether the change had been gradual and unper-
ceived or sudden and deliberate. How had that
dowdy charity-boy become transformed into this
flashy, resolute creature with both feet upon the
earth? He went on: "Doing well, too. Booked
for three months ahead. Twelve quid a week.
And chance of better money when these bookings
are through."

This was a second shock. "Twelve pounds a
week?"

"Ah. Twelve golden jimmies a week. 'Course,
it isn't much as prices run to-day, but I'm making
me way. And I got people after me, too."

This hurt me a little. I had assumed prosperity
from his clothes, and had placed it at five pounds a
week. But twelve! Gold Flake—the pale, unconsidered bungler—on the stage, becoming famous, a
man in the public eye, one who was Doing Things,
and earning actually twelve pounds every week.

I murmured something about his having done
well, and altered a lot since the Hardcress days.
"Have I? You haven't. You're just the same.
Only about two inches taller. That's all. . . .
Well, feeling better after that? Let's get up West
and have a snack somewhere, and see if we can do
anything for you. I'm only half-awake just yet—
having to get up so early and come all down here to
the Court. . . . But come on—here's a 'bus."

Gabbling and spluttering, he pushed me on to
the 'bus, and all the way to the Strand he splashed
me. I discovered on that journey that, despite his
bodily growth and his success, he hadn't changed

much: he was as delighted at finding me helpless and taking command of me, as he had been on the day I entered Hardcress, and all his talk was what he could do to put me on my feet. "No home? No job? No money? Only what you stand up in? Blimey, you've been having a time. But we got to put that right somehow. I'll think o' something before lunch's over." In the Strand he looked round as though he owned the Strand, and then said: "Let's go to Gatti's."

I said: "Gatti's! No—not there. I'd rather not. Couldn't we go to an A.B.C.?"

"A.B.C.? Blimey—what for?"

"Well, my clothes—Gatti's——"

"Lorlummy, boy. Clothes don't matter there. You comerlongwimme."

Again I was pushed through a swing door, and found myself in Gatti's. Even had I been earning five pounds a week, I would never have dared to enter the place by myself, but Cosgrove strode in as though Gatti's were an everyday place. My head was still not clear, but clear enough for me to be conscious of bewilderment at being there. There were white tablecloths and napkins, and flowers on each table, and swift waiters, and an array of knives and forks and spoons and glasses at whose office I could only guess. I had the feeling that everybody was staring at us, but Cosgrove stood in the centre of the main room, and looked carefully round for a table, quite at ease. He knew just what to do; how to talk to the waiter, what to order, and how to order it. He called the waiter Antonio, and the

waiter paid attention to him. "Now, then, boy—
what d'you fancy?" He handed me a blue-and-gold
menu, and I stared at it, trying to pretend, before the
waiter, that I was studying it. *"Hors d'œuvres*—
eh? Or what about some oysters, and then
some——"

I said: "Oh, something light for me. Anything.
Just a——" I had no idea how to finish the sentence, but he did it for me.

"Ah, you want feeding a bit, y'know. After
last night. You better have some soup, and then
an omelette, and then a cutlet. Got that, Antonio? Oysters for me; and then one of your
fillets; and then we'll see. Now—what are we
drinking?"

"I don't think I could."

"Ah. P'raps you're wise. Now then—let's hear
all about it."

As well as my confused state would allow, I told
him; but half the time I was looking about me,
trying to tell myself that I was really lunching at
Gatti's. I felt small and abashed at being there,
and being in the company of a rich young man who
earned twelve pounds a week, and had a joyous life
of half an hour's interesting work in the evening,
and the whole of the day to himself. I had no right
to be sitting with him. He had got on. I was
nowhere.

Then the meal came, and I realised the sublimity
of the material. It was for me a fleshly poem.
The soup—Crême de Tomate—which mocked the
Brick Lane soup as Gatti's mocked Brick Lane

itself: a ruddy pool making a gloria to the eye and
a benediction to the mouth. The omelette—yellow
as buttercups. The cutlets—dark brown and wearing little white collars. And the cheese—a cheese
I had never tasted before. I had not known that
there was more than one cheese, that cheese could
be other than white and waxy. I thought cheese
was just cheese. This was called Camembert, and
was enclosed in a thin brown skin, which you peeled
off; and the cheese itself, hesitating between cream
and solid, between old ivory and daffodils, was as
cool as a dairy and as soft and rich as country fields.
I ate all—soup, omelette, cutlets, and cheese, and
talked to Cosgrove between eating and listening to
him. A week ago my poetic ear would have winced
at his rasping voice and his street phrases, but soon
I found myself talking easily the same language,
and happy with it.

"So you write stuff for the papers, eh? *Ally
Sloper*—eh? That's an idea, now. If you can
write for *Ally Sloper,* you ought to be a useful man,
y'know. You might do some stuff for me or one
of the other boys. Lyrics, y'know. I want a good
song to foller the one I got now. Lemme see, now.
. . . D'you want coffee? No? Right. Let's
go along to the Cavour. Just thought o' something.
Chap I know—manages the Resplendent, Lavender
Hill—he's losing his money-box man next week.
Wonder if you could do that. Expect he'll be there,
but if not, sure to be a few of the lads there. They
may know o' something."

After that meal, following long hunger and last

night, I felt like weeping on his shoulder; but I only said, "It's awfully good of you to take all this trouble. It isn't everybody that'd——"

"Good Gawd, it ain't any trouble. At present you're down and I'm up. Some day may be t'other way round. Then I shall come down on you. Besides, fer the sake of the Old Days. . . ." He waved his hands.

"How did you come to get on the stage?"

"Gawd knows. On'y a year or two ago. I got a job in a hall as electrician's assistant—on the limes, y'know—and I useter imitate the turns. And one night the manager come round and caught me at it, and told me to do it again. And do one or two other people. And then he arst me if I'd like a trial. *I* never knew I could do anything, but just for a lark, I said Yes. So 'e give me a Sat'dy night trial—you know—extra turn. And I got 'em. I got 'em, me boy. They kep' me on ten minutes. Wouldn't hardly let me go. Well, after that, he give me a booking, and put me in the reg'lar bill, and told me I oughta work up an act of me own. So I done it. And here I am. My act's just a couple o' songs, and then my speciality dance. You must come along to the show to-night, and see it. And o'course you'll have to stop with me till we find yeh something. I can fix up a shakedown for yeh. I live with my sister—just off Clapham Common. Funny, ain't it, that I got to pick up with you at that school 'cos you come from Poplar; and then we meet again at Poplar. There's some queer things about life—eh? Come on, let's get along to the

Cavour. You'll like the boys. They're nice boys. Oh, jolly good boys, all of 'em."

Still dazed, I was taken to the Cavour, and entered a world of which I had never dreamed; a world of laughter and friendship and cheer and all the softer virtues: a world from which everything sensible or solemn or austere was resolutely barred; a little world that lived in and by itself, taking no thought of other worlds. For the first time since childhood I felt warm. This splendid leisurely company around the bar, all of them apparently friends of Cosgrove's, seemed pleased to see me, and treated me affably and on the level. And when Cosgrove took one of them aside, and introduced me, and told him, in a phrase that I had not heard before, that I was up against it, he said, "Hard luck, ole man. Hard luck. What yeh drinkin'?"

Drinks were served, and Cosgrove prodded his friend, the manager of the Resplendent, and spluttered over him, and said, "Look here, Billy, he's a chap you could do with. Shorthand. Typewriting. Money-box. And *writes*. Writes for *Ally Sloper*."

"*Ally Sloper*—eh? Looks very young."

"Ah. Same age as me, though, really, all but a month or two. He could brighten up your bills for you. Write good snappy bill-matter. And good press-stuff, too. I've known him fer years. He's no fool. And as young Merrick's going, I thought maybe you could fix him up with something. He's had a rough time last few months, and I got to get him fixed somewhere. What about it?"

Billy, the splendid manager, looked at me, then

at the floor, then at the end of his cigar. "Well, seeing he's a pal of yours, Freddie, I dessey I could work him in. Depends how much he wants. No doubt he'd be useful."

I was about to say, "Anything as long as I get a job," and had got as far as "Any——" when Cosgrove snapped at me, "You're not drinking, boy. Go on—make a mouth at it." Then, to Billy, "Well, what'd he be worth to you?"

Billy again consulted his cigar. "Two quid a week's about as much as it'd run to."

I nearly dropped my glass in excitement; but Cosgrove stepped in with: "Two quid! Gorstrewth, guv'nor. That ain't like you. Just because I told yeh the lad's up against it. Two quid! Jesus! Ticket-office and writing ads. for yeh, and letters and everything. Two quid. If he ain't worth three he ain't worth nothing. Come orf it?"

The guv'nor considered again. Then said: "Oh, all right. Three quid. Seeing he's a pal o' yours. Come in Monday, boy. But you'll have to get a decent rig-out by then. Them clothes . . ."

Cosgrove said: "That's all right, guv'nor. I'll fix him."

I managed to find a voice to say, "What are the hours?"

"Hours? Hours? Good Gawd, boy, we don't have hours in the theatre. You'll work when you're wanted to work. Maybe three hours a day, maybe twenty-four. All depends. Come in Monday round about twelve and just look round and get the hang of things. Don't quite know yet where'll I use yeh. Never been in the business before?"

"No."

"Ah. Well, Freddie'll give you a tip or two. Drink up, Freddie, and have just one more. Then I must go."

So it was done. In five minutes I had risen to affluence and position. It was a wonderful world, if this was the way they did things. Remembering the City, and the cross-examination, and the references, and the "state age, experience, and salary required," and the formal interviews where one sat at the other side of the desk, and said "Sir," the whole thing seemed a dream. Sixteen shillings a week for six days' dreary work among dreary people in dreary offices; and three pounds a week for delightful work in a music-hall, issuing tickets or writing about comedians. Truly a wonderful world.

When the guv'nor had gone I wanted to dance round Cosgrove, and load him with thanks. I was near to delirium at this sudden uplift, but my streak of caution saved me, and Cosgrove dismissed the matter with a casual "That's that, then. Glad I got you fixed up so quickly. You got a start, anyway."

I said, "Yes, a wonderful start. If it hadn't been for you——"

"And once you get inside you may be able to pick up a bit here and there by writing patter and that. . . . Hullo, Dan!"

He turned to greet a little fellow, shabbily dressed and so sharp-faced that he looked as though his state were mine of yesterday's. A shrill voice answered him. "Hullo, Freddie!"

"What you having, Dan?"

"Thanks, old man, I got one. How're things?"

"Oh, fine!"

"Who's that?" I asked.

"That's Dan."

"Dan who?"

"Dan who? How many Dans are there? Dan Leno, o' course. One o' the best. No side with ole Dan. Always the same to everybody. . . . Hullo, Joe. What's your news?"

"All the best, boy. Ain't seen yeh for some time. Where are yeh this week?"

"Acme. Blackwall."

"Good houses?"

"Packed every night, boy, except Tuesday. Packed. What you having?"

"I was just going to ask you. And Dan. Hullo —Dan—what you having?"

"Thank's, ole man, I got one."

I stood outside all this, watching, and trying to sort out the events of the last twenty-four hours. Here I was—among The People—with three pounds a week coming to me and a friend who would look after me and steer me as he had steered me years ago. And though, with my shabby clothes, and my awkwardness, I was out of it, I felt at home there. In this atmosphere I began to have a better opinion of myself, and to wonder what the poor creatures of the Lime Street office would think if they could see me hobnobbing with famous names

in a West End bar. My skin was titillating. This
was air that I could breathe, and when, during a
break in the throb of talk, I overheard Freddie
telling Dan that I was a writer—wrote for *Ally
Sloper*—and Dan looked at me, I went agreeably
hot. Then I was drawn into the circle again, and
Cosgrove pointed to a short man, wearing a wide
sweeping hat over his yellow curls. "See that bloke?
He's an author. Often see him here, but don't know
his name." I had seen that face in photographs,
and I knew his name; a name so august that I could
hardly believe that this was its owner, standing in
a bar and drinking a little green drink. I turned my
ear from Joe and Dan and Freddie to listen to him.

"You're right," he was saying. "I never read
such bloody poppycock in my life. That silly devil,
Martindale, took it seriously. Said it was an Event
in Literature, and asked me if I'd write something
about it, as 'e can't get it noticed at all. Shouldn't
bloody well think 'e could. I told 'im so, too. God
damn it, if that's literature. . . ."

So that was the famous B——, was it? That
creature, as course and flashy as the music hall men.
After all the trouble I'd been taking with my h's
and my accent and my language, this was how dis-
tinguished authors talked. I had imagined that
all authors were public-school men and scholars,
with delicate manners, silver tongues and fastidious
voices. And here was B——, a poet and novelist,
whose name was always in the literary papers, talking just as I talked; swearing, too.

Well, well—this was surely my day of surprises.

I turned my ear from him to others. From the talk around me, I learned that I was in a world of light, among the good and true. The music-hall profession was unique: there wasn't a single dull or mean fellow in it. They were all Good Fellows, Dear Boys, or Fine Chaps. There were brisk men and heavy men and fat men and little men. There were men who slopped over the bar and men who stood with the poise of athletes. There were men who talked in monosyllables, and men who talked with their hands, like Cosgrove—"My boy, listen. Listen, my boy." Hand raised to side of head, fingers spread. Tap on the chest. "What you want to do is this." "Now listen. You want to go to him and say——"

Each newcomer, as he entered, said, "Hello, Dan. What you having?"

"Hullo, ole man. Thanks, I got one."

They seemed to be divided into the Established, the Had-Beens and the Will-Be's, and the great talked to the little without the merest shadow of magnanimity. I was among men who had earned a hundred pounds a week, men who were earning a hundred pounds a week, and men who, if this and that were "fixed up," were going to earn a hundred pounds a week. These last were filled with the rapture of the forward view: the kingdom, the power, and the glory, were always to descend next month. With the Has-Beens, everything was retrospective. "Now, my dear boy, if you'd only asked me last week I could have done it. But this week . . . I'm out."

But all were cheerful and in love and charity with all men. "Yes, my boy—me—me that played Polonius to the old man, where am I? Going on tour next week—on tour—with one of Worple's damned smack-bottom farces. But there you are, my boy. What? Eh! . . . And what are you doing?"

"I'm off next week, too. *Hearts of Women.* Number One Tour. But the second act, my boy. The second act's a scream. The entrance! I got a magnificent entrance. Mag-nificent. It's worked up, y'see. He's got her down. She's screaming for help. He says something like this, 'Scream, damn you, scream. Screaming won't help you. Nothing can save you now.' See? That's my cue. Then—chord on the brass, I smash down the window and enter with, 'You lie! British pluck and courage will save her!' God! Don't it make your heart burn, playing stuff like that? But what can yeh do?"

At half-past three Cosgrove told everybody that he had got to rush away, and he pushed me before him into Leicester Square. "Now, boy, we'll get down to Clapham Common. I could do with a bit of shut-eye before to-night's show, getting up so early in the morning. Thank God I ain't on till ten, and on'y working one hall. If I get a booking with the Syndicate—and I think I shall—I'll have to work two halls. I got a good agent. Finkelstein. One o' the best. Now about them clothes. My sister'll fix yeh up with something fer the night, and to-morrow you better go and get a rig-out."

"But I got no——"

"I know you haven't. I'll fix that. A fiver'll about do it, I reckon. You want to *look* all right—that's the main thing. You can't afford to be dressy yet awhile. But in this business you must Look Right. It pays, ole chap. It Goes. I'll stick up the fiver, and you can pay me back bit by bit, as you can. Or else write me a good song. It's quite easy for a feller with ideas, who can write lyrics. You don't want only short words in it, y'know—easy words—some'ing that Gets Over at once. And the rhymes don't matter much. You better meet an ole pal o' mine—Jimmy Hayhoe—he can hash out the music all right. And if you get together, you oughta be able to fix me with some'ing. P'raps—if I get on the Syndicate, as I hope, and go all right—they might let me put on a sketch. There's a lot o' money in sketches, if you could do that sort o' thing. You know—the sort o' thing Joe puts on. Nothing in it—but plenty o' laughs. I got an idea that you and me'll be able to do something Big together. Fancy you going in for being an author. But you was always one o' them quiet ones."

.   .   .   .

I had felt in harmony with the atmosphere of the Cavour, but in Cosgrove's home I felt that at last I had found my place.

It was the untidiest home I had ever seen, and to me at that time full of happiness. It was at once easy and bright and alive; all cigarette smoke and music and laughter and litter. His sister, Miriam,

greeted us by pulling her brother's nose; then, seeing me, she giggled, heard my story in a few sentences; said, "Oh, you boy!" smacked me on the back
and said: "Never mind—we'll put you to rights.
Come on—tea's just ready. Go in and cut yourself
a slice of cake. May's here and young Connie.
Jimmy's coming in later." Then I was in the front
room in a whirlpool of chatter.

After five minutes' fumbling, I found a word for
it all. These people were evidently of the sort that
I had read about—Bohemians. That was the word.
Clever people—yet not stuck up with their cleverness, but free and easy with everybody. Nothing
"put on" about them. Just being themselves without caring whether they were right or not. They
had no misgivings, no envy of and no respect for
those with more brains, more social grace, or more
money than themselves. No desire to be any better than they were. The parlour was furnished
in a slapdash way, but it had a note of what I took
then to be Culture, which I couldn't connect with a
music-hall comedian. On the walls hung brown
prints of Rosetti, an original pen-drawing by Phil
May, and a mask of Beethoven. There was a piano,
its top strewn with ragged music-sheets, comic songs
mixing with Schumann and Chopin. The fireplace
was littered with cigarette ends. On the mantel-
piece were a number of signed photographs of dis-
tinguished-looking men and women, all shiny hair
and teeth. Two or three numbers of *The Encore*
were lying on the floor. And there were books—
modern six-shilling novels—about a dozen of them

lying on the sofa and on the side-board and on the floor.

Without introduction, May and Connie drew me into their talk as though I were an old member of the party, addressing me or Cosgrove impartially, while Miriam fussed with the tea. At first their frocks and furs a little awed me, but soon I was talking to them as to Cosgrove. The lunch had cleared the stupor and fatigue of last night, and I felt bright and clear. They talked in leaps and gushes, of this and of that, and of people whose names meant nothing to me; as though they must unburden themselves and had only five minutes in which to do it.

They interrupted each other, and Cosgrove interrupted both, and Miriam, flashing in and out, brought new topics up. They Said Things, and giggled; things, it seemed to me, that were often more funny than they were meant to be, so that each was doing a mental sprint to catch up with the laughter on her own jokes.

When Miriam had said that "young Connie" was there, I had expected to see a girl of fifteen or sixteen, but May and Connie were of equal age, of the robust sort; matronly. They had masses of yellow hair and big bold faces and thick limbs; and their bodies and their voices seemed to fill the room. They were so much alike, and talked and (apparently) thought alike, that even a year later I couldn't determine which was Connie and which was May.

"They're Dear Girls," said Cosgrove to me afterwards. "Dear Girls. Straight and clean as

they make 'em. They do a double act—Sisters
Marigold. Smart girls. Workers, too."

They heard my story with motherly interest and
many exclamations; and when Cosgrove spoke of
the circumstances in which he met me, they cried:
"Oh, you men! You're all alike!" I had never
been called a man before. I grinned, and allowed
things to be understood. Then Connie said: "So
you're going into the Resplendent—eh? You'll
have to keep your eyes open if you go there."

I asked, "Why?"

"Well, if you don't, old son, you won't see anything!"

Into the shriek of laughter, May thrust her word.
"Talking of the Resplendent, I was just telling
Miriam, when you come in, Freddie, about old
Mame."

"Oh? What's she been up to?"

"Only after one of the programme-girls."

"Strewth! Don't seem that no girl's safe from
her. What did yeh do?"

"Oh, I got hold of the girl and put it to her
straight. Took me a long time. She'd been giving
the girl frocks and a necklace and chocolates and
things, but I told her. I said: 'Don't you be a
fool, my girl, or you'll find you've opened the wrong
parcel. You're only one of dozens. She finds a new
one every month, and when she's done with you,
she'll hate you, and you'll be down and out.' Wanted
the girl to chuck up her job, and go as her companion
and dresser, and the kid was all for it. I says to
her, I says: 'If you're so innocent that you can't

understand what she's after, I'll tell you.' So I told her."

"And what did *she* say?"

"Oh, howled at first. Said she loved her Dear Mamie, and would give anything to be always with her. That Dear Mamie was a real Lady. Said that nobody had ever been so wonderful to her as her Dear Mamie. Mame has certainly got a way with her with the flappers. Then I put it to her straight; and told her how many dressers she'd had, and why they all left of a sudden. Then she began to understand, and showed me one of her Dear Mamie's letters to her. *You* know—one of her Heart to Heart letters, calling her Little Mignonette."

"I know."

"But I think I settled her at last. And to-night I'm going to get hold of Mame and give her hell."

"That's the style. If I was a woman I'd do some'ing more'n *talk* to Mame. Which programme-girl is it?"

"That little dark one. You know—Kitty—what's-er-name? Girl that come from some teashop or other."

"Oh, I remember. You told me about her some time ago. Ah—nice kid. I remember her last year when I was playing there. One of the orchestra was after her then. I rather fancy she led him up the garden."

Connie pricked up. "Eh? What's that? What's all this?"

But Cosgrove for once showed tact. "No—'tain't fair to tell tales out o' school. I'd forgotten all about it, but your speaking about her brings it all back."

"Oh. But who was he and what's this about a garden? Seems she ain't as innocent as I thought."

"Never you mind, Connie. It wasn't anything, anyway. I never knew the girl—only by sight. Pretty kid. Dunno what she's like now, but I wouldn't like any girl to get into Mame's hands. What do you say, ole man?"

I said "Oh, rather not!" but who Mame was, or what she was going to do to Kitty I didn't know. It seemed to be something bad that everybody understood except myself; but there were so many strange things in this coarse kind world into which I had been dragged. I was still puzzling and wondering what this was and who that was, and where I was and why, when Cosgrove asked:

"Ever come across any of that sort?" Before I could think of the right answer, he went on: "There's a lot of 'em in the West End, but you've been the other end mostly. 'Tain't so popular there. Make a good dancing act, wouldn't it— The Six——"

His sister reached round the table and boxed his ears. "Shut up, Freddie. You *are* a filthy beast. Talk about something else. Here—you haven't told us about the murder. How did it go off?"

"Oh, I wasn't there more'n ten minutes. They only took evidence of arrest and eye-witnesses, and

I come out soon as I'd spoke my lines. And then run into this chap. . . . Hullo, there's Jimmy."

With the coming of Jimmy Hayhoe the atmosphere changed. Jimmy had an air of course distinction. He was more quietly dressed than Cosgrove, but carried himself with a similar swagger. His features were thick, and he had a mass of brown hair brushed back from a high forehead. His eyes were bright and restless as though bella-donna'd; his skin was puckered; his hands were the hands of a workman. I had seen somewhere a portrait of Kubelik, and Jimmy Hayhoe looked like a debased and battered Kubelik. He took no notice of anybody, but sat down, drank tea, and talked at large. In an aside, Cosgrove said to me: "Clever chap. Writes all my songs. I'll get him to play in a minute." Drinking his tea, Jimmy told two indecent stories that he had picked up that morning, asked about the murder trial, damned the women, said that he was lunching with George Edwardes to-morrow, and had we heard that new thing of Debussy's?

"Fine stuff. I'll show yeh. Lemme see—I can only remember one or two themes. Listen to this one."

He went to the piano, cleared the top with a sweep of the arm which littered the floor with twenty pieces of music, lit a cigarette, and sat down.

The Debussy themes conveyed nothing to me; but when they were done Connie said: "Play that Schumann stuff we had the other night." He played the Schumann stuff. He played two Nocturnes of Chopin. He played the Prelude to Tristan. He played the Hungarian March. He played Liszt, Grieg, Schubert, Brahms, Dvorák, Berlioz.

Would there ever be a day like this again? Or was this my Day of Days of eastern legend? Chopin —Debussy—Schumann—in a front parlour. Front parlours, in my experience, were places for harmoniums on Sundays. I had thought that all these beautiful things were understood only by educated and wealthy people. I had thought that music-hall comedians were vulgar brutes, interested in nothing but drinking and backing horses, and composers of comic songs something even lower. Yet here was the fact. Here was I in a front parlour, listening to music that I had heard only at Queen's Hall, played by Jimmy Hayhoe in a manner that, to me, placed him on a level with the pianists who gave concerts at select halls in the West End. But all my ideas were being thrown down to-day; famous novelists dropped their h's and swore, and comic-song men played the piano like Paderewski, and held me enthralled in the presence of power and beauty. I regretted my first impression of him. After he had played those Grieg pieces, I could only stare at him in wonder and worship.

And this—this (I learned later) was the composer of "Mother's Caught Her Tongue in the Mangle," "The Randy, Brandy, Strand-y Boys," "Can You see Baby's Eyes in the Stars, Daddy Dear?", "Ain't It Nice to 'Ave a Bit of Garden?", "Hold Tight to Your Tiddler, Father," "Say a Prayer To-night for the Boys in Blue," "I Don't Mind Him Kissing the Missus, but He Eats Me Breakfast too."

Jimmy Hayhoe, now tense and grave, with hair falling over his face, making that piano surge and sing, and making himself my hero. Then, abruptly, he stopped and said, "Oh, heard that one about the bishop in the lavatory?" and for ten minutes poured out more indecent stories.

．　．　．　．　．　．　．　．　．

At nine o'clock, after Miriam had prepared a room for me and laid out one of her old night-dresses, and Cosgrove had lent me a clean collar, which was a size too big, we started for the Acme.

There I saw a new Cosgrove, and began to understand his twelve pounds a week.

I went behind with him, and then down to the wings, and watched two of the turns, and discovered that I enjoyed music-halls as much as grand opera or Promenade Concerts or poetry. I began to envy, as I had done when a boy, those clever people who nightly held the stage and received the clapping hands and laughter and welcoming eyes of the public. It was exciting to think that I was going to be in this world, and to get three pounds a week for being in it.

Then it was Cosgrove's call, and, directly he was on and at work, I saw that he had more in him than he knew himself. It was a ridiculous act, but it "went" with all parts of the house. Standing in the wings, he had been Cosgrove—vacuous face, drooping shoulders, wandering hands, and splutter. In his dressing-room he had been drinking stout and eating fried potatoes, and exchanging bawdy stories with one or two other turns. But the moment he

was out there, a change came over his face, his bearing, even the lines of his body. He started with an
insane song—"If I Can Have the Crackling, You
Can Have the Pork"—then some patter, and then
the Speciality Dance; and as I watched him I had
the feeling of watching a complete stranger. I could
hardly believe that this was the man I had been with
all that day. For, by some quality which I could
not name, he turned all this sorry stuff into a sort
of wild poetry. He did not make his audience laugh :
he tickled them. He was at once madly comic and
infinitely wistful. He used his legs puppet-fashion,
and through all his contortions kept his face dead.
With his legs he approved, desired, gibed, exulted,
despaired, and . . . But one can no more present
the idea of a clown than one can describe a sunset.
I can only say that as I stood there I felt an affection
for him, and a longing to know him better, and to do
something for him.

But I never did know him better. Off the stage
he was off the stage : just Cosgrove. Only once did
I perceive some hint of the creature who lived "out
there." In an expansive moment, when we were
walking across Clapham Common one midnight I
began to tell him of my "moments"—of Quong
Lee, and Fosdick, and Old Kent Road, and discovering books, and Caruso and the broken toys,
and he said:

"I know whatcher mean. I've had that feeling,
too. Sorta feeling that you've seen something—
something new—only you dunno what it is. Sorta
feeling drunk only not drunk. When everything

seems Right and clear, and you're full of—full of—
you feel that you couldn't possibly be any happier
than you are then.   You feel something wonderful's
happened to you, only nothing has, and you can't
tell anybody about it.   Know what I mean?"

I did know; and I knew that when he was singing
his idiot songs and dancing his idiot dance he was,
though perhaps he didn't know it, trying to tell
people about it.

It was two o'clock in the morning before that day
ended and I went to a real bed in a real bedroom.
There was supper when we got home (not bread and
mustard), and a long "jaw" with his sister, and
whiskies-and-sodas, and much pottering and fiddling
as though bed were an unpleasant duty.   But at
last I was alone, half-drunk with unaccustomed talk,
and with a head packed with the events of an ordinary year.

I was now on the way to anything.   I was out of
the dead City, with my foot inside the world of
living people, and with my hand on three pounds a
week.   I talked myself to sleep with it—three
pounds a week—three pounds a week—to the air
of "Three Blind Mice."

And all from Cosgrove, the despised Gold Flake.
He was feeding me, sleeping me, clothing me, lifting
me out of my slough, and setting me on my feet.
Why?   What had I done for him?   What splendid thing could I ever do for him in return?   Nothing.   He had meant nothing to me; at school I had
not even considered him while Fosdick was about;
nor could I have meant anything to him.   Why was

he doing all this for me? But there was no puzzle in it. The answer was simply—Because he was Cosgrove. It was his way always to go blundering through life, being excitedly kind to everybody, and then forgetting all about it; never expecting, and seldom getting, thanks.

.   .   .   .

And now I turned another corner, and began to live, for the first time, among clean, well-dressed people.

For the next few days I was filled with a light-hearted vigour which was wholly new to me. I knew all the joy and surprise of the convalescent as life creeps into him in waves of light. Those days—until Monday—were holidays, and I went about with Cosgrove discovering London in the morning: the fountains in Trafalgar Square, which I had never seen playing; the flower-girls in Picca-dilly Circus; Oxford Street in sunlight instead of lamplight; the morning sparkle of Kensington Gardens. The mere sense of being in London in the morning was an intoxication. The first thing I did was to break into the five pounds which Cosgrove advanced—"Oh, here y'are—you better have this five quid for yer clothes and 'bus rides. You can get a decent suit to measure at McGregor & Epstein's at Clapham Junction"—and redeem my box of treasures from Mrs. Flanagan. The next was to take a morning 'bus ride into the City, tasting, on the way, the moist perfume of the parks, and the leisurely bustle of the West End, where business seemed to be taken with a touch of the fingers instead of the solid grab of London Bridge. Then, right through the City, looking down into the offices. How I pitied the poor wretches grubbing over grey ledgers, and imprisoned, save for the hurried lunch-hour, all through the shining day. Better ten bob a week, I said, and the day to yourself, than twenty pounds a week in the City.

That 'bus-ride was a private triumphal progress, and by it I felt that I had got out of the City what it owed me. The vision I had long cherished of going into Lime Street office and speaking my mind, had no attraction now. I saw myself as a spiteful little beast snapping at people who had treated me as justly as I had deserved. It seemed silly and mean even to laugh at them. I was out of their world, and could not evoke the faintest feeling about them. They were shadows. In the splendid world to which Cosgrove had helped me, men were men. I was no longer the slave of the clock. I could wake up each morning with a sense of freedom. Until twelve o'clock I could do as I pleased: get up, or lie in bed, go out for a walk, or lounge the morning away in the parlour with books and gossip.

When Messrs. McGregor & Epstein had done with me I had, for the first time in my life, a suit that fitted me, and I had money to spend. I could go here or there. I could go into a restaurant now instead of tea-shops. My clothes were fit for any place. I need not shrink from being looked at, for I was, I felt, correct; not, as when I bought my suit in Newington Causeway, correct in parts, but correct all over. New suit, new hat, new boots, new shirt, new tie; and Cosgrove had even insisted upon gloves and stick.

My first week's work at the Resplendent was nothing like work, as I had known it. Each mid-day, when I arrived, the guv'nor called me into the office, gave me a cigarette, and gossiped about Things. An amazing procedure to me—to be taken casually into his room, to lounge in an easy-chair, instead of standing respectfully before him, to be given a smoke, to be talked to chattily and humorously, and to call him "Guv'nor"—it was a holiday and a tonic. Under such treatment I blossomed, as I had grown for awhile under Mylchreest. My step became firmer and my voice clearer. I lost my diffidence and grew confident of my abilities, and wrote billmatter as easily as I talked to the stars of the week. I picked up the work quickly, and it was such work that if there had been thirty hours in the day I would have put in thirty hours for the guv'nor. Generally, I was that nondescript figure that is found in every theatre—the general utility man, working behind and in front, at all hours; and after a week I felt that nothing would come amiss to me. I felt that I could write a song or a sketch, or "fix" an act, or work up a man's "business," in the odd half-hours of my day. I felt this because the guv'nor felt it. I showed him my cuttings from *Ally Sloper*, and they made him laugh, and he called me a Great Lad, and took me to lunch with him. With me, to be told that I can do a thing is to be able to do it; to be told that I cannot do it is to be robbed of every shred of confidence. Some men, under praise, grow slack, and, under blame, are spurred to greater effort. With others, it is the reverse: they take blame for truth, while praise only fills them with desire to deserve it by better work.

To this holiday atmosphere Cosgrove and his circle contributed. He decided that I should continue to live with them, and when I asked what I should pay his sister, he said: "Oh, rubbish. You'll want all that three quid. You ain't in the way here, and you don't eat much. You stay on here, and shut up about it. Then we can get together and see if we can't work up that sketch."

So I stayed on, and learned to laugh and to take part in that life at which I had only peeped. There were lunches, little dinners in Soho, rambles, rides home by cab at midnight after the show was done, suppers with Jimmy Hayhoe and the guv'nor (I had always to be at the guv'nor's heels) and meetings with all manner of semi-celebrities. At home there was cheap wine with supper, and supper was prepared jointly by Miriam and Cosgrove (who was a dab at omelettes and trifles) and coffee and cigarettes followed until supper burgeoned into breakfast-time. From Miriam and Connie and May I learned to laugh at all the things that I had once hated—at pomp, at solemnity, at superiority, at the pride of wealth, the pride of birth, the pride of cleverness; and to look kindly upon other people's sins. I began to form new views of what mattered in life, and I decided that good manners mattered more than intellect or spiritual grace and that the only good manners were kindness and consideration. I forgot my books, my poets and essayists: I was too busy living with immortal souls to dally with the creatures of fancy; and after all, I had got little from them but refreshment. All that I knew of life I had got direct from life.

I forgot Quong Lee, too; I was in a world he couldn't reach. Once or twice, in the heat and noise of some jaunt or some feast, my mind was filled with a picture of the Causeway, and of the shop, and of himself sitting in the window; and following it came a gush of something like home-sickness. Myself in Romano's, and Quong Lee sitting on his wooden tea-chest in the Causeway. And the lunch and the occasion went suddenly insipid. I did not want to get up and rush to the Causeway; I wanted to *be* there.

But those moments were few. Most of the time I was "in" everything, and with appetite. There were Sundays at Richmond and Maidenhead and on the Surrey Hills; wild impromptu excursions, invented at eleven o'clock and started ten minutes later. There were Sunday-night "doings," when friends and strangers dropped in, and sang songs and played little sketches that the English stage would not pass; and Jimmy Hayhoe played Schumann or accompanied Cosgrove's raucous songs, as called upon. And always there were new people to be met and absorbed, and, with each meeting, the wild hope that perhaps in *this* meeting one would find the ideal friend or the charmed circle; and always the disappointment.

I went into the Resplendent every mid-day with

a skip, often before my duties called me there. Even so, I had a feeling that I was getting money for nothing. It seemed so unfair to be getting three pounds a week for pottering and amusing myself, when poor devils were getting fifteen shillings a week for slavery in underground offices. Certainly I was working longer hours than they, but the work was pleasure, and was broken by lunches, teas, chats; and I was not bound down to one seat at one desk. I inspected bills, I interviewed people when the guv'nor was engaged, I took the ticket office at opening time, I checked the house, I heard complaints, I invented interesting stories about the star-turns for the local paper, and I made many friends among the minor turns by expounding our audience to them and supplying them with local allusions that would "go."

I became good friends with Jimmy Hayhoe, and found him delightful company. He had taken two rooms in South London, and whenever I was tired I would go there, and he would go to the piano, with face transformed, and fill the room with crash and chime and thunder, bringing to life the thought of dead magicians. Jimmy, like many composers of "tripe," was a full gold-medal executant; but as he said: "What's the good? I'd like to do serious work, but what's the good if it isn't Big? And I'm not big. Oh, I can write nice little studies and impressions, concert-pieces and all that, but the best that I can do looks so damn silly by the side of the Real Stuff. My songs are sheer ghastly poppycock, but they don't pretend to be anything else. So I do

what I can do—write stuff that people sing and whistle for a month and then forget all about. Mind
you, I started with serious stuff—had it done at
students' concerts and all that—but I had sense
enough to see there was nothing in it. I knew I
didn't carry any guns. I know what music is, all
right, and I knew that I wasn't big enough to do it.
So when I first met our pal, at Rule's, one night, and
he asked me if I could knock-up a tune for some
words he'd got, I went to it. Been at it ever since.
I found my line there. And I will say that of its
kind my stuff's good, because I do know orchestra-
tion, and I can produce melodies. Vulgar melodies,
perhaps, but I don't pinch 'em from Handel and
Wagner and Puccini, like some fellows."

He was frequently moody: he had all the irri-
tability which the popular imagination credits to the
great creative artist under the title "artistic tempera-
ment." But it is seldom possessed by the artist of
achievement: it belongs mostly to the thwarted
artist. And that was Jimmy's state. He saw, far
away, the work he wanted to do, and knew that he
had not the power to do it; and his pretence of
acceptance of his present "line" was the gesture of a
restless soul.

.   .   .   .

Once, during this magnificent year, I did visit
Quong Lee. I was in town one Sunday morning
on the guv'nor's business, seeing an agent who lived
in a mansion flat on the Embankment; and when
the business was done I came out to the Strand just

as a 'bus, labelled for the East, drew up. The sight of it brought the face of Quong Lee into my blank day, and as it moved on I boarded it.

I reached the Causeway at noon, and found his window as it had always been, and himself sitting at the counter, looking out. But . . .

When I went in and stood before him, he looked long at me without expression. He looked at my brilliant grey suit, at my neat collar and tie, at my soft hat, at my light cane. Then he smiled—a long, slow smile. Then he turned about, fished in a jar, and, still smiling, and with the gesture of twelve years ago, held out a piece of ginger.

I grinned, and took it, but the grin wasn't quite certain of itself. Was the ginger a touch of humour? Or a reproof? Or a hint of—what? He set me thinking, as he always did. I stayed an hour with him in the back room, and drank tea; and he sat before me with hands folded in his linen coat, smiling. For the first time the sense of fluent peace that I had known there was interrupted by little prickings. I had a feeling that I was giving him private amusement, and I left him in a mood of self-inquiry.

When I got back to Clapham Common the atmosphere jarred. I was dissatisfied with it and with my surroundings and with my idle life. Cosgrove was working, Jimmy Hayhoe was working, May and Connie were working. I was doing—nothing. And I felt there and then that I must do something. I must write. I must do something for Quong Lee.

So I began to write. I went early every morning to the Resplendent, and used the hours before midday in writing. I wrote in the form of the short story, and sent out what I wrote to the illustrated magazines. They came back, and went out again, and again came back. But one day, scarcely thinking what I was doing, I sent two of them to a serious monthly review. And to my amazement they were accepted. With that acceptance I became absorbed in writing. I was doing what I wanted to do, and what I wanted to do was approved by the mighty Bax Mycroft Milligan.

I was so absorbed that when Cosgrove moved on to other worlds, and invited me to accompany him, I refused. Had I gone with him I should not to-day be worried about the rent, and I should not be riding on the top of the 'bus on wet days. Still, Cosgrove found happiness in his work and I in mine, and though my rewards are slender and his are prodigious, each of us has got what he wants.

It happened this way.

One Sunday afternoon a Mr. Rosenbaum arrived at Clapham Common noisily and wetly demanding Mithter Cosgrove. He was a short, stout man, not over-clean, and not, in appearance, over-prosperous; but his talk denied his clothes. He came darkly, as one with the message of the philosopher's stone.

". . . and I seen yer show, boy, and I said to meself, that's the chap that'd make a hit on the pictures."

"Pictures? What yah mean—pictures?"

"Why, you know, boy, you know. The Bioscope. The cinematograph."

"Oh, what they call animated photographs. I know. I've seen 'em about. They show 'em at church halls, don't they? Like they used the magic lantern?"

Mr. Rosenbaum spluttered, and spluttered as Cosgrove had never done. *"Magic lantern!* Magic lantern me backbone! Listen, boy!" He leaned across the table with his mouth almost on Cosgrove's ear. "Listen! Let me tell yeh something. The Pictures is going to be a Big Thing."

"Big Thing? How?"

"Listen. . . . D'you know they're going to build places specially to show 'em in? Going to build picture-theatres and give all-day performances."

"Picture-theatres? All day? Who the hell d'yeh think's going to sit in the dark all day and look at moving photographs?"

"Oy-oy-oy! You wait, me boy. You'll See Things. Americans ain't fools. And City men ain't fools, and Rosenbaum ain't a fool. And the City men are coming into this game, me boy. Oh, yes. They're coming in. Coming in fast. America's in it already. It's going to be Big."

"But, dammit, there's nothing in it. I saw one of 'em once—express trains running—horses galloping—old men running after their hats."

"Finished, me boy. Finished. Listen—we're getting stories. We're going to have plays specially written for 'em. By big authors. Real stories. Dramas. Comedies. Human Interest. Listen—what yeh think of this for an idea? Take a book—a book like, say, *Uncle Tom's Cabin.* See the

idea? Tell it all in pictures—see? From start to
finish. Yeh can't do it on the stage, but yeh can
do anything with pictures. Show anything. Got
it? And for them that gets in early, there'll be
chances. Chances, did I say? My boy—it won't
be twenty quid a week. It won't be a hundred a
week. It'll be five hundred a week? See? You
put yourself in my hands, Mithter Cosgrove, and
I'll Make yeh! I'll make yeh! I know what I'm
talking about. I'm talking about five hundred a
week."

"Five hundred a week for me?"

"Not at first, boy. Not at first. But that's what
it's going to be. You chuck up vaudeville and come
with me, Mithter Cosgrove."

Cosgrove twiddled his hands and looked into the
fire. Then said, as though changing the subject:
"Is my tie up the back of me collar, Mr. Rosenbaum?"

Rosenbaum looked at him. "No, Mithter Cosgrove. No. You're all right."

"Well, what is it about me makes me look such
a bloody fool?"

"Eh? Eh? What yeh mean? What yeh mean?"

"You come here and ask me to chuck up a certain twelve quid a week, and probably twenty, and
maybe thirty 'fore long, to go into the blinking
magic-lantern business. Blimey!"

"Oy-oy-oy! Oh, my boy, you'll be sorry some
day. You'll be sorry if you turn me down."

"But how are yeh going to do these things?
Where are yeh going to do it?"

"Do it? All over the world, me boy. Indoor stuff in the studios. Outdoor stuff wherever the scenery is—China, India, Egypt—anywhere. *Anywhere!*" His voice rose to a squeak.

"But it's so damn scrubby. I got a reputation now and a name. I'm known."

"Boy! Boy! I'll make yeh known all over the world."

"But how can an actor be known if he ain't seen?"

"Why, boy, you'll keep yer name. We're going to give the names of everybody taking part in a picture. And boom 'em, too. We're going to make Stars. People'll go to picture-theatres to see *you,* same as they go to see Forbes-Robertson and Martin Harvey and Bernhardt and George Alexander and Sir Herbert. Ah—and before long we'll have *them* in the business, too."

"Here—chuck it—Forbes-Robertson in a magic-lantern show!"

"Oh, the smart boy! Will ya believe me if I tell yeh that this thing's going to kill vaudeville? And kill the theatres?"

"No, I won't. I'm damned if I'll believe fool-talk like that."

"All right. All right, me boy. Live a little longer, and you'll see. Then you'll look back to that Sunday afternoon when Mithter Rosenbaum called on yeh. And your name'll be Mithter Thorry. Hein? . . . Once again, boy—come with me and I'll Make yeh. This time two years I'll have yer name everywhere. I seen yer show, and there's nothing like it for the pictures. That tumble o' yours. Never been done. It's new, me boy. It's *new*. And that bit o' pantomime with the lamp-post on the back-cloth——"

"What bit o' pantomime?"

"Oy-oy! Pretending yeh don't know. Here— have any o' the others been after yeh yet? Is that why yer shying? As man to man, now—have they?"

"Any of what others?"

Rosenbaum lifted his hands and played pianos in the air.

"Oh, he's a deep 'un! Listen—I'll make a firm offer. Never you mind the others—they'd tie yeh down and spoil yeh. I ain't gointa tie yeh down. Not me. Rosenbaum knows talent when he sees it. Once you learnt the tricks of the business, I shall leave y'alone, and let yeh go your own way. I'll give y'a contract now—thirty quid a week for twelve months. That'll be three pictures. But you'll have to chuck yer vaudeville. We're putting up a studio in Cannes—South o' France—must have the sunshine—and you'll be there with us. We got backing. We got plenty o' backing. Yer agent can look into it as deep as he likes. And he'll see it's all square. Now—what d'ya say? I hope yer not going to be a fool. Oh, fer yer own sake, boy, I hope yer not going to be a fool. I tell yeh—this time two years you'll be asking me six hundred a week. Yes, me boy, six hundred. And what's more, I shall have to give it yeh—to keep the others from getting yeh. They'll all be after yeh.

And the public—I tell yeh—people what never go to vaudeville will go to the pictures. You'll strike a new public altogether. They're running up palaces all over the country—better'n any music-halls —as good as the Empire. And cheaper. Thrippence to one-and-a-kick, me boy. And not England only. France—Italy—Germany—Spain—China— they're all building picture-theatres. And with the stuff we shall give yeh to do, they'll eat yeh. You'll be the Dan Leno of the world, me boy. Of the *world!* And you'll look back to this Sunday; and you'll say, 'Oh, God, thank you for sending Solly Rosenbaum to me!' Now then—what d'yeh say?"

.   .   .   .

And so I lost Cosgrove. Nothing could stand against Mr. Rosenbaum, and though Cosgrove felt that he was doing a mad thing, he gave way. But Rosenbaum was not far wrong. A year later, the three pictures, supported by the press-agent and an advertising campaign, came one by one before the public, others followed, and then there came a Cosgrove boom, and Cosgrove went about among his friends with an air of "What the hell's all the fuss about?" Exhibitors reported full houses. People who had never entered a picture-theatre were drawn in to see him. Even those who didn't go could not pretend ignorance of "Goggles," the children's joy. It didn't last long, though. Rivals sprang up, and soon a greater than Goggles arrived, the greatest of all; and the Goggles boom ended. But it left him, Cosgrove, with a fortune and an assured position as a producer.

Chapter X

CICELY

FROM the day I parted with Cicely at the western corner of Kensington Gardens to this day,
I have never seen her; and, though I so loved her
then, I find it impossible now to visualise her. I
cannot recall her eyes, her hair, or her expression;
I remember only that she was dark; and if we met
now in the streets I might pass her a hundred times
without knowing her. The thing remains only as
a romantic episode having no contact with a living
creature.

It's very sad that these tempests of youth should
leave so little in their track. One would expect to
find fallen boughs, mounds of perished leaves, up-
rooted trunks. But no—nothing: one would never
guess that there had been a storm.

And she—where is she now, I wonder; and has
she ever thought since of the fumbling clerk who
so loved her and berated her and bewildered her?
I wonder if she remembers that first outing when I
took her for a threepenny ride on the tram-car, and
afterwards to a two-shilling seat in a suburban
theatre? And the cab-ride from Oxford Street to
Greenwich; and how I paid him off at her door,
and she tried to recall him because I should not
pick up another at that time of night; and I urgently

274 THE WIND AND THE RAIN

restrained her, saying that I always knew where to find cabs? How should I have handled the situation if she *had* got him back, since he had got my last penny, and I had to walk home to Lavender Hill? And would she remember the evening in Richmond Park when, for half an hour, I tried to show her that my folk were not animals, and how a month in Bethnal Green would do her good? And that afternoon in a Lyons' tea-shop, when she told me that she thought more of me than anybody, and that I was wonderful, and was sure to get on; but that It was impossible, because I wasn't . . .

I try to see her, to breathe her presence as I breathed it that terrible Sunday, when it was at last ended, and I was working in my back bedroom in Lavender Hill to earn a guinea or so for the next week. But I cannot. All that day, between me and the paper, floated her face; and between my mind and my work came the thoughts: "What is she doing now? Starting from home to church? Meeting her friends? A party to lunch, perhaps? In the afternoon, the drawing-room, the piano, callers, the parlour-maid bringing in tea."

But I cannot recapture it. It is nothing. I say her name to myself, seeking its old magic; and it is nothing. Nothing. If we met to-morrow, it would be no more to me than meeting an old office-acquaintance. But we never shall meet, for she is rich; so rich that she can speak of herself as belonging to the New Poor.

I am writing these pages at Monaco, trying to look back to that November Sunday at Lavender

Hill; and the windows of my *pension* make a frame
for a scene of colour profuse and wanton. Above
me a sharp white-and-blue sky; before me a sea of
violet; and rising from it the rock and the gardens,
with their palms and flowers—lakes of vermilion,
sweeps of green, and thrusting foams of lilac carven
out of the crystal air. Below, on the right, I can
just see the little café at Beausoleil where, six years
ago, I sat with Caruso and Pierre Boutteville and
the little Italian dancer. The morning sunshine
loads the room with light. There are canaries on
the balcony, the odour of coffee in the air; and a
cleaner in the garden below is singing *Core 'ngrato*.
I am in Monaco; on the edge of her world again;
padded with the luxury that was her necessity. My
feet are sunk in the pile of the yellow carpet. My
writing-table is gilt, glass-topped, and under the
glass is a silk brocade of eighteenth-century pattern.
My clothes are not ragged, and if it rains my boots
will not let water.

I am in her atmosphere, but I cannot remember
her. I can only get, faintly, the smell of boiled
cabbage in a back bedroom of Lavender Hill.

.   .   .   .

With Cosgrove's departure with Mr. Rosenbaum
there followed changes. The guv'nor of the Resplendent got the sack—a sack that covered me;
and, after some weeks of looking about, he was
offered a hall in Yorkshire. He asked me to go
with him ("Though it won't run to three quid,
boy"), but in those few weeks I had had another
story accepted; and I declined. I took a bedroom

in a hilly street leading from Lavender Hill, and hired a battered typewriter at five shillings a week, and there, all day, I wrote. I wrote what I wanted to write and what I didn't want to write. I found that I could write the sort of rubbish that the monthly magazines would pay for, so I divided myself into two parts, doing this work with one part, and cherishing, in the other, the stories that I would do when things were easier. I wrote at a chest of drawers, at a washing-stand, at a bamboo table whose top was smaller than the width of the typewriter, and sitting on an upturned box with the typewriter on the bed. A chest of drawers makes an indifferent writing-table. There are two ways of using it—either to sit sideways in your chair, with legs crossed, or to open the bottom drawer, put your feet inside, and splay your knees outward. This is the better way; and I wrote many thousand words in this position. The bamboo table was the worst: one had to be so careful how one hit the typewriter, lest the balance were upset.

I was getting on well with these arrangements, earning an average of thirty shillings a week, and was content with my estate. Then, as always happened, my content with makeshifts was broken by a sudden thrust of beauty from above.

I met Miss Cicely.

I was taking a lonely walk along Regent Street at dusk, when I ran into a feather boa. I murmured apology, and was moving on, when the girl said, "Hi, young man!" At first I thought she was one of the Regent Street girls, until she said,

" 'Scuse me, ain't you Mister Battershell's boy?
That useter be at Greenwich?"

"I said, "Yes. Why——"

"Don't remember me, do you?"

I looked closely at her. The face was familiar,
but I certainly didn't remember her. She noted
my perplexity and giggled. Then I remembered.
With the giggle came a flash of the Big House at
Greenwich and Anne the kitchenmaid. I blushed
and stammered and apologised. "Oh, that's all
right. I guessed it was you, though. Glad you
haven't quite forgotten me. Well, and how you
getting on since you left school?"

"Oh, pretty well."

"What you doing?"

"I'm writing."

"Writing?"

"Yes. Writing for the papers. Articles and
that."

"Reely? Well, now. Fancy that. Writing for
the papers, eh? Well, now. . . . Very sad about
your uncle, wasn't it? So sudden, too. I've left
Greenwich, y'know. Got a good place at Glou-
cester Gate—just near Regent's Park. Housemaid. We often useter talk about you at The
Gables. You haven't been there, I suppose?"

"No—I never thought——"

"Well, they're all there still. 'Cept me. You
should go. They'd love to see you. They often
talked about your funny songs. But there—I
mustn't stand gossiping here. I gotta be in by ten.
They're awfully nice people to work for, but they're

very strict on that. . . . Well, I'm awfully glad to seen you. And do go down and see 'em at The Gables. They'd think a lot of it, y'know. And even if you did see the Old Woman, she can't eat you. Goo-bye!"

With a bright nod she flitted away.

I continued my stroll, thinking about the Big House and Uncle Frank and cook and the parlour-maid and the garden; and it seemed that I owed them a duty. I had been forgetful and ungracious.

I went the next Saturday afternoon, and had a rich welcome in the kitchen, and stayed to tea. They stood round me and surveyed me, and agreed that I had grown a bit, but hadn't altered in the face, except that I was thinner and paler. I slipped into it as easily as though I had left it yesterday, and when cook spread the table, as for an annual tea, I felt ready to sing them a comic song if they had asked for one.

Towards the end of tea something white in the garden caught my eye. I looked, and saw the white hat of a young woman. I said: "Who's that in the garden?"

"That?" said cook. "Surely you know who that is. Look again."

I did. I saw a dark head and the profile of a proud face.

"Well, now. . . . Don't you remember who used to play with you out there? And climb the apple trees and all? That's Miss Cicely."

"Oh!" All the years between faded. I saw a sweep of lawn, roses and fuschias, the silken win-

dow of the morning room, and a little girl; and
through the window came a string of broken toys,
buzzing and stinging at the face of a gardener's
boy. Then the flash was gone, and we went on
talking.

"No, she doesn't live here now. She only comes
to see her Aunt nows and thens. They don't hit
it off very well, y'know. Miss Cicely lives with a
friend in a flat at Kensington. Her aunt don't half
like it—thinks it a little—you know—Fast. But
Miss Cicely just does what she wants to do. Like
most girls to-day."

Then the parlourmaid, who had gone upstairs,
came back and said: "You're wanted upstairs,
young man."

"Me?" I said. "Upstairs? But . . ."

"You needn't be frightened. Miss Ingram's out.
Otherwise I wouldn't have let Upstairs know you
was here. You're no favourite of *hers*, I can tell
you. Not coming to see her. Come on—I'll take
you up. Miss Cicely wants to see you."

I could have refused flatly, but I didn't. I went.

I went into the drawing-room, where I had so
often bowed and repeated "Tex." There was
little change in its features, but to my eye it appeared less august; even shabby. The pictures—I
cast an eye at them and felt superior. They were
expensive reproductions of "story" pictures: "The
Railway Station"; Cromwell going for That
Bauble; Doré's "Christ at the Praetorium." The
books—no poems; a set of Scott; all the rest religious stuff, bound volumes of *The Sunday at*

Home and *The Leisure Hour. The Christian World* was lying on a table, and on the sofa was *The Quiver.* But it was still a drawing-room, where I had bowed, and I had no hope of owning a drawing-room or of sitting at ease in one.

And Cicely was there.

She came in from the garden with two young men, and greeted me as an old friend. "*Awf*-ly glad to see you. Collins told me you were here. Why—you're hardly any different from when you went away. I thought you'd be quite grown up. And how are you after all these years? She told me you're writing now. What are you writing for?"

I gave the names of the weeklies and monthlies where I had appeared.

"Oh, ripping! I *am* glad." Then she laughed. "Oh, this is Captain Hornby and Mr. Grant. . . . This is my old playmate. D'you remember the day when the bough of that cherry-tree snapped and I came down?"

Did I remember?

"And what are you writing now? The friend I live with writes a little, you know. But hers is chiefly for the stage. You must come round and see us some time. Quite close to Earl's Court. Come to tea one afternoon." She turned to the two alert young men—looking at them I thought of race-horses, taut yet quivering—"Tommy writes, you know."

"Really? By Jove, that's awfully jolly. I wish I could write. It must be awf'ly jolly to write.

I've seen such a lot o' things, here and there, y'know, in India, if I could only write 'em. I envy any feller who can write."

They looked at me with something that was almost wonder.

Then two girls were announced, and I lost myself, and could say hardly a word. I sat back and absorbed the atmosphere: the cool talk and the cool tinkle of tea-cups; the smell of violets and of Turkish cigarettes. What was I doing there? Ten minutes ago I had been in the kitchen, the friend of the cook and the parlourmaid; and now I was in the drawing-room, and they were deferring to me, asking my opinion on this or that review and on modern books. But I could not meet them: I could only see them with the eyes of the kitchen. Even to-day, when servants are in the room, at a lunch or a dinner, I suffer an insane temptation to turn and talk to them, and ask them: "Well, Collins, what do you think of this lot? Pretty ordinary, aren't they?"

But they were charming people; so charming that they made me think about myself and feel disgust with myself because I couldn't be charming. They made me remember that I thought meanly and lived meanly and bilked 'bus-conductors. I thought how kind they were to take this notice of me, on the level; and on top of it came the thought that to their minds such a thought would have seemed ignoble. But then they hadn't been to Hardcress. These men and women had lived all their lives along one level line; never derailed,

never even shunted. They lived with those who
talked and thought as they did, without clash or
heat or flourish. They were clean and gracious
and securely poised in their right places. Life
lapped about them. How delightful I thought, to
be like them. In parting, Cicely took my hand,
and said, quietly, "I'm awf'ly glad I've found you
again. And you *will* come to tea, won't you?"

I came away in that mood in which I left
Covent Garden after hearing Caruso, bewildered,
delighted, and melancholy. I didn't want to go
back to Lavender Hill. I couldn't face that back
room in the autumn twilight. I walked as though
on a wager. Nothing had happened to me; no
change; but as I walked, I found myself walking
to, "I'm going to see her again. I'm going to see
her again." Now why on earth that? What put
that into my head? I didn't know. Cicely? What
was she to me? Nothing but a young lady at a
Big House. And yet I was excited because she had
asked me to tea.

Idiot!

.   .   .   .

A week later I went to tea at the Earl's Court
flat. Her friend was out—called away to a rehearsal—and, except for the maid, we were alone.
The flat was the usual flat of well-to-do Kensington
people, but it was the first of the kind that I had
seen, and I received an impression of flowers and
soft carpets and bright walls and sleek living: the
right setting for Cicely. Cicely was not beautiful,

but, like Gracie, she had charm. Men do not fall in love with physical beauty: beauty is too rare for love; and a truly beautiful woman is as extraordinary as genius—and as lonely. But a woman with a crooked nose—and charm—will never lack lovers. Cicely had much charm, without ever being charming. It was with her a spiritual essence.

Once I had got over my consciousness of the luxurious appointments of the flat (and the feeling, "What on earth am I doing here?") I found that Cicely was not the worshipful Young Lady of years ago; not the remote Miss Cicely; but an ordinary lively companion, with feet on my earth; like most of her class interested in the lighter modern literature, the lighter theatre, and the lighter music. The Chesterfield was strewn with *The Tatler, The Sphere, Vanity Fair, The English Review*. In attitude and outlook I discovered a sympathetic spirit, and soon I was talking to her as freely as I had talked to Gracie, and we were laughing over mutual jokes about her aunt. I found that a word, pointed by a look, conveyed my meaning instantly. Was it possible that I had found my true friend in this wonderful girl from a remote world? Now and again that world came between us, as when she spoke of dinner-parties, boxes at the theatre, Henley, Ascot, tea at Rumpelmayer's, polo at Hurlingham, as casually as I spoke of tram-cars. After privately debating whether I should be polite, and say, "Oh, yes"; or honest, and admit that she was talking of things that I didn't understand, I decided that she was a friend with whom I could be open, and I said, "What's Rumpelmayer's?"

"What's Rumpelmayer's? Why, Rumpelmayer's —you know. . . ." Then—"Oh, Tommy, I'm sorry. I forgot. I forgot you've been working outside these things, while I've been playing. It's the tea-place in St. James' Street—*the* tea-place. You must come there some time. Why not Thursday? Can you meet me there Thursday?"

"Oh, but—I don't think I——"

"Don't think what?"

"I mean—if it's the sort of place you say, I—I'm —not used to that sort of place."

"Oh, nonsense. You'll have to get used to that sort of place."

"I—I'd like—it'd be nice to have tea somewhere, but—but not there. You see——"

"Why on earth not?"

"Well, I—I—I——"

"Look here—I shall shake you if you talk like that. What is it makes you so shut up? I noticed you at auntie's the other day. You'll have to come out of your shell. And you've *got* to come to Rumpelmayer's with me on Thursday. Now then. I'm very interested in you, you know. I meet so few people who are Doing Things."

"Yes, but a place like that, and—the sort of people who go there, and——"

"What's that to do with it? You've got as much right to go there as anybody else. I got those reviews you mentioned, and read your story, and so did Marjorie. That's my friend. You're doing jolly good stuff, old boy. We both think so. I shall be awf-ly interested in your work."

I ought to have taken the warning. I ought to have remembered the broken toys, and what "taking an interest" meant. But I didn't. After tea, when I prepared to go, she said she would walk a little way through the Park with me. On that walk we discovered mutual enthusiasms, similar tastes, similar shapes of humour. And I knew then that I loved her, and had loved her ever since that first day in the Greenwich garden. Could it be that she—— I was hypnotised. Why was all this? Why had she, who hadn't seen me for ten years, suddenly taken me, the gardener's boy, to herself? Without a word of explanation, it seemed, she had had me sent up from the kitchen, picked up our childhood acquaintance, and taken command of me. Where was I? What did it all mean? Or did it mean nothing? But was it nothing to go to the trouble of ordering back numbers of magazines in order to read my stories? Nothing to have me to tea at her flat and take me to tea at Rumpelmayer's?

What was I thinking about in letting her take command of me; in going into a world where I didn't belong? I wasn't thinking at all. I only knew that in those few minutes in the Greenwich drawing-room I had filled my empty heart with the idea of her as a far-away dream. And in that walk through the Park the dream came closer and took life.

And so the wretched business began.

I went home thinking: "Oh, God! Supposing a girl like that cared for me? What couldn't I do? If she did—how I'd work. How I'd try to be different, to be something that she wouldn't be ashamed of. I would show her how I could range myself. I would show her that although I came from down there, I could, for her, stand on my feet in her world."

Then came the thought—"Idiot! How could you meet her on the level? You haven't got one decent suit. You wouldn't know how to wear evening clothes. You can't take her out—you don't know how to do it, apart from the fact that you haven't got the money to do it with; and precious little hope of getting any."

But the thing grew; and at last—after a month of weekly meetings and long companionable talks —came the thought—"Well, it's no good. There's no hope. You can't stand in her world; but you can get the misery off your chest and tell her. Tell her the whole thing, from the broken toys onward. Have that one rapturous moment; and then go right away."

I did. I knew at the time that I was doing a foolish thing, that I was putting a knife into myself, but I could not stop. After tea at the flat one summer afternoon, I told her.

I don't know what reception I had expected; something, I think, like this: "Yes, I understand, Tommy. I'm sorry. Very sorry. But——"

It wasn't at all like that. She said: "What?"

And then a sharp, "Oh!" And then, "Oh, Tommy. Oh. . . . You *are* sudden, aren't you? When on earth did you think of this?"

I said, "Years ago." She said nothing to that, but sat looking at the floor. It seemed that I had somehow crushed her. Then she said very quietly, "But do you mean——"

I said, "Yes. I do."

And then she was neither Miss Cicely nor the jolly companion; but a frail and weak little girl, and I was beside her, holding her, and she was letting me hold her, yielding to me. Her voice was a feeble whisper. "I don't know. I don't know. I couldn't. . . . Oh, Tommy. I'm awf'ly fond of you. I always was. And when I saw you again, last month, in the drawing-room, directly you came in, I felt that—I felt that—that I'd known you quite a long time, and that we. . . . Oh, but I couldn't——"

"Is there anybody else? I'm not going to worry you. I'm going in a minute. But is Captain——"

She laughed then, and laughing brought tears. "Oh, goodness, no. There's nobody. I never thought. . . . I wish you hadn't. . . ."

"I'm sorry. I'll go now. But I had to tell you. I couldn't go on like this. Perhaps I oughtn't to have said it. But I've said it. So now I'll go. And you can forget about it."

"Oh, but you mustn't go. I don't want to lose you now. We get on so awf'ly well together. And I like you better than anybody I've ever met."

"But what's the good? It isn't any good, is it? We couldn't meet after this, like we used."

"I don't know. You see——"

"*Is* it any good? If I came back in six months?"

"I don't know. I don't know. You see—there's—there's so many things. There's auntie."

"I thought you took no notice of her?"

"I pretend I don't. But all the same, she's there. And she does matter—to me. And then—you see, if you had a position, it might be different."

"I know. I know it was damned impudence telling you this. I know what I am, and where I come from. I know all about the difference and——"

"Oh, it isn't that. But auntie—and all my friends —and—and—you *do* understand, don't you?"

"Oh, yes, I understand all right. I've had plenty of chance of understanding."

"Well, will you—will you let us go on as before? And then—later—perhaps—I don't know—but. . . ."

I accepted, and accepted a year of torment. But I see now that it had its purpose, for it led me back to Quong Lee, and there I learned at last the secret of right living.

She wouldn't let me go. She held me by a thread of half-promises, dancing me up and down the pit, until, in agony, I cut the thread. Often, during that year I wished I had never thrust my head out of Bermondsey, but had stayed there peacefully, in loneliness and hunger. All through that year she poisoned me. By her attitude towards me she pulled my little world to pieces and tumbled me down with it, and left me with nothing. She made me ashamed of all the things I had loved, and of all my enthusiasms. All that had served me with delight and interest became, in her presence, mean. She took me in hand, kindly and delicately, and showed me, without a word, that everything I did was wrong and vulgar. Everything I liked was cheap. All my friends were vulgar. Even in daring to love her I had been vulgar. Often I tried to escape and wrote to her to say that it was better to part; but each time she wrote me a letter whose words hinted at something unsaid, and so brought me back.

Once, when I was out with her, we met Jimmy Hayhoe; and Jimmy raised his hat—a little too elaborately—and smirked; and when he had passed on, she asked, "Who's that?" I told her. She said "Oh!" Just "Oh!" But I knew her tricks of speech and their implications and by that "Oh!" and a faint quiver at the corner of her mouth, I knew what she was thinking. And I thought—"Good Lord! If only you could hear that man play. If only you could understand what he does night after night all over England—all over the world in camps and settlements and barracks—with his songs. You think George Alexander's wonderful and you sneer at Jimmy Hayhoe."

But, of course, she was right. She was always right. While she was rich, being rich was the right thing, to which I could never attain; and penury was despicable. If she were ever to become poor and I rich, then again I should be wrong. Poverty would be correct and comfort would be vulgar. To think of her and Jimmy Hayhoe was to think of a Spring morning and fried fish. To think of her when I was writing a column of *Ally Sloper*—God, it was awful! Under this daily reproof of blood and state, my soul wilted a little each night. She could abash me with a look, push me down the pit with a word. Under my newly grown skin of assurance, grown during the Cosgrove and Resplendent days, she thrust at the Hardcress boy, and found him. Across my world she slashed the soul-destroying words: "Not good enough." My manners were vulgar, my clothes were vulgar, my work was vulgar, my ambition was vulgar. She pitied me for what I was, and pitied me for loving her.

And still she was right. I had brought all this upon myself by my presumption in telling her I loved her.

Centred as much upon myself as upon her—there is nothing so selfish and so altruistic as youthful love—I fell to wondering how much more she would have found me wanting if she could have seen me in my daily life. Writing at my chest of drawers. Lining up at the gallery door of a theatre. Lunching at the counter of a pub. off Guinness and Welsh rarebit at a penny a time. Eating fried potatoes out of a bag with Jimmy Hayhoe. Listening to dirty stories with a few of Hayhoe's friends. My God, what would she think? And all the time I was loathing the world where I belonged, I was feeling that if only I could, by some magic bridge, enter her world, I could be at ease with it and with myself; aware of rightness, holding my head up with no shames or concealments or disgusts. But she kept my head well down.

The ridiculous things I did for her. Taking her to tea at a Lyons tea-shop. Saving up two shillings and buying four carnations for her, and walking to Kensington, at an hour when I knew she would be out, and leaving them on the mat, and walking home to Lavender Hill. Cadging free stalls for her from theatrical pals. With two pounds that I had received for a story I printed twenty copies of my poems in booklet form for her. Taking her for rides on the top of the 'bus. Buying her chocolate from an automatic machine. All these things she took as though they were gifts beyond words.

As surely as I wrote or telephoned to her to say that it was useless, and that I couldn't meet her again, so surely there would come a bright letter from her, telling me not to be silly, but to remember that there was nobody but me; that it was a serious matter for a girl; and that it wasn't fair to catch her up in a whirlwind. I began to take a morbid interest in the postman. I began to turn sick at the sight of an envelope addressed in her writing, fearing to open it. She wouldn't leave me alone. Once, for three weeks, following a letter of mine, I never saw her or heard from her; and I felt glad that it was at last over, and I settled down contentedly to work. Then came a telegram:—"*Must see you Thursday. Have been very miserable without you.*"

Ha! She did care, then? I did mean something

to her? She couldn't be so damnably cruel, knowing the torment that the mere thought of her, let alone her presence, meant to me, as to do this out of idle habit? She could, though. I kept the appointment, and found that she had been unhappy without me, and would I go with her to a dance at the Empress Rooms?

As I walked home, I wondered whether I couldn't hire an evening-suit and somehow learn dancing and all the other teasing graces of her set. Perhaps if I learnt dancing, and danced well, perhaps that would. . . . But it cost money to learn dancing. And time. A month, perhaps. A month's time, and a struggle for the money—but weren't they worth an evening with immeasurable beauty? Yes, but what then? Only another opportunity for making a fool of myself; more time-serving, more self-disgust, more heart-ache, more failure.

Again I told her that I was finished, and set my mind steadily towards work, and again she dropped chatty letters on me, and filled me with nausea. Hour after hour, instead of working, I would sit with one of her letters, and wonder, "What does it mean? Does she really, after all, care for me— perhaps unknown to herself?" Once at her bureau she had discovered, in my presence, a number of my letters, and I had noted that they were tied with blue ribbon, each in its envelope. Would she have kept all my letters (in their envelopes) if she didn't care? Or was it mere callousness—or lack of understanding? Was there some occult love-language, of which her letters and telegrams and gestures were a part, which I ought to be able to interpret? Was she thinking me stupid because I didn't rise to them and respond? Was she trying to say something to me, or was she just blundering without purpose?

I gave it up, and wrote one final letter, demanding Yes or No. I waited four days. Then the answer came. By telegram.

Yes.

I can't remember how that day passed. I couldn't see her because she had gone to the country with friends, and would be away three or four days. And I couldn't work. I went out. I walked and walked and walked. I sang songs to myself. I felt clean all through, purified and poised, in harmony with all life. You know the feeling. I saw a London that I had never seen before: a London shot with spiritual beauty. I grew light-headed, and, in a moment of sense, being afraid of this exaltation, I decided to beat it down. I went to the Cavour; and there met Jimmy Hayhoe and others of his set. Jimmy said: "Hullo, boy, you look all lit up. Where've you been?" I said nothing, but took the drink he handed me. Later I told him privately and quietly, that I was engaged. He said: "Good boy! Splendid! Delighted to hear it. Here's everything of the best. There's nothing like it, boy. It'll do wonders for you. Make everything worth while, and set you working so's you won't know yourself. This knocking about's all very well —*I* know. I've had plenty of it—but the right girl and a home—that's the main thing, my boy. That's the main thing, my boy. That's the thing to go for. But I missed it. I missed the boat, just as I've missed everything else. . . . Well, on an occasion like this—what about it? Drink up!"

All that afternoon Jimmy stayed with me, fatherly. He told me how he had "missed it," and he told me portentously about marriage, and its awkward corners, and the right way to take them.

It was about eight o'clock when I got home, still in a state of cloudy effervescence. A second telegram was lying on the bed. I opened it. It read *"Ring Dorking* 8609." With many internal quivers of bliss, and, I daresay, an idiotic grin, I went out to Clapham Junction, and rang Dorking 8609, and heard the precious voice. It said:

"I'm awfully sorry. But—I've got something I must say to you to-night. I can't go on with it. I wish I could. I want to so much. But . . . I can't. It's no good. I'm sorry. You've been perfectly sweet and patient about it, and I've been a selfish beast. But I can't do it."

I said, "Oh? I see. It isn't you that's been selfish, though. It's me. All right. . . . Well, . . . good-bye."

"Good-bye, dear."

I came out of that telephone-box, and stood in the noisy, crowded passage of Clapham Junction, with a buzz in my ear and a buzz in my stomach. Her message did not stun me or leave me gasping or bowed down. I did not reel under the blow. There was no break of time between putting the

receiver back and getting into the passage. I knew
this was the end: I knew that I was suffering as I
had never suffered before; but its only effect was
a feeling of nausea and a tendency to giggle. Standing there, I got the railway-station feeling; the feeling I always have when seeing people off: there
is no place like a railway-station for inducing sen-
tentiousness and sterility. "Well," I said, and I
said it aloud, "that's that. Life's a bloody funny
thing. Why on earth has this happened? Why
on earth did I ever go to tea with her, and what on
earth made me fall in love with her, and what on
earth made me tell her? I *am* a fool! Wonder
where Jimmy is? If I can find Jimmy. . . . I can't
go home. I can't go home."

By a happy accident, I did find Jimmy. He said,
"Oh. . . . Oh. . . . Well, y'know, it sounds rather
rough, perhaps, but I felt when you told me that
it'd Never Do. I think you'll be glad later. But
cut it out, boy. Cut it right out. There's nothing else
for it. Let's go along to the Resplendent; if yeh
don't wanter see the show, we'll have a drink. Cheer
up, boy. Here—heard the one about the sailor
and the emu?"

I awoke next morning in ache and sourness from
which there was no escape. Some day, I supposed
I should be myself again, but just then I was not
whole. I had surrendered for ever my independ-
ence. I had given my soul into the hands of another,
and never, I thought, should I get it back again.
Henceforth, wherever she went she would carry with

her part of me; and if I were near her in a crowd, though I could not see her, I should know that she was there—possessing part of myself.

But even then, I was not suffered to hide. A week later, I found on the mat a letter, and at sight of the writing I went cold. An inner voice said, "Burn it! Don't open it." Of course I opened it. She would like to see me again, to try to explain. I tore it gently into halves, quarters and eighths, and threw it in the fire. And again, of course, that evening I answered and fixed a meeting in the Park.

We talked for two hours, the usual bitter and tender things that are talked by youth on these occasions.

"I ought not to have brought you here. But . . . somehow I couldn't . . . couldn't let you go like that. I—I'm afraid to let you go. I feel I'm doing something that—something I shall——And yet. . . ."

"Well?"

"Oh, if only things were different."

"You mean if I were different?"

"No, not that. But—you see, our lives have always been so different, and——"

"I know. It's all very silly. You've always been accustomed to so many things that I know nothing about. I feel I've—soiled you, somehow. But, anyway—I want to ask you one favour. Let this be the finish, and never, never write to me again."

"Oh, but . . . I don't know. I——"

"You must. It must finish. Unless——"

"Oh, I want to. But—you see, I don't know

what they'd say. All my friends would—— And when a girl offends all her friends, and hasn't any others—— It isn't as though you had any friends. Or any place. Or any—— It's horrible to think of losing you, but, you understand, don't you? It would be hard on both of us. I'm sure they'd never accept you as—as——"

"I see. Well, in that case, we'd better say Good-bye. And leave it at that."

We stood still, looking up and down the path, or at our feet; and now and again, straight at each other. And at each of those looks I saw something —something concealed that seemed to be begging. We had nothing more to say to each other, but she wouldn't go and I couldn't go. We lingered. It seemed that we had never moved from the moment when I stood in front of her on the lawn, looking down at a heap of broken toys. Then I turned away a few paces, stopped, and looked back. I felt even then that if only I could find the right words, she would forget her friends, and we should come together on common ground. Some little word, some fragile thread, some small action, would, I felt, do it. But we never found the touchstone. In the moment of going I turned back and swooped at her, and held her, and made a last foolish declaration to her. For ten seconds the shadow of her friends lifted. I felt the air clear.

"Tommy!"

"Cicely!"

Then I broke away. "Good-bye, Cicely."

"Good-bye . . . Tommy."

Then the shadow came down.

And so we parted.

Yet, even then, in my self-centred mood, I saw it from the outside, and felt that it wasn't a true parting. Every lover's parting I had ever heard of had been beautiful—tinct with twilight rapture: touching of hands, averted heads; lifted from earth by the dignity of inevitable grief. There had been nothing of that: scarcely even grief; only an abominable physical nausea. I felt that I had been cheated all ways. I wanted to go back and do it again. But it was a parting, sure enough. I never saw her again.

The next day was Sunday, and all that day I sat in my bedroom, laughing, and talking to myself. "Nobody loves you, old son. Garden . . . worms." Then: "Oh, for God's sake, don't try to be funny about it. You can't, you know; and it doesn't make it any easier. You only keep coming back to it, and finding it hurts all the more." Then: "Oh, well—go on. Laugh, if you think it's so funny. Anyway, it's a good thing it's over. You could never have made her happy. You'd only have pulled her down. (No, I shouldn't.) She wasn't your sort at all. (Liar!) She would never have understood you. (Yes, she would.) And you'd have been hurting her all the time. (No, I wouldn't.) You never saw her properly. You made her something that she never was. You dressed her up in poetry and sentimentality. (Liar! Liar!) I loved her. I loved her. And she's gone.

"Oh, all right. Keep on laughing, then, and kill

it. It's got to be killed some time. Kill everything of her. Every thought of her and all her
letters. Ah, you can burn letters, but you can't burn
thoughts.

"Anyway, you're not the only fool, my boy.
There are thousands like you walking about London,
seeing a lost face in every face that passes, and
thinking that the world is ended, and the sun's
stopped shining. Smile—damn you, smile. Go and
see Jimmy Hayhoe and get drunk."

All the time I was trying to write, for I was down
to five-and-sixpence in cash and nothing to come.
But wherever I looked I saw her face. Every two
minutes the pen would stop, and I would hear her
voice, and see her hair, her movements, the colour
of her clothes. Her face was on the wall, on the
paper on which I was writing. If I looked up, the
sky taunted me with her. Every passing figure in
the street had some touch of her; and through my
head all day went the silly tune of a song that was
then on the streets:

> "What is the use of loving a girl
> If the girl don't love you?"

I looked forward to next week with horror—
horror lest, in the streets, or in turning a corner, I
should see her. I imagined myself coming suddenly
upon her as she came out of a theatre or a restaurant, and the thought made me sick.

Thereupon I left my work and gathered together
all her letters, and stowed them in the fireplace,

laughing all the time, and set a match to them. All that Sunday afternoon, amid the cries of muffins and winkles, and the jangle of church bells, I laughed knowing all the time that the laughter and the self-mockery were fraudulent. Cicely was gone, and had taken my spirit with her: my youth, and my joy in work, and my capacity for work. The thing that sat in the back bedroom, throwing letters on the fire, was not me, but a mere husk. She had taken spirit from body, and body was sitting over a paper fire in Battersea, while spirit was miles away—a prisoner in a Kensington flat. In time, I said, I shall get used to it, and laugh honestly at it; and the world will be just the same and as happy as it always was.

But I didn't believe it. And all next week I writhed in misery inescapable, unable to work, unable to stay indoors, and even when a letter came from a literary agent, to whom I had submitted some work, asking me to call and see him immediately, I had not the heart to answer. I sat and mooned and moped; until, at the end of the week, looking round an empty world, I remembered my city of refuge and saw a way of escape.

I would go back to Quong Lee. I would go back to his shop and stay there always. I was done with grace and beauty and the clean world. My place was in the obscurity of Quong Lee's shop, among the unconsidered things. There I had once touched the skirts of happiness, and there I would touch them again. I would leave Lavender Hill, and I would never look at Kensington Gardens again. I would

give up all atempts to write, all attempts towards
the things that had seemed so desirable; and I
would get a job of some kind down there, and live
as Quong Lee lived, from day to day, without
thought or striving. An hour later, with a small
bag, I was on my way to him.

Chapter XI

CAUSEWAY

I WENT back with my sickness to the Causeway and to Quong Lee.

But this time there was no Quong Lee.

It was late when I arrived. I entered from the river end. Hooters and whistles came from the river, and far away, the headlight of a departing vessel moved across the sky. The Causeway was a wad of shadow, broken by the two lamps that shivered in the wind. The air was strong with tar and dried fish. From a distant court came the murmur of a guitar and the beat of a drum. Shuttered windows all around me enclosed strange life and alien thought. Quong Lee's windows, too, were shuttered, and the door fastened.

I knocked, and waited.

There was no answer.

I knocked again, and kicked, and hammered with the flat hand.

No answer. Then a neighbouring door opened and a man whom I recognised as Ho Ling came out. He peered at me, and said: "Quong Lee he go."

"Go?"

"Huh! He go pleece mans."

For a moment I did not understand. Then I said, "How long?"

"He go long time."

"A long time ago? Or gone for a long time?"

But Ho Ling couldn't follow that: he could only repeat that Quong Lee had gone pleece mans; and as I could get nothing more from him I turned away. Then I remembered "The Barge Aground" and the station housekeeper. It was only eleven o'clock: they would still be open, and if the house-keeper were not there, somebody there would probably know something.

Again I surprised Mr. Sturt by my return after two years; and was quickly introduced into the Wheelhouse, where the "regulars" were assembled. The man I wanted was in his usual corner, and I put a direct question to him. "Oh, ah. I know. Quong Lee. Ah, yes. . . . And how long've you known him—eh?"

I told him that I had known him in the days when I had sat there eating heart-cakes."

"Oh, you did, did you? You kept it pritty quiet, then. Nice friend for a kid. Wonder what your uncle would a-said?"

"But what's the trouble with Quong Lee? I want to know."

"The trouble with ole Quong Lee was six months. *And* to be deported."

"Deported? Has he gone, then?"

"He ain't. And if you want to see him so bad you're only just in time. He finished his time a week ago, and they been holding him for a boat. He'll be put on board t'morrer."

"Oh. But what's it all for?"

He looked at me. "You know very well what it's for. Eh?"

"Well. . . . I did see something—last time I was there."

"Well, that's it. He's bin at it fer years now. They been waiting a long time to git him, and now they got him. Lucky you wasn't there when they raided him. You might a-got into trouble. And was he reely a pal of yours?"

I explained briefly; then asked "Could I see him somehow before he goes. I do want to see him. Only a personal matter. Could you fix it?" Somewhere inside me was a feeling that if I couldn't see Quong Lee just once before he went, life would be impossible. My city of refuge was barred and bolted. The one thing to which I had clung in all moments of distress was now taken from me. But if I could only get one peep at it. . . . .

"Well, what you want to mix yourself up with that sort o' thing for, I don't know. Still, you know your own business, I suppose. I dessay I can fix it. Faulkner's got the job. He's handing him over at Albert Dock t'morrer. Faulkner's a decent chap, and I dessay he'd let you go down with 'em. Come round to the station—about half-past seven."

Ever since that November morning I have hated November mornings. It was dark, but not dark enough for street-lights. Here and there an early shop had put its lights on, making the succeeding stretches more miserable. The streets were muddy, and a thick drizzle was falling, and a warm wind came stickily to one's face. Buildings, houses, pave-

ments and sky looked sick and bleared. I reached
the station at half-past seven, and there I found
the housekeeper and, a few minutes later, was introduced to Faulkner. I knew him by sight, and he
knew me, but after a friendly nod, he became official,
and wanted to know why this and why that, and
what my relations with Quong Lee had been: questions which irritated me because it was impossible to
explain the inexplicable to anybody: least of all a
divisional detective. But at last he grunted, and
said, "All right, then. Of course, it's outside regulations, but. . . . Come on."

Then Quong Lee was brought up. He was im-
passive; even dignified, and, dirty as he was, and
shabby as his clothes were, it seemed to me that
there was only one man there. Faulkner's height
and the housekeeper's bulk faded into shadow
against this bent and withered figure from the East.
He gave me a slow smile; then stood with hands
folded and face expressionless.

There was a cab to Canning Town; then a train
journey to Manor Way. Under the light of that
November morning I could imagine nothing nearer
to hell than the country through which that dockside
railway passes—Tidal Basin, Custom House, Central, Manor Way—flat, marshy, and ashen; all
litter, refuse and open spaces. Once on the journey
I spoke to Quong Lee.

"Why you do it? Why you do that smokee?"

He answered gravely: "I do for make cash go
back my own country. . . . Huh! Now your country pay ship take me back. Veh good!"

He took no further notice of me until we reached the dock. There Faulkner led him to the boat, myself following some paces behind, sent for the captain, delivered him into the captain's charge, and took a receipt for him as though he were a parcel. As I saw him standing on the deck, I was sensible of utter desolation. An old and dirty Chinese, no different from a thousand of his fellows; a shopkeeper in a dirty street, who ran an opium room, and had been to prison, was being kicked out of the country. Yet it seemed that with his going I had lost everything, and my life would come to a stop, and I must begin all over again. There was no going back and no moving on. I must turn aside and find other ways. What he had meant to me I never knew: when I came to make account of it in terms of ideas, the answer was Nothing. Yet there was the fact of my spiritual desolation.

Faulkner let me go on deck with them, and as we stood there I said, for the sake of saying something: "It's very dark. Very cold, too."

"Ee-yess. It is veh dark cold. But in my country all flower."

There was a bell; some voices; business with ropes and gangway; the throb of the engines. Quong Lee put his hand into his pocket and said, "Eere. I giff you," and handed me something soft. As we stepped off the boat, Faulkner reached out and snatched it from me and opened it. He ran it through his fingers, looked at it all ways; then grunted and gave it back to me. It was an old black silk cap.

There was a scream from the whistle, and she slowly drifted from the side, set herself to midstream, and dropped down the river. Quong Lee stood with his back towards us, looking straight ahead of him; and I stood, with a feeling of nakedness and intense hunger, and watched him till he was beyond vision.

Then, in a mood that was of the morning's weather, I thanked Faulkner, said I would walk back, and parted from him. All that day I walked, thinking now of Cicely and now of Quong Lee, until at night I found myself back in the Causeway. There I lingered, having no purpose, yet reluctant to leave it; and at last I went into Ho Ling's, next door to Quong Lee's shuttered shop, and there I took tea and a meal of fish and noodles, and tried to pretend that I was sitting next door. After the meal I sat at the upstairs window, looking into the narrow street, listening to its music or talking broken talk with Ho Ling, until eleven o'clock; when, too slack to move, I arranged with him for a bed.

I stayed the night there, but I slept little. All night, until the first hooters of five o'clock, I lay thinking; or, rather, thoughts and fancies moved through a mind that could not comprehend or command them. Quong Lee was gone. Quong Lee was gone. Everything was gone. My hopes were gone, and my last city of refuge had collapsed. Was it any good beginning again? Was it any good rebuilding?

At last I slept.

What happened in that sleep I do not know. I only know that at ten o'clock next morning, I awoke to a state that I could only remember in childhood— clear, fresh, steady. Something had been lifted from me; something else had entered into me. It seemed as though all the little specks of wondering and doubting and wanting had come together and crystallised themselves into something hard and enduring.

I went out into the shimmering Causeway, and mingled with the calm faces there in a mood of Springtime; the mood that had held me at the first moment of knowing Quong Lee. But this time something told me that this was no flash, but a burning lantern that would always keep alight. In those fourteen years I had given and gathered much in attrition and adhesion. I held something of all the people I had met, and each of them held part of me; and that morning I felt, in the colloquial phrase, a new man.

Two hours later I knew that visions fade; that seeking here and there is folly; that my world was not the rare world but the little world of stress and the laughter of common people; and that all my journeys to the street across the road were vanity. For at twelve o'clock I went to the "Blue Posts," and there in a corner, looking more like Irving than ever, was Creegan. And after greetings, Creegan asked questions, and I answered them; and then, led on by his interest and my morning mood, I unburdened myself of all my silly sorrows.

He didn't laugh at me for being twenty-three.

He didn't laugh at my attitude towards the world. He took my sorrows seriously, and talked to me. For two hours we sat in that corner, he talking discursively and drinking Guinness, I listening. It was mainly platitude, I think, but the sort of platitude that is astonishingly new to twenty-three.

He showed me that I must go back to Lavender Hill and go on writing, and stop being a damned young fool. That all living is hunger, and that without hunger we perish. That each man's city of refuge must be built within himself—of broken toys. That the only people who truly live are those who are always beginning again. That it was not I, or Cicely, who mattered, but love itself: not my suffering that must be eased, but love that must be served. That only by love do we come to understanding and truth. That the mocking magic that comes and goes is the lamp that is lighting us to beauty. That this beauty is the happiness of God, and is not in clouds or on hill-tops, but everywhere about us.

Creegan said this, but I felt that it was just what another man would have told me, could he have spoken English. And as I rode back to Battersea, I knew that I had turned another corner—this time into the straight.

THE END.